'Bec… all that is … is y…

Terror fought with … could not speak, fe… she had managed … death.

'What is it, Becky? Is it that you do not know me?'

'Pip…Pip Hurst?' she managed to croak.

'Aye! When I saw you leaving I determined to make myself known to you.'

'I'm surprised you should recognise me after so long a time. I am much changed.'

'Indeed you are…' His blue eyes washed slowly over her face and then slid to her slender neck and throat, before pausing a moment as they took in the swell of her bosom in the tight bodice. They skipped lower, scanning her narrow waist and the curve of her hips to finish their exploration at the sensible shoes protruding from beneath her grey skirts. 'You're very much a woman now.'

Rebecca drew herself up to her full height and said in a prim voice, 'It would be strange indeed if I were not, *Master Hurst*. After all, like you, I have seen twenty-four summers. Your appearance has certainly changed, although your habit of putting me to the blush remains!'

'H… vanished. 'But yo… gotten th… een…'

June Francis's interest in old wives [illegible]nd folk customs led her into a writing career. History has always fascinated her, and her first novels were set in Medieval times. She has also written sagas based in Liverpool and Chester. Married with three grown-up sons, she lives on Merseyside. On a clear day she can see the sea and the distant Welsh hills from her house. She enjoys swimming, fell-walking, music, lunching with friends and smoochy dancing with her husband.

More information about June can be found at her website: www.junefrancis.co.uk

Previous novels by this author:

ROWAN'S REVENGE
TAMED BY THE BARBARIAN
REBEL LADY, CONVENIENT WIFE
HIS RUNAWAY MAIDEN
PIRATE'S DAUGHTER, REBEL WIFE
THE UNCONVENTIONAL MAIDEN

MAN BEHIND THE FAÇADE

June Francis

All the characters in this book have no existence outside the imagination of the author, and have no relation whatsoever to anyone bearing the same name or names. They are not even distantly inspired by any individual known or unknown to the author, and all the incidents are pure invention.

First published in Great Britain 2012
by Mills & Boon, an imprint of Harlequin (UK) Limited.
Harlequin (UK) Limited, Eton House, 18-24 Paradise Road,
Richmond, Surrey TW9 1SR

ISBN: 978 0 263 89267 3

Harlequin (UK) policy is to use papers that are natural, renewable and recyclable products and made from wood grown in sustainable forests. The logging and manufacturing process conform to the legal environmental regulations of the country of origin.

Printed and bound in Spain
by Blackprint CPI, Barcelona

MAN BEHIND THE FAÇADE

Chapter One

Oxfordshire—September 1526

Rebecca Clifton rested her aching back against a tree and bit into an apple without taking her gaze from the players on the green. A saucy riposte from the one disguised as a hag caused laughter to ripple through the crowd a few yards away. The happy entertainment brought back memories of her girlhood and a particular day she had passed at a boatyard, in Deptford, when she had accompanied her father to his current place of work. A master-carpenter, he had been employed by the Hurst Boatyard to work on a ship that Henry VIII had commissioned for his navy. It was a place they had visited every summer since she was eight years old, as it was then the boatyard was really busy. Then, as now, she had remained in the shadows, listening to a story unfold. Reminded of the guilty pleasure she had experienced as she'd watched Phillip Hurst, nicknamed Pip, the youngest of the Hurst brothers, wielding a hammer under her father's tutelage, a grim expression on his face. The muscles in his arms and back had rippled in the hot sun and perspiration had darkened his mane of flaxen hair.

Although naïve to the ways of the world, even then she had considered him almost too handsome for his own good, with a silver tongue that he used to good advantage when he had a mind to do so. His honeyed words had set her heart aflutter and for weeks she had shyly followed his every move that summer ten years ago. Well, she smiled to herself ruefully, she had been young and impressionable then and those years were behind her.

But what was she doing letting her mind wander? She had missed the character's next sally which had raised another gale of laughter. She must concentrate because she had stayed behind to enjoy the entertainment. Life held too few of these pleasures to pass them up so lightly. The performance came to an end and the actors took their bow, their eyes scanning the crowd, smiling, as they were applauded enthusiastically. The actor who had played the hag caught her gaze and gave her a cheeky wink, which made her blush and look away, moving her attention to a youth who was doing the rounds with a hat. She dropped a coin into its depths, wishing she had more to give. Soon there would be more feasting—another roasted hog being on offer as well as other tasty morsels. But she was hesitant to remain here in Witney much longer. The sun was setting and she must return to Minster Draymore, a short distance away, before dark.

She had passed the church of St Mary on the very outskirts of the town when she heard her name being called. The voice was slightly breathless, as if its owner had been running. Her pulses quickened as a hand seized her shoulder and whirled her round. Sapphire-blue eyes outlined by kohl gazed down into hers. 'Becky Mortimer, by all that is holy, it is you!'

Terror fought with vague recognition, but she could not speak, and feared a recurrence of the nerves she had managed to conquer since her father's death. 'What is it, Becky? Is it that you do not know me?' The man before her removed the wig, revealing a thatch of damp, darkened flaxen hair. She watched, transfixed, as he thrust the wig beneath the cloak he carried over his arm and wiped the carmine from his lips with a rag he dragged from his sleeve. 'Do you recognise me now?' he asked softly.

'Pip…Pip Hurst?' she managed to croak.

'Aye! When I saw you leaving I determined to make myself known to you.'

'I'm surprised you should recognise me after so long a time, I am much changed.'

'Indeed you are…' His blue eyes washed slowly over her face and then slid to her slender neck and throat before pausing a moment as they took in the swell of her bosom in the tight bodice. They skipped lower, scanning her narrow waist and the curve of her hips to finish their exploration at the sensible shoes protruding from beneath her grey skirts. 'You're very much a woman now.'

Rebecca drew herself up to her full height and said in a prim voice, 'It would be strange, indeed, if I were not, *Master Hurst.* After all, like you, I have seen twenty-four summers. Your appearance has certainly changed, although your habit of putting me to the blush remains!'

'Ha!' he laughed. Then the smile vanished. 'But you're not blushing and I have never forgotten that you were the prettiest maid I had ever seen.'

'You flatter me, just as you did then.'

'I spoke the truth.'

He sounded so sincere that her heart seemed to flip over as she recalled once more that distant memory, which now seemed like only yesterday. Pip's father's employees had taken time out from their work to eat their midday meal of bread and cheese and, as her father, Adam Mortimer, had also left the yard, they had called upon Pip to tell them a tale. The tension that had been so present in his features when under her father's eye had relaxed and he had become a different person as he began to spin a yarn.

'I remember that day when you told the men your own version of the ballad of Robin Hood, acting out the parts and putting on different voices,' she murmured. 'You caused much merriment and I kept praying that neither of our fathers would return before you had finished.'

'I am glad I amused you, because you were far too serious a child,' said Phillip, his blue eyes alight with remembrance.

'I thought I had cause to worry that day,' she retorted. 'You knew that the king was expected later and that tale had been banned. The nobility was convinced that it might encourage the commoners to take it into their heads to imitate

Robin and his merry men by robbing the rich to feed the poor.'

Phillip shook his head at her. 'One can't prevent a good tale from being retold time and time again, Becky, but I recall you didn't approve of my ending.'

She felt the blood rise in her cheeks. 'You said I could be honest in my criticism.'

'So I did! Fool that I was, I convinced myself that you would be kind,' he said mournfully, his gaze holding hers as if he could read her thoughts.

She remembered how, back then, he could pierce her to the soul with one of his intense looks, causing all sensible thought to desert her. She had believed herself to be a plain mouse of a creature because her father was so critical of her appearance, and she had been in need of love and affection. 'My comments were fair,' she said stiffly.

Phillip's fair brows drew together above his fine nose and he folded his arms. 'You began by stammering out that you could find no fault with my skill as a storyteller, but then you added "as for the plot ending it was unbelievable."'

She bit her lip. 'You—You looked at me as you do now and you barked at me "No, it isn't!"'

'And you squeaked "B-but it isn't true to life!

I've listened to several of your tales and too often you wander into the realms of fantasy!"' Phillip mimicked her voice to perfection.

The roses in her cheeks deepened. 'I told the truth, never expecting that it would make you so angry,' she protested. 'I was shocked when you said that I would obviously prefer an unhappy ending and gave me an alternative one with Robin dead in a dungeon and Marion raped by the Sheriff of Nottingham.'

Phillip had the grace to apologise, but spoilt it by adding, 'But be honest, Becky, at the very least you'd have had Robin going off on another crusade and being killed in the fighting. Marion would have taken the veil and ended her days in a nunnery. You had no faith in our hero making her happy and providing for her at all!' His manner was teasing but, somehow, Becky was unable to respond in kind.

'It's my experience that there are few heroes in this life, but I will say you have an excellent memory,' she said tartly.

'I need it to remember my lines,' he riposted.

'And you have been fortunate to realise your dreams and live the life of a player; I remember how much you disliked the work of shipbuilding.'

He stared at her intently. 'Ah, yes, that was

proper men's work, was it not? I remember how you used to blush and flutter your eyelashes at my brother Nicholas.'

'Of a surety I did not! It was just that I was more conscious of your brother because he had worked in the yard before he went travelling,' Rebecca replied, hotly, and, deciding it was time this conversation came to an end, she bid him good day and strode off.

'Be honest!' he called after her. 'You believed that being an explorer made him a hero. You were madly in love with him.'

'And what if I was?' she said recklessly, preferring him to believe such a thing, rather than that she had ever lusted after him.

He caught up with her and grabbed her arm. 'But you clearly married someone else! You didn't wait for him,' he said, indicating the band upon her wedding finger.

Rebecca sighed. 'That was because Giles asked me to marry him. Master Nicholas had no real interest in me, he had his own dreams to pursue. And if you don't mind, you are bruising my arm!' She pulled away.

A frowning Phillip slackened his grip. ''Tis a pity women can't be strolling players as well because you'd never forget your lines.'

'I do not know what you mean, Master Hurst.

I have to reach Minster Draymore before dark. Good day to you, sir.' Rebecca moved away from him and put on a spurt as she walked along the path which now led on to open country.

'Perhaps I should remind you,' said Phillip as he caught up with her. Taking her by her upper arms, he brought her close to him. 'You said that being a player is not the stuff of which heroes are made.'

Her grey eyes did not flinch beneath his blazing blue ones. 'Well, I beg your pardon, *Master Hurst,* if you deem my words uncalled for at the time. As it was, I only had your best interests at heart, believe it or not! You are to be congratulated in making your dream come true. I remember seeing you perform before the king as you vowed you would that day, and I applauded you for your achievement.'

He looked surprised. 'When was that?'

'When my husband was still alive. My musician brother, Davy, saw to it that we were invited to the entertainment during the Christmas festivities at Greenwich Palace.'

'Why didn't you come and make yourself known to me?'

She could not bring herself to say that she had feared he might not remember her and that would have been too embarrassing. 'You had enough admiring women around you and I had no intention of joining their number,' she replied lightly.

He frowned. 'And no doubt your husband would not have approved. Do you still believe me a fool for becoming a player and deem I should be building ships for His Grace?'

'I don't remember ever saying you were a fool, but it is true that I consider boatbuilding a steadier and more secure occupation.'

'I wasn't looking for security then, but adventure. As it was, I had to wait until my father died before getting my wish,' said Phillip, releasing her. 'I suppose it was the same with you? Your father's death freed you to become the woman you are now.'

'Freedom has its price, Master Hurst.' She turned and walked away without waiting for his reply. She had known Pip Hurst had not immediately been able to have his wish because her friend, Lady Beth Raventon, had told her so. His eldest brother Christopher had inherited the family business after their father's death and he had insisted that his youngest brother finish his apprenticeship. His elder brother, Nicholas, had followed his own dream after inheriting a goodly sum of money from his godfather, which had enabled him to be financially independent of the family business. It was only seven years since Pip had been set free to do what he wished. This had happened shortly after her own father's death, which had resulted in her being reunited with her brother, Davy. Five years older than Becky, it was several years since she had seen him as he'd quarrelled with their father over Davy's refusal to complete his apprenticeship as a ship's carpenter. Desiring to pursue his musical talent, she learnt that his knowledge of carpentry had enabled him to earn a living whilst performing at fairs and the church on feast days, where he had been fortunate to find a patron, which had resulted in his eventually performing before the nobility.

It was her brother who had decided she needed a husband and provided a small dowry, so enabling her to marry Giles Clifton, a stonemason. A young man, a kind man, he had died unexpectedly in an accident when a wall had come crashing down and crushed him, leaving her grieving, childless and almost penniless. During that time Davy had found a position at Queen Katherine's court and so Rebecca had decided to accept an invitation to live with Giles's sister, Jane, who had married a widower. Simon Caldwell was also a stone mason and had two daughters from a previous marriage. He and Jane now had a son, and she was with child again. The family lived in Oxford.

'Where are you going?' called Phillip, interrupting Rebecca's thoughts.

She ignored the question, thinking she should have left the Witney feast with Simon and the children. Even when she heard a muffled curse, she managed to resist turning to see the cause for those shocking words. She had said all that she was going to say to Pip Hurst. Besides, she must make haste or it would be dark before she reached the house at Minster Draymore.

'I have noticed that you have managed to control your stammer,' said a voice closer than she had thought it should be. She almost jumped out of her skin and barely managed to control her jitters to say, 'I only ever stammered, Master Hurst, when my father addressed me or I was rash enough to speak my thoughts aloud. A lesson I learnt much earlier than the day I first stepped foot in your father's shipyard. You should never have encouraged me to be honest that time.'

'I can understand your fear of your father.'

Now she did turn and stare at him and the picture he presented caused her to lose her train of thought. He was still wearing the gown and had not quite removed all the paint from his face. She itched to reach up and remove a patch of pink from beneath his arrogant nose, but she controlled the impulse. 'Of course, you were often on the receiving end of my father's questionable wit,' she muttered.

'Sarcasm.' Phillip's brow clouded. 'The times I had to resist the urge to punch him in the face, although I admit your father was an excellent ship's carpenter. Fortunately I only had to put up with his moods a few months at a time. Trouble was, I never knew when one of his dark moods would suddenly take him. Or why!'

'He—he blamed the Devil for many things, but women also came in for much criticism,' said Rebecca, her eyes darkening. 'You—you're probably unaware of the fact that my mother deserted us when I was a very young child. My brother, Davy, told me that our father always had a temper, but he became embittered after she left and would seldom allow me out of his sight. That was why he took me with him wherever he had work, which surprised me. My mother having rejected me, I could not understand why he should fear I might run off in search of her.'

Phillip frowned. 'I didn't know any of that! I presumed your father was a widower. Do you know why your mother deserted you?'

'I used to ask that question and once I was told there was another man involved. I received a clout for my pains and never dared ask again. I do remember crying myself to sleep and wanting my mother when I was very little, only to be told that if I mentioned her name again then I would be whipped.' She shuddered. 'It seemed like a bad dream and I grew to hate her. I have no idea where she is or whom she is with and part of me does not want to know.'

'I can understand why you feel so angry. I find it difficult to imagine growing up without a mother's warmth and affection. Whenever my father beat me when I was small—even then I did not conform to his standards—I knew I could always find comfort at her knee. He thoroughly disapproved of her encouraging me in my playacting and love of storytelling. She died three years ago and I still miss her.' He paused to remove the last of the paint from his face and changed the subject. 'It's a fact that I did not appreciate your honesty at our last meeting. In truth, your words stabbed me to the heart and my pride took a beating.' There was a hint of self-mockery in his voice. 'You see, I always considered myself something of a hero when I took on a role.'

She smiled. 'That does not surprise me, Pip

Hurst, because even at fourteen summers you had the build and countenance of what I imagined a hero to look like.'

Phillip rolled his eyes. 'There's no need to go overboard with your flattery in an attempt to compensate for what you said years ago.' He paused. 'You know, I'd almost forgotten you had dimples. You should smile more often because you are far more attractive when you do.'

'Now you are determined to put me to the blush again,' she said, lowering her gaze, 'although I'm not quite certain if I should take that remark as an insult rather than a compliment.'

He said seriously, 'It's a compliment. Not many girls would have dared criticise me to my face, but despite your having a habit of shying off whenever I approached, you showed amazing courage for the mouse-like creature you were then. And because of what you said, I determined not only to become a successful storyteller and player, but do something heroic, as well.'

'Why heroic?'

His eyes met hers. 'You should not need to ask. Nicholas, of course. He was my hero, too, and so I wanted some of the fame that came his way.'

Her smile deepened. 'You were not playing the part of a hero this evening.'

'No.' His lips twitched. 'Although it takes a certain kind of courage for a man to don feminine garb.'

She bit on her lip to prevent herself from laughing, remembering his gesticulating and pouting, his mincing walk and the falsetto voice he had adopted several times. 'You were very convincing in the part.'

'So you were at least entertained?'

'I would not deny it.' Her curiosity moved her to ask, 'Do you always play women's roles?'

He screwed up his face. 'Not now, although I did when I was younger. Today one of our players fell ill and so I stepped into his shoes.'

'You are to be commended, Master Hurst.' she said, inclining her head.

He curtsied.

She laughed out loud. 'You became that hag and the beauty as well! I would never have recognised you had you not approached me.'

He seized on her words delightedly. 'So my disguise succeeded. I always told you it was a god-given talent.'

'And you make such a fine woman!' laughed Becky.

Phillip grew serious. 'I tell you truthfully that I prefer writing to disguising, but I am not bothered about my friends seeing me dressed thus, although it disturbed my father when I adopted feminine guise and he would make himself scarce, so if it disturbs you also then I will strip off.' Before she could say a word to prevent him from doing so, he dropped his cloak and dragged the bodice of the gown from his broad shoulders.

'I am not embarrassed, Master Hurst,' she said. Nevertheless, she could not take her eyes from the width of those powerful shoulders that she remembered wielding an axe and hammer.

She watched him wriggle out of his skirts, the breath catching in her throat, for there was no mistaking he was all man as he stood there in tight-fitting hose that lacked a codpiece. She could not look away, telling herself that it was not as if she was a virgin, bashful because she had never seen a man's private parts before. Despite being childless, her husband had been desperate for a son and had been ardent in his attempts to get her with child.

Phillip cocked an eyebrow at her before bending and picking up his cloak. He swung it about his shoulders and it fell in folds to just above his knees, concealing, in the main, the garments beneath. He tied it at the throat before gathering up the gown and stuffing it beneath his arm with the wig. 'So where is this Minster Draymore and why does your husband not escort you?'

The questions took her unawares and her head shot up. 'But I am widowed, Master Hurst. I thought you must have realised that was so.'

He said slowly, 'Forgive me for not expressing my condolences earlier. I had heard that was so from mutual friends of ours, Sir Gawain and Beth Raventon, but it had temporarily slipped my mind.'

She shrugged. 'Why should you have remembered? We have not spoken for an age until this even and if we had not met now, no doubt you would not have given me another thought.'

His brow knit. 'You belittle yourself. Surely you must have gathered from our conversation that you proved unforgettable.'

Rebecca flushed, believing him to be flattering her and determined not to fall under his spell again. 'I had forgotten your family was acquainted with the Raventons,' she said hastily, wishing to change the subject.

'They did mention that you were living in Oxford, so why do you go to Minster Draymore?'

'Simon Caldwell, my brother-in-law, and his children are staying there and will be expecting me. I have no need of an escort, so if you wish to hurry back to the feast, then please do so. I know the way and it is unlikely that I will be set upon. Cutpurses and such ruffians will find better pickings in Witney this evening.'

'Well, I'm not going to allow you to wander the countryside all alone when it'll soon be dark, however unwilling you are for my company,' said Phillip crisply. 'And please, do not call me *Master Hurst.* It reminds me of your father.'

'But that is your name,' she protested.

'I would not deny it, but I would prefer it if you called me Phillip.'

'Phillip!' She moistened her lips. 'It would not feel right calling you Phillip. After all, your father was my father's employer.'

He swore under his breath. 'Becky, we are old friends and have no need of such formality—please call me Phillip.'

'Then you are an unusual man, because in my experience most men prefer to keep a woman under their heel,' she said roundly.

'I thought you had realised by now that I am not your usual man. I do not wish to squash you. Tell me, was that how your husband behaved?'

She took a deep breath. 'My husband, Giles Clifton, was a kind man, a good companion; we were happy for the short time we had together. It is just that men view the world differently from women, so why should I have deemed you would be any different?'

'I confess I find it difficult to get into the head of a woman,' he said ruefully. 'You don't reason like us and are moved too much by your emotions.'

'Men have emotions, too! They just pretend that they don't,' protested Rebecca.

'Damn it, of course they do and I make no pretence about it,' he said.

Her lips twitched. 'Actors are always pretending.'

He protested, 'That is not true! I think we should change the subject. So, where is your sister-in-law?'

'She stays in Oxford because she is expecting another child and is needful of a rest from the children. Knowing that the Witney feast was taking place today, it was considered an excellent notion that the children and I visit and stay with their father for a short time,' said Rebecca. 'We have been here two nights so far and I am sure he is already wearying of the children's company. They are boisterous and proving a distraction, I fear.'

'What kind of man is he?' asked Phillip.

She eyed him carefully. 'A decent man, one to be trusted. A stonemason, like my husband, and he has a commission to make repairs to the vacant Draymore manor house. And what of yourself, Mas—Phillip? Do you have a wife?'

'I have no room for a wife in my life,' he said shortly. 'The travelling life is not one that most women find to their taste.'

Why did such news cause her relief? wondered Rebecca. 'So such a life does have its drawbacks,' she murmured.

He slanted her a long estimating look, thinking that meeting her was causing him to consider how a wife would mean changing his way of life in so many ways. 'I am well aware that I would need to provide a wife with a certain standard of living and a covered wagon would deter most, if not all.'

She raised her eyebrows. 'But surely you don't sleep in a covered wagon during the winter? And what of your entertaining the king? Does he not provide you with lodgings? My brother, who is now employed at Princess Mary's court, has living quarters at Ludlow Castle. Lady Salisbury is her governess and has ensured it.'

'I know of Lady Salisbury—she is a great friend of the Queen. It is true that the Master of the King's Revels provides such quarters for me and my troupe, but only when we are performing at court. Last year was a particularly bad year for all of us, with the plague raging in London and its environs, and we have had to spend more time on the road this year.'

'Tell me, how did you cope with such a setback?' she asked, her expression concerned.

Her interest was obviously genuine, so Phillip told her. 'I worked in my brother's shipyard for a while and I also went abroad. It was not so for the troupe. We had hoped for occupation during the Christmas festivities, but the king and his lords did not make merry during that period for fear of the plague. They retreated to the countryside and did not allow anyone in or out. No doubt Davy escaped the worst of the plague at Ludlow?'

She nodded. 'Although I've not had news of him for some time. I wish I could visit him.'

'Then why don't you?'

Rebecca hesitated. 'If you must know, I do not have the means. Giles was only a young man and had yet to make his way in the world.'

Phillip frowned. 'I see. Did you love him?'

She flushed. 'My feelings for my husband are none of your business, *Master Hurst!* Now, if you don't mind, I must make haste. Goodnight!'

She was not to get away from Phillip so easily and he kept pace with her. 'Couldn't Davy send you the money?'

Her head shot up. 'I would not ask him! If the king was to decide on a change in his daughter's situation, then it is possible my brother would need to look for another position, so he needs to salt away all the money he can. He was kind enough to provide me with a dowry, for my father did not!'

'That was remiss of your father and must have caused you pain. But surely your brother would help you again now you are a widow? I have heard that he is an excellent musician, so it is unlikely that he would be long without a position,' said Phillip, reassuringly.

'That is as may be, but I do not wish to be a burden on him,' she said, agitated by such talk. 'I must make haste. Simon gave me leave to linger in Witney to watch the play, but young James will be missing my putting him to bed.'

Lucky James, thought Phillip. 'Then let us quicken our pace,' he murmured.

Why could he not leave her alone? She did not want him asking her any more questions about Giles. Phillip had roused memories of her marriage that filled her with guilt. Although she had not been in love with her husband, they'd had a warm and friendly relationship. She missed him and it grieved her that no child had resulted from their marriage.

* * *

As it was, she did not need to fear Phillip's questioning. They walked on in silence until they arrived at Minster Draymore. Phillip noted aloud that some of the houses were in a bad state of repair, being constructed of wattle and daub and roofed with thatch.

'Simon has commented that they need to be pulled down and replaced with houses of stone and slate,' said Rebecca, pointing to one of them. 'Apparently the man who now owns them and the manor house has been out of the country for years and has only just returned.'

'At least it explains their neglect,' said Phillip.

'Come winter, I am certain Simon will return to Oxford, for the damp will play havoc with his rheumatics and he has a commission in the town to complete that means he can work indoors during the worst of the weather,' said Rebecca, not loath to talk about the Caldwells' business.

'Is he much older than your sister-in-law?' asked Phillip.

'Aye. The girls are from his first marriage, but James is his and Jane's son. The difficulty is that there is little to occupy the children here. Simon came to visit Jane a few days ago and escorted us here, but he cannot spare another couple of days away to accompany us on the return journey and he will not allow us to travel without a man's protection.'

Phillip made no comment for she had now stopped in front of a house that was larger than the others in the village. 'Here we are,' she said with a sigh of relief.

He stuffed the gown and wig behind a tub beside the door and followed her inside. There was no sign of the girls, but a child could be heard crying. A grey-haired man was seated at the table, but on their entry he jumped up, almost sending the plans spread out on the table flying.

'Who is this?' he asked, placing a hand over the plans as he stared at Phillip. 'I did not ask you to bring anyone here, Rebecca.'

'Simon, this is Master Phillip Hurst, who knew my father. We met in Witney and he kindly escorted me here,' she replied. 'Phillip, this is Master Caldwell, my brother-in-law.'

The two men shook hands. 'Rebecca's father used to work at my father's shipyard most summers,' said Phillip as way of introduction, wondering why the other man's hand trembled so much.

Simon Caldwell nodded jerkily. 'I recognise the name Hurst. Your father is dead, is he not?'

'That's right. My brother now has charge of

the yard. I believe you are a stonemason, Master Caldwell,' said Phillip politely.

'If you'll excuse me,' interrupted Rebecca quietly, 'I'll just go up to the children. I bid you good even, Phillip.'

'Good night, Becky,' he said, taking her hand and pressing it gently. 'Perhaps we'll see each other again before too long.'

She flashed him a smile, withdrew her hand and hurried out.

There was a silence after she left and Simon Caldwell fiddled with a drawing implement on the table. 'So, what are you doing in this area, Master Hurst?' he asked after a moment or two.

'I am just travelling through, but I might have need of a master mason to do some building work for me in the near future,' he said impulsively, 'so when Becky mentioned your name and occupation I was interested to meet you.'

'I see.' The other man ran a shaking hand through his iron-grey hair. 'I cannot make any promises. It might be best if you looked for another mason.'

Phillip was relieved, wondering why meeting Rebecca had caused him to broach a plan of action that he been considering this past year, but had decided was not feasible for at least another two years. 'Unfortunately, just like ship's carpenters, they are in short supply, so I am prepared to wait,' he said easily.

'If you are not in a rush, then that makes a difference.' Simon Caldwell's manner thawed but Phillip thought he still appeared a little on edge. 'You would recognise Rebecca's father if you saw him?' asked the older man abruptly.

Phillip was startled by the question. 'Aye, but Master Mortimer is dead, so I don't understand why you should ask such a question.'

Simon Caldwell cleared his throat. 'Master Hurst, do you believe in ghosts?'

Phillip's eyes narrowed. 'Obviously, you believe that you have seen one if you ask me such a question,' he said slowly.

'Have I seen a ghost or was it a figment of my overtired brain?' muttered Simon Caldwell, drumming his fingers on the table. 'You have to understand that I only met the man twice. He was most difficult to deal with, as you undoubtedly know, having served as his apprentice.'

Phillip nodded. 'All I can say is that I would rather he didn't come back from the dead.'

'Agreed,' said the other man, now gripping the table. 'Yet I cannot ignore the sighting. If the labourers were to believe Draymore Manor is haunted, they'd be off. You know what they say about ghosts?'

'That they have unfinished business here on earth,' said Phillip, understanding why the man should be so nervous. 'I presume Becky and the children have not seen this apparition?'

'Saints' teeth! You think I'd allow them to play around the manor house?' said the other man fiercely. 'Parts of the building are highly unstable. I'm thinking it's a mistake I ever brought them here.'

'Then send them home,' advised Phillip.

Simon Caldwell frowned. 'Rebecca is a woman of good sense, but she is only a woman and wouldn't be able to defend herself and my children against ruffians, Master Hurst.'

There was a short silence and then hesitantly Phillip said, 'If you would allow me to make a suggestion, Master Caldwell. On the morrow I will be travelling to Oxford as I have business there. If you are willing to entrust them to my care, I will provide them with my protection on the road.'

Master Caldwell looked relieved. 'That is generous of you. I must warn you that my son is an imp. A lovable lad, but an imp none the less.'

'I am certain Becky copes well with him,' reassured Phillip, although he had no idea at all if that were true or not but he felt this man was in need of help. 'Besides, I have nephews and a niece of my own and so am accustomed to children,' he added.

'Then I accept your offer with gratitude, Master Hurst.' This time when Simon Caldwell shook Phillip's hand, it was with enthusiasm.

Phillip decided there was little chance of seeing Rebecca again that evening to see if she approved of his actions and, as it was now dark, that he should make haste to Witney. 'I would appreciate it if you could inform Becky that I will call for her and the children shortly after dawn. I need to make an early start.'

Simon Caldwell thanked him again and escorted him to the door.

As Phillip left the house, he pondered how Rebecca would accept the news that he would be escorting her to Oxford. She might resent his interference and not wish for his company, as it was obvious that she had cared for her husband. It seemed that Giles had replaced Nicholas in her heart, although now her husband was dead, she might wish to marry again. When his brother eventually arrived home, it would be best if he took a wife and settled down. Phillip frowned, remembering how he and Nicholas had discussed women, love and marriage whilst in their cups on the Greek isle of Rhodes. In truth, they had wagered two gold pieces on which of them would marry the first—the remaining one being the victor. Worryingly, it was some time since there had been news of Nicholas and he could only pray that he was safe.

Phillip was halfway to Witney when he remembered he had left his costume stuffed behind the tub beside the front door. Hopefully it would not rain during the night. Maybe Becky would notice it and take it in? *Becky!* He was glad he would be seeing her on the morrow. What would they talk about on the journey? What would she think of Master Caldwell's mention of having seen her father's ghost? Somehow he could not imagine her dismissing it lightly, but it was not for him to discuss the matter with her. Even though both of them, no doubt, preferred him to remain buried in the past.

Chapter Two

Rebecca had spent a restless night and woke from a dream in which she was wiping the paint from Pip Hurst's almost-perfect features amongst other things. The intimacy of the vision unsettled her and she wondered why the Almighty had decided that now was the time for their paths to cross again. Whilst married to Giles she had prayed that she would forget Pip and had managed, most of the time, to put him out of her mind. Then she had seen him at Greenwich Palace and the desire she had felt for him had been reignited and he had figured prominently in her thoughts after that. She felt hot and bothered thinking about those times. Now here he was, but still as unattainable. Despite his flattering words, he'd made it plain there was no room for a wife in his life. It also appeared that he believed that she had been in love with his brother, Nicholas, until Giles had come along. Obviously, he did not suspect that it was Pip, himself, that she had lusted after. It was true that she admired the older Hurst brother, who had kept a journal of his travels in the Americas. How excited she had felt when she had held a copy and read the words for herself! Pip and her friend, Lady Beth Raventon, who had inherited her father's printing-and-stationery business in London, had shared the preparation of getting the journal into print as a birthday gift for Nicholas six years ago.

The book had sold well and, after Rebecca had blurted out how much she wished she could read the book for herself, Beth had taught her to read and write. It had proved a task that had given them both great pleasure. But however much she had enjoyed the book, Rebecca had never considered Nicholas Hurst, explorer and merchant, as a possible husband for herself. After Beth had married her guardian, Sir Gawain Raventon, Nicholas had sailed away and disappeared from Rebecca's life.

A sigh escaped her and she turned over in bed. It was at times like these that she had missed Giles during those first weeks after he had died. A child would have been such a comfort. Fortunately her desire for children had been partially satisfied in helping to care for her young nephew and his half-sisters. But now Phillip had re-entered her life, she could not deny that he affected her still in a way no other man had ever done. Yet would she ever see him again? By the time she had left James sleeping, Simon had gone to bed and Phillip had vanished, just as her mother had done, without any words of hope for her to cling to that they might ever see each other again.

Rebecca felt that sense of rejection experienced on waking as a child, knowing that her mother had not loved her enough to want her company. She sighed, knowing there was nothing else to do but to get on with life. She noticed that it was getting light. Time to get up. She dressed swiftly and as silently as possible and, lifting the latch with care, slipped through the gap between door and jamb. She went downstairs and outside to fetch water from the butt by the door. She had a drink, then she spotted Phillip's gown and wig. She felt her pulses quicken. He would be needing them that day, so perhaps she should take them to him. It should not be so difficult to find the covered wagon he had spoken of.

She fetched her cloak and set out towards Witney, hurrying up the hill, past a stream that dashed over rocks on its journey to the valley floor. The water was so clear that one could see the pebbles at the bottom and darting fish. It was as she rounded the foot of the hill that she caught sight of Phillip going up the hill in the direction of Draymore Manor House. Her heart leapt. The house was situated a short distance from the village of Minster Draymore and hidden by trees. How odd. Before she could call out to him, he disappeared from her sight. Had he come to collect the gown and wig and taken the wrong path? She set off in his wake. When she reached the brow of the hill she could see the surrounding area as far as the church spire of St Mary's in Witney, but there was no sign of Phillip. She dithered, trying to decide whether to remain where she was and to watch out for his return or to walk to the manor house.

Several birds flying up from the trees below made her think they had been disturbed by Phillip's passing and she set off in that direction. She passed through the copse until the trees opened out to reveal an overgrown garden and a path in need of weeding that led up to front door of the manor house. It was a heavy door with studs on it and she had not really expected it to give way when she gripped the sturdy metal ring set in the wood, but the door creaked open. She hesitated before entering, remembering that Simon had told her to stay away from the house and not to take the children there as it was not safe. Even so, if the door was unlocked, that meant he must have forgotten to lock it yesterday.

She placed the gown and wig in the corner behind the door and gazed about the hall. It was small in comparison to the one at Raventon; there was a pile of rubble and one of the walls appeared to be crumbling in places. She guessed that the building dated back maybe more than two hundred years ago to the time of Edward II who had married a French princess, Isabella. This royal lady had taken a lover called Mortimer, the first Earl of March, who had lived at Ludlow Castle. That Rebecca and her brother shared the same surname had caused Davy to wonder aloud whether they were descended from Mortimer and Isabella, who, if she had been a man, would have become the ruler of France. Such ancestry was what caused King Henry to fund the Holy Roman Emperor, Charles, betrothed to Henry's daughter, Mary, to fight the French in the hope that at least his descendants would sit on the throne of France if Charles was the victor in that conflict. Rebecca was of the opinion that the closer one was to the throne, the more dangerous life could be. Mortimer, lover of Isabella, had been executed for treason, although she and their offspring had been pardoned by Edward III. She wondered what Phillip thought about King Henry and his ambitions in France and whether one day he would write a play about such stirring royal events from the past.

She came to a decision and walked carefully across the hall to a door at the far end, noticing that some of the walls were blackened with smoke. She was startled by a shout and her first instinct was to head straight back to the front door and outside. Then she heard a banging and a crash; hesitating no longer, she ran towards the sound, almost tripping over a clump of fallen stone, thinking perhaps that Phillip might be under attack from ruffians. She came to a small chamber. The door was half off its hinges and on the opposite wall was shelving. Possibly it had once been a still room. There was a smashed jar on the uneven floor and a couple shrouded in cobwebs on a shelf. The room appeared to be empty, but cautiously she went inside to make certain, stepping over more rubble. The next moment she felt an arm go round her throat. Fearing she would be choked to death, she sank her teeth into the wrist of her attacker. Her captor released her and she wasted no time in trying to escape, but he seized hold of her again. With fists flying, she aimed for his chest, only to realise that it was Phillip.

'Damn it, Becky, what are you doing here?' he said harshly, seizing both her wrists and holding her arms aloft.

'I was searching for you, but I didn't realise that my attacker would be the person I sought!' she cried. He released her abruptly and she fell against him. Instantly, she was aware of the hardness of his chest and the heat emanating from him as his arm slipped around her. 'What a fright you gave me!' she gasped. 'I was convinced you were about to throttle me!'

'I thought you were the ghost,' he said drily. 'As soon as you bit me, I knew better.'

'Ghost! What ghost?' She glanced about her.

He hesitated. 'The one Simon Caldwell believes he saw. I caught a glimpse of a figure a short while ago and called out to it, but then it disappeared, so perhaps there really is a spirit abroad.' A faint smile played about his lips.

'But you attacked me and I'm obviously no ghost,' said Rebecca reasonably.

'That's because I heard footsteps and I thought *only the living could be responsible for that and maybe it was someone who could intend me harm.*' He lifted his wrist and inspected the marks left by her teeth and cocked an eyebrow.

'I'm sorry I bit you but it did the trick, didn't it?' She placed her hand on his and gazed at the red indentions. 'I don't think I'm poisonous, but perhaps some salve on the wound?'

He made a noise in his throat. 'At least I know you can defend yourself if necessary.'

'Very graciously said,' she murmured, looking thoughtful. 'I wonder why Simon made no mention of a ghost to me.'

'He did not want to frighten you,' said Phillip, removing her hand. 'Be careful where you step,' he warned.

The words were no sooner out of his mouth than Rebecca tripped over the pile of rubble and ended up flat on the floor. 'Ouch, that hurt!'

He went down on one knee in front of her and his blue eyes were dark with concern. 'Are you all right?'

'Just help me up, if you please,' she groaned.

He took her hand and jerked her to her feet without realising his own strength so that she was catapulted against him. This time he almost lost his balance and for several moments they swayed back and forth on the uneven floor, their bodies pressed against each other and their faces only inches apart. It was strangely comforting, thought Rebecca, in no hurry to have him release her this time.

Then he kissed her.

The temptation to taste her lips had been irresistible, thought Phillip. Her lips were as cool as spring water and as she made no attempt to pull away, he deepened the kiss and delved between their moist softness and captured her tongue. It was a while since he had kissed a woman and never had he found it so arousing. Then he remembered that she did not think much of a player's way of life and dropped her like a hot brand and walked away.

It was several moments before a now-seething Rebecca recovered her equilibrium and was able to pick herself up off the floor. Giles had never kissed her in such a thoroughly penetrating fashion, but neither had he ever used her so roughly. How dare Phillip kiss her and then cast her aside as if he couldn't bear to look at her! Obviously he had no thought for her feelings at all. Hurt and anger coursed through her veins and, after taking several deep breaths, she marched out of the room, careful to avoid any obstructions.

He was nowhere to be seen. Had he left her alone in this place, prey to ghosts or vagabonds? She made for the front door and there she found Phillip resting against the door jamb. She waited for him to speak, but after what seemed a long time, she came to the conclusion that he was not going to refer to what had happened. Well, she was not going to allow him to ignore the episode. It might be true that she had enjoyed the kiss, but if he was now regretting what had happened, she was not going to let him know that. Most likely he had kissed lots of women over the years and had enjoyed doing so. Lackwit that she was to think that just because the kiss had set her whole body alight, that it had done the same for him. Misery threatened to flood her, but then she remembered that part of a man's anatomy that had trouble sleeping. His had flared into life as he had kissed her and flaunted itself against her belly. A definite indication that he had desired her, if only for a moment, before rejecting her.

'I should have slapped your face,' she said.

'I'm amazed that you didn't!' He straightened up. 'I didn't intend to behave so, but you were irresistible.'

'Was I? Well, that's good to know,' she replied, taken aback. 'I—I presume you're not going to make a habit of it?'

He gave a ghost of a smile. 'Probably not, you'll be pleased to know.'

'Good, because we both know that we wouldn't

suit. You're not in the market for a wife and I have nothing to bring you that would be of help in making your way in the world. Although I am not such a fool to believe that kissing a woman means a man must feel compelled to propose marriage.' She dimpled at him in an attempt to reassure him that she had decided to make light of the situation, despite the fact that she ached to be held in his arms again.

Phillip found those dimples bewitching and experienced a further rush of desire, but it was obvious that she saw no future for them together, so all he said was, 'I'm glad that we've got that sorted out. Shall we go?'

She nodded, picked up the gown and wig. 'You forgot these last even.' He took them from her, thanked her and closed the door before heading towards the trees. 'Was the ghost the reason you're up and about so early this morning or were you on your way to collect your costume? I saw your gown and wig and decided to bring them to you. I was doing so when I spotted you.'

'And your curiosity got the better of you when you saw me?'

'I can't deny it.' Her brow puckered. 'Do you mind telling me about this figure you thought you saw?'

'I do not doubt what my eyes saw, Becky, but

I didn't get close enough to make out the identity of the man.'

'Then can you tell me what Simon told you?'

Phillip's eyes locked with hers, but still he hesitated.

'Please, of your courtesy, I would like to know. There is obviously some mystery here that needs solving. I do have a talent for such.'

'If I do tell you, I want you to bear in mind that he believes it possible that his mind was overtired and he might have imagined what he saw.'

She nodded. 'That goes without saying.'

Phillip took a breath. 'He thought he saw your father's ghost.'

Rebecca felt a peculiar sensation shoot down her spine and the ground appeared to rock. The last thing she wanted was her father to return to haunt her from beyond the grave—why should he appear to Simon? And why here, of all places? It had to be a figment of his imagination. 'I don't believe it!' she said, a tremor in her voice.

'Neither do I,' said Phillip firmly. 'But it's interesting, isn't it? And why should he appear here? Is it possible that your father has kin living in the area?'

Rebecca took a deep breath. 'As far as I know he had no kin. At least he never mentioned any to me, but then he never saw any reason to discuss anything of importance with me,' she said bitterly. 'I was only his daughter.'

'My mother would have loved a daughter, so don't pull yourself down. Your father was a fool not to appreciate your worth.'

'You're just being kind,' she muttered. 'Anyway, we've strayed from the subject.'

He frowned. 'Think the worse of yourself then, woman! Tell me instead, is it worth asking the people who live in Minster Draymore about your father?'

'Surely Simon would have thought of that? Unless he didn't want to look a fool. Besides, could he be looking for me?' She looked up at him from scared eyes.

'Then why come here? Why not seek you out in Oxford?' he asked reasonably.

Rebecca forced down her fear and smiled. 'You don't know how much your saying that relieves my mind.'

Phillip returned her smile. 'Maybe there is no ghost and it was a real person I caught a glimpse of?'

'He could have been a vagabond and reacted violently. My next question is—do you think we should speak of this to Simon? He's normally a man of good sense, but if he mentioned this to you, then it really is playing on his mind.'

Phillip was silent a moment, then said, 'The person who might know if your father had other kin is your brother.'

Rebecca's eyes met his and she nodded. 'But how am I going to get a message to him? I'd have to pay a messenger and I don't have that kind of money.'

'I would go myself if I had the time, but—'

'I would not ask it of you,' said Rebecca hastily. 'He might get in touch with me himself before Christmastide, so perhaps I should just wait a while. In the meantime I will see what I can discover here.'

'I don't think that will be possible now,' said Phillip, taking her arm. 'I'm leaving for Oxford this morning and I offered to escort you and the children home.'

She felt that peculiar leap of the heart. 'I—I can't believe you'd want the bother of three young children as well as myself on the journey.'

'No, I don't,' he said, straight-faced, 'but I could see their poor father was desperate and, as I am heading in that direction, I thought it would be good for you to experience the travelling life, albeit briefly.'

She gave him a severe look. 'I deem you are

teasing me. You are forgetting, Phillip, that I do have some experience of such due to having travelled about with my father for his work. Still, it is generous of you to make such an offer and I accept it gladly. But why is it that you go to Oxford? I cannot believe that you do it purely for my benefit.'

'God forbid! Why should I want to travel with you, knowing that you can be a shrew at times?' he said in a mocking voice. 'You must have forgotten that it is St Giles's fair today. We plan to perform there. Also, I have been asked by the Raventons to take a look at a vacant property in the town with the idea of setting up a print room, stationer's and book shop there.'

Rebecca's eyes lit up. 'I had no idea. But why would they ask you to do that?'

'I act on behalf of Nicholas, who has shares in the Raventons' business. It is some time since they and my brother and I have heard from him and so—'

Her smile faded. 'When did you last hear from him?'

The muscles of Phillip's face tightened. 'Ten months or more, but you must not worry. It is not the first time he has left it for a while before getting word to us that he is safe.'

She placed a hand on his arm. 'But still you must be anxious.'

'It would be dreadful, indeed, if there were to be no more tales of his adventures,' said Phillip lightly. 'But let us not lose hope. Tell me, by what means did you travel here?'

Rebecca accepted the change of subject and removed her hand from his arm. 'On horseback. I had two of the children up with me and Margaret, the eldest, rode pillion with Simon.' She bit her lip. 'I've just realised he will need his horse and mine cannot bear four of us.'

'I suggest the two youngest children travel in the wagon where Tabitha can keep an eye on them.'

Rebecca seized on the mention of a woman. 'Tabitha? You have a woman in your troupe?'

He smiled. 'I couldn't manage without her. She cooks for us and takes care of the costumes, as well as telling us exactly what she thinks of our performance. She also acts as a prompter if any of us should forget our lines. She is good with children and I'm sure the pair of you will rub along.'

Rebecca felt a pang of envy that he should think so highly of this woman. 'What is she like?'

'Young and pretty. She was in dire straits

when we came upon her in Coventry, a couple of years ago. Some quick action was called for and we carried her off. It soon proved that we had made the right decision.'

Rebecca found herself almost hating this paragon of virtue despite never having set eyes on her. 'I look forward to meeting her,' she said stiffly, thinking that although Phillip had told her there was no room in his life for a wife, he still had a man's needs. Really he should not have kissed her if he had a mistress! The pleasure she had felt earlier at the thought of travelling to Oxford in his company evaporated, but she could hardly say that she had changed her mind about doing so.

'Shall we make haste?' said Phillip. 'It's a good four leagues to Oxford and I want to be there in plenty of time to make ready for this evening's performance.'

When they reached the house, it was to find Simon talking to the woman from the neighbouring cottage. When he saw Rebecca and Phillip, he brought the conversation to an end and approached them.

'There you are! I was wondering what had happened to you, Rebecca. Has Master Hurst divulged our plan to you?'

'Indeed he has,' said Rebecca, deciding to make no mention of her father's apparition. 'I will go and see if the children need help getting ready.'

She went indoors, thinking she must also don a pair of riding breeches under her skirts. She was greeted by eight-year-old Margaret, who was fair-haired, with a spare frame and a fussy manner. 'There you are, Aunt Rebecca! Father says that we are going home today.'

'Indeed, we are, love,' said Rebecca, forcing a smile. 'Are you not pleased?'

The girl nodded. 'I hear we are to be travelling with a Master Hurst who owns the shipyard where your father worked.'

'It is his brother who owns the shipyard,' corrected Rebecca, 'but the rest is true. I'm sure you will like him.'

'Is he the man who is with Father now?' whispered Elizabeth, the younger daughter who was small and chubby.

'Aye, it is. You and James will be riding in a covered wagon. Is that not exciting?' said Rebecca.

'What d'you mean a covered wagon?' demanded Margaret, pausing in the act of fastening her shoe.

'Master Hurst is a member of a troupe of travelling players and they are going to Oxford to perform at St Giles's fair,' answered Rebecca.

'How exciting!' cried Elizabeth. 'Will he drive his wagon right up to the house, so Mama can see us arrive?' she asked, her brown eyes sparkling.

'I—I—I want to go home,' said four-year-old James, pressing himself against Rebecca and hugging her knees. 'I—I—I mith Mama.'

She lifted him up on her knee. 'I know, sweeting, and I would have risked the highway on our own to take you there, but your father would not allow it. Fortunately, Master Hurst is to escort us, so all is well.' She kissed his rosy cheek. 'You do know that you must be on your best behaviour? I do not want Master Hurst regretting his offer.'

'I be good,' said James, nodding solemnly.

If only I could believe that, thought Rebecca wryly, aware that four leagues was a long journey for a small boy. Well, she would just have to hope for the best. Few women would like to have two boisterous young ones thrust on them for such a journey, but hopefully this Tabitha would accept the situation without complaint.

After a breakfast of bread, butter and eggs, washed down with small ale, they made their way outside. The horse was saddled up and, after taking their farewell of their father, the two youngest children were lifted on to the back of the horse by Phillip. He took it upon himself to lead the beast before Rebecca could protest that she was quite able to do that herself. She pecked Simon on the cheek and he slipped several coins into her hand, saying they were for anything the children might need on the journey.

She thanked him and set out to walk beside the animal with Margaret next to her and Phillip the other side. Elizabeth chattered to her sister in a high voice that informed Rebecca that she was a little nervous about being up on the horse without Rebecca to cling on to.

They had not travelled far when Phillip suggested that the children might like to hear a story. Instantly they chorused agreement, as did Rebecca, who was far from averse to listening to one of his tales to while away the journey. She was surprised when he launched into the fable of the tortoise and the hare. By the time he had finished they had arrived at the church in Witney and James was clamouring to get down and wanting to be a tortoise.

'And the moral of this story is—?' asked Rebecca.

'You tell me,' responded Phillip, raising his eyebrows.

'Don't be over-confident or look down on others who appear less able than yourself. This isn't one of your own creations, is it?'

Phillip's eyes narrowed. 'You've heard it before?'

She nodded. 'If I'm not mistaken, it was written by a Greek slave hundreds of years ago and you won't find it in any book written in English.'

'I wager Beth Raventon told you that. I know she stocked a Latin translation in the London shop and she is extremely well read.'

Rebecca smiled. 'I wouldn't deny it. I have a lot to thank Beth for. She has been extremely generous with her time and sharing her books with me.'

'I was told the story by Frederick, who was my mentor when I first left the shipyard. You'll be meeting him soon and it'll probably surprise you to hear that Frederick was a scholarly cleric who has travelled widely, including to Greece and its islands. He translated the story for me to turn into a play, as well as some of the Greek tragedies.'

'Tragedies?' She pursed her lips. 'There doesn't sound much to amuse one in such plays.'

'You'd be surprised,' he said with a grin.

'There was also comedy in the Greek theatre, but it didn't really become popular until after the Peloponnesian Wars and was known as the New Comedy.'

She was impressed. 'You surprise me, Phillip. I never expected to hear of such from your lips. Do all strolling players know of the Greek plays?'

'No, but I have visited Greece and one of its islands myself,' he said, doubly taking her by surprise. 'But some like Frederick studied at Oxford. Here he comes now,' said Phillip.

Rebecca turned to see an elderly bald man limping towards them. 'About time you made an appearance, Pip,' he grumbled. 'We need to be on our way. The road will be busy and we don't want to be held up.' Even as he spoke, his rheumy eyes were on Rebecca and the children. 'These are them, are they? They look a motley crew. Let's get the young 'uns inside the wagon and they'd best behave themselves.'

Elizabeth gazed up at him nervously and James clung to Rebecca's skirts and sucked his thumb. 'Come, children, no need to be frightened of ol' Frederick,' said a woman, poking her head out from beneath the canvas flap of the hood. 'He's got no authority in here. It's me that says what's what.'

'May I introduce Tabitha to you,' said Phillip, lifting up one of the children. 'Tabitha, this is Mistress Rebecca…' he hesitated before adding '…Clifton—and her nieces and nephew.'

Tabitha nodded a welcome as she seized hold of Elizabeth. 'Pleased to meet you, Mistress Clifton.'

'Thank you for your help,' said Rebecca hastily, taking in the other woman's appearance. She was not in the least like how she would have expected a mistress of Phillip's to look. Beneath a man's cap, she wore her fair hair frizzed on her forehead and about her ears. She had a fresh complexion and was clad in a garment that appeared to be a man's shirt. The draw strings at its neck were unfastened to reveal a generous expanse of cleavage. Suddenly there came a baby's cry from the wagon's interior and Tabitha jerked her head in that direction. 'There Edward goes again, but as soon as we get moving he'll quieten down and won't be any bother.'

'You have a child?' blurted out Rebecca. *Was it possible that Phillip had fathered a son?*

'Aye, has Master Phillip not explained our situation?'

'No, I haven't, Tabitha,' said Phillip, glancing at Rebecca. 'I didn't see any need for anyone else to know what is your private business.'

'Fair enough,' said Tabitha. 'But Mistress Clifton might like babies and will wish to see him, and the children will certainly want to play with my manikins.'

'What manikins?' asked Elizabeth, clinging on to Tabitha's shoulder, her eyes alight.

'You'll see soon enough,' said Tabitha kindly. 'Now, what about your little brother?'

Rebecca was aware of Phillip's eyes on her. His mention of *private business* had made her feel the outsider she was, but that did not make it any easier for her to accept. She glanced at the woman's hands and saw that she wore no ring. The child must be Tabitha's bastard, but was it Phillip's? How could Tabitha smile so easily in such a situation and how did she cope with a baby and the travelling life? She allowed Phillip to take James and lift him up, so enabling Tabitha to seize hold of him and hoist him into the wagon.

'Can't I go in the wagon, too?' asked Margaret wistfully.

'If you don't mind being squashed, then you're welcome,' said Tabitha, beaming down at her. 'Here's Jack and Ned now. We'll soon be on our way.'

Margaret stood on the rim of the wheel and was helped up into the wagon. Rebecca turned to her horse, but before she could hoist herself up on to its back Phillip had seized her by the waist and lifted her off her feet and dumped her on the saddle. She was caught unawares, so that she slipped sideways. She jumped as he placed a hand beneath her bottom and pushed her back into the saddle. She had to bite back the rebuke that hovered on the tip of her tongue, hating the thought of his being intimate with the other woman. She did not know how she managed to smile so sweetly when Phillip introduced her to the two other members of the troupe.

They had returned with loaves of bread and something savoury smelling in a napkin. One was the youth who had passed round the hat last evening and was called Jack and he looked a little wan. The other appeared to be slightly older than Phillip and was named Ned. They nodded in way of greeting. Then Ned handed up the food to Tabitha before going to the horse's head, whilst Jack had a low-voiced conversation with Phillip before helping Frederick up into the wagon. Phillip mounted the other horse and gave the signal to walk on. As the other two men were on foot, they kept the horses reined in.

For a while Phillip and Rebecca had not spoken. She was pondering on the duplicity of men, when he said abruptly, 'No doubt you have noticed that Tabitha does not wear a wedding ring, even though she has a child.'

'You do not have to explain. You made it quite clear that it was no business of mine.' Rebecca's voice was cool and she did not look at him.

'Even so, I do not wish you to draw the wrong conclusion. It isn't at all what you might think.'

Rebecca's hand tightened on the reins. 'I deem it a shameful situation for a young unmarried woman with a baby to have no proper home to raise that child. You mentioned the troupe having no winter quarters. Could you not ask your brother, Christopher, to take her and the child into his household when the weather worsens?'

'I would if the father did not object to it,' said Phillip.

His words took her unawares and she spoke without thinking. 'Aren't you the father?'

He shot her a glance and snapped, 'You really shouldn't jump to conclusions. Ned is Edward's father, not me.'

She felt her cheeks burning. 'I do beg your pardon.'

'At least I know what you think of my morals,' said Phillip in a hard voice.

Her colour deepened. 'I admit I was wrong

to judge you. Your private life really is none of my business.'

'No, it is not.' He felt deeply hurt that she should think ill of him. What had he ever done that she should think so badly of him? Surely that one passionate kiss he had pressed upon her earlier was not the cause? Suddenly he remembered what she had said last even about seeing him at court surrounded by ladies. Perhaps she thought he had set one or even two of them up as his flirts as well! If only she knew how he never knew what to say to them when he was just simply Pip Hurst, playwright, and not Phillip Hurst, actor. Suddenly he noticed that her hands trembled on the reins and instantly knew he had to take the sting out of their exchange and searched for the right words. He cleared his throat. 'Yet I suppose by my offering to help you, I have invited you into my world and left myself open to your judgement. You do seem to care about Tabitha and her baby, but I am presented with a dilemma.'

'Are you wondering how to bring pressure to bear on Ned to marry her and provide them with a home?'

Phillip shook his head as if in despair. 'You're doing it again. Jumping to conclusions. Tabitha and Ned married once the child was on its way, but he cannot afford to buy her a wedding ring. Its lack matters to them both. I offered him the money to buy her one, but met with a refusal.'

'I see,' said Rebecca, feeling mortified. 'Again I beg your pardon for reading the situation wrongly. I wish I could help.'

'As it stands, all the money he makes goes on living expenses and putting a little by for winter. Soon he's going to have to decide whether, with a wife and baby, he can continue the life of a travelling player. Yet I know it will break his heart to give up acting. I wonder…' He hesitated.

'What do you wonder?' asked Rebecca.

'Whether your sister-in-law has room for a serving maid and if she would hire Tabitha and be prepared to accept the baby as well? Just for a short time whilst I sort lodgings out for the winter?' His blue eyes met hers.

Rebecca thought that here was a way for her to make amends for misjudging him. 'I am certainly willing to put the idea to Jane. At the moment she is not the easiest person to live with, but, as she is with child, allowances must be made. Have you spoken to Ned about it?'

'I have only just thought of it.' Phillip's brow knitted. 'It's possible he will refuse to allow it, even if your sister-in-law agreed. Let us hope we make a decent sum this evening. Now the nights are drawing in, there won't be many more performances, unless some lord asks for the troupe especially. It is different for me. Not only do I have my writing, but I can always return to shipbuilding. I am not short of ways to make money.'

'You are fortunate in your brothers,' she said earnestly. 'And this year it has been a good year?'

'For me, aye. If it were not that I was worried for Nicholas's safety, I could almost be happy.' He paused before adding, 'If I receive news of him when next I visit the shipyard, then I will find a way of letting you know.'

She thanked him, thinking that Phillip still seemed to be of a mind that she cared for his brother. She should never have agreed that she had been in love with him when they were younger.

They both fell silent.

An idea suddenly occurred to her, but it remained unspoken. Rather she wanted it to come as a surprise and she thought he might prevent her from acting in a way that he might consider foolish in the light of her own situation. In the meantime she must consider what to say to Jane, to persuade her to hire Tabitha and allow her to have her baby with her. Maybe she might also be willing to hire Ned, temporarily, to do all those tasks around the house and in the garden that were more suited to a man.

Chapter Three

'Will you be in the audience this evening?' asked Phillip, passing a sleeping James up to Rebecca. They had reached Oxford, the wagon coming to a halt on one of the vacant plots just inside the city walls, close to the North Gate, the other side of which was St Giles Street.

'I shouldn't think so, although I would like to watch another of your performances. I assume you'll still be here on the morrow if you're visiting the property in which the Raventons are interested?' she said, carefully settling the boy into the crook of her arm.

'Aye, but I won't be putting on another play. I must make for Greenwich soon.' He noted her softened expression as she gazed down at the slumbering child and wondered how she felt about not having a child of her own when she had the task of caring for her nephew. For the first time ever, he wondered what it would be like to have a son.

Rebecca glanced at him and the expression in his eyes caused her to feel slightly breathless. 'What is it? Is there something else you wished to say to me?'

'Will you mention Tabitha's situation to your sister-in-law?'

'Aye. I am certain I can persuade her to meet her,' said Rebecca, an idea occurring to her which she decided to keep to herself.

'Thank you.' He suddenly appeared to feel awkward. 'I don't have your direction and I will need it if I am to visit you with news of Nicholas.'

'Of course, your brother,' she said, her voice subdued, 'I do hope you have good tidings of him soon.' She gave Phillip directions to the Caldwells' house and added, 'I must have a word with Tabitha before I go. If I don't see you again, I pray that you have a safe journey and I thank you again for your escort.'

'It was my pleasure,' he said, placing a hand over hers and pressing it gently, before turning away and going to speak to Frederick.

For a moment she stared after him with an odd little ache inside her and then she called over to Tabitha, who was speaking to the girls. She hastened over to her. 'Is there aught else you wish me to do for you, Mistress Clifton?' she asked eagerly.

Rebecca smiled and removed Giles's wedding ring and held it out to Tabitha. 'I no longer have need of this and I would like you to have it.'

The other woman stared at the silver ring with a mixture of emotions warring on her pretty features. 'I can't take it. It's far too precious!'

'Please, do have it!' urged Rebecca. 'I only wish it were gold.'

Tabitha reached out and gingerly took the ring. 'I don't know what Ned will say but I confess I'm hoping it will fit.'

'You can always wrap some thread round the back of the ring if it is too big,' said Rebecca, 'and that will make it a better fit.'

But Tabitha did not need to take such a precaution as the ring fitted securely enough not to slip from her finger. 'I do thank you, Mistress Clifton!' she said, beaming up at her. 'It's truly generous of you. As I've said, I don't know what Ned'll say as he's a proud man, but this ring is staying put until he can buy me one himself,' she said firmly, 'then I will return it to you.'

Rebecca smiled down at her, delighted by her reaction. 'I pray that all goes well with the performance this evening.' She delayed no longer, but called to the girls and told the horse to walk on. Margaret asked if she and Elizabeth could run on ahead and Rebecca gave her permission. Despite it being a fine evening, she doubted that Phillip and his troupe would get the size of audience that they had in Witney. Oxford had lost some of its status. In the past it had thrived as a manufacturing and market town, as well as playing an important role in government. Then the spinners and weavers had migrated to the countryside as more colleges of learning had been founded, increasing at least the town's reputation as a place of scholarship. The latest colleges were Brasenose and Corpus Christi, founded in the last fifteen years.

Rebecca kept the horse to a walk along Broad Street and past Balliol College before turning into a street near the opening to Lincoln College and thence into High Street, where the university church of St Mary the Virgin was situated. She thought of Simon and the alterations he was to oversee inside the building before too long. Thinking of him, she pondered on what Phillip had told her about her father's so-called ghost and of the kiss he had pressed upon her at Draymore Manor. She was obviously more desperate than she would have believed for that physical contact that she had missed since Giles's death. The remembrance of that kiss sent a pleasurable warmth through her and also a yearning to be held in Phillip's arms again and for them to take up where they had left off and go much further.

She sighed. How could she contemplate such activity when she had believed him capable of having more than one mistress? She might have misjudged him, but she had seen with her own eyes how attractive he was to the women of Henry's court. She felt a stab of jealousy and knew she must not obsess about him. She glanced about her, thinking she might catch sight of Jane amongst those who had come into town for the fair. In two months she would be confined to the house, preparing herself for the birth of her child, but there was no sign of her now.

Eventually Rebecca caught up with the girls, a short distance from their home. The house was constructed of the yellowish stone of the Cotswolds and had been designed and built by Simon and his team of labourers. The front garden would soon be a mass of those purple daisies named for that leader of angels called Michael, whose feast day was at the end of September.

Rebecca called down to Margaret to take James. The boy woke as she passed him to her niece and instantly he struggled to get down. The front door opened as Rebecca dismounted and Jane made an appearance. Despite being six months' pregnant, she lifted her son up into her arms and smothered his face in kisses, demanding to know how it was that they had arrived home earlier than she expected.

'We came home in a covered wagon, Mama,' said Margaret smugly.

'And Tabitha allowed us to play with her manikins,' said Elizabeth, dancing around her stepmother. 'They had jointed wooden arms and legs that I could move.'

Jane glanced at Rebecca. 'What is this all about? Where is Simon?'

'He is still at Minster Draymore,' replied Rebecca. 'And you should not be lifting James. He is far too heavy for you in your condition.' She reached out and took the boy from her sister-in-law and set him down. 'Besides, it will be good for him to stretch his legs.'

Jane gazed at her from lively brown eyes. 'I assume my husband has his reasons for packing you all off so soon and in a wagon.'

Rebecca pulled a face. 'We proved to be a distraction and he is determined to complete his task there before winter sets in. As for the aforementioned wagon, that belongs to Master Hurst and his troupe.'

'Master Hurst?' enquired Jane.

'The girls will tell you about him whilst I see to the horse.'

Jane fixed her with a hard stare. 'I would rather hear it from you!'

Rebecca lifted a hand in acknowledgement as she led the animal away to the stable to the rear of the house. After she had unsaddled the horse, despite her aching back, she made certain there was fresh straw, water and hay for the animal before returning to the house. There she found Jane and the children sitting in front of a blazing fire in the kitchen, eating thick slices of bread and butter.

'Where's Maud?' asked Rebecca, helping herself from the loaf on the table. 'Is she as unreliable as ever when I'm not here to chase after her?'

'At home with her mother,' replied Jane, glancing up. 'I hope you are not going to scold me in place of Simon. I really do not have need of her whilst I only have myself to care for. It has only been four days. I don't know why he insists on hiring her when she does as little as she can and has a habit of vanishing just when I do need her.'

'You know why,' said Rebecca softly. 'He doesn't like you being alone in the house.'

Jane rolled her eyes. 'He fusses too much. I am perfectly capable of taking care of myself. Now tell me, is the Master Hurst you spoke of the same person who wrote the book from which you read to me a while ago?'

Rebecca shook her head. 'No, that is Master Nicholas Hurst; this is his younger brother, Phillip. He will be appearing in a play here, in Oxford, this evening.'

Jane pulled a face. 'A player!'

'I know what that look means,' said Rebecca, spreading butter on bread. 'And you are mistaken. He is utterly respectable,' she said blandly. 'He and his troupe. Is there any ham?'

'No, I ate the last of it at midday,' murmured Jane, frowning as she watched her. 'Where is your wedding ring?'

Rebecca had given no thought to what to tell Jane about giving away that precious piece of jewellery and knew that she had to be careful how she answered because Jane had dearly loved her brother, Giles, and she had it fixed in her mind that Rebecca had felt the same and would never want another man. 'What would you do, Jane, if you met a young married woman with a child whose husband could not afford to buy her a wedding ring?'

Jane fixed her with a stare. 'You haven't!'

'I thought it was what Giles would want me to do. He so wanted a child, as did I, but we were not as fortunate as you,' said Rebecca, her voice uneven.

Jane's eyes filled with tears. 'I prayed earnestly that God would grant you the gift of a child, but it was not to be. Yet my brother loved all children and would want what was best for them.'

'I so agree,' said Rebecca. 'How well you knew your brother's generous spirit.'

'So who is this woman you have gifted his ring to?'

'Her name is Tabitha and I would like you to meet her,' said Rebecca. 'She is married to Ned, one of the travelling players.'

'A travelling player's wife!'

'I know exactly what you think about travelling players. I felt the same when Phillip Hurst first told me that was his dream. I thought he was quite mad wanting to write and act when he could earn a good living shipbuilding in his father's yard. But now I have seen him disguised and acting out several parts, I admit I was wrong. I can assure you, Jane, his troupe is well worth watching.' She bit into the bread and butter, chewed and swallowed. 'Phillip has also performed before the king.'

Jane sighed. 'I am not sure Giles would have approved of his ring being worn by a player's wife. Did Simon know Master Hurst was a player and not a shipwright?'

Rebecca did not immediately reply, but took a larger bite out of the bread and chewed in a manner that suggested that she was thinking deeply about the question. In a way she was vexed that Jane should still refer to the ring as belonging to Giles when it was hers to do with as she wished. Yet she knew how difficult her sister-in-law had found it, accepting the loss of her beloved brother. 'She is a mother just like you, Jane. Is that not more important? Phillip spoke to Simon and so it is likely that he mentioned his way of life whilst I was taking care of the children. They appeared quite easy in each other's company.' She dropped her voice. 'So much so that your husband told Phillip that he had seen a ghost. Of my father, would you believe?' Her throat felt suddenly tight, remembering her father's bouts of anger when he would tell her to get out of his sight.

The children glanced up at her. 'Papa didn't

mentioned a ghost to us,' said Elizabeth, her eyes widening.

'You weren't supposed to hear, Big Ears!' said Rebecca, having forgotten the children were there. 'I deem your father is working too hard and his mind played tricks on him.'

Jane looked worried. 'I'm sure you're right. He won't listen when I tell him that he should be taking life more easily now. I suppose having a young family makes him feel he must work as though he was in the first flush of youth. Still, it's very odd that it should be at Minster Draymore that he sees a ghost of your father. I remember your brother telling me that your father was born there.' She took a deep breath. 'Anyway, we've digressed. Your wedding ring—'

'You say Father was born there?' interrupted Rebecca. 'Davy never mentioned that to me. I wonder what else he hasn't told me,' she added crossly.

'I think you would like Master Hurst, Mama,' interrupted Margaret as she licked butter from her fingers. 'He has a face like one of the statues that Papa sculptured and placed in the garden.'

Jane said sternly, 'Are you saying he looks like a Greek god? I'll never understand why your father should wish to sculpture such images. Anyway, you obviously believe I am impressed by outer appearances. Let me tell you both that too many young ladies have been misled by handsome men, believing they are as good on the inside as they are on the outside. I hope you are listening to this, too, Rebecca!'

Rebecca cut herself another slice of bread. 'I'd have trouble not listening, Jane. But don't you consider it a mistake to judge a man purely by his appearance? Anyway, you have yet to meet him. Why don't you go and see him in the play this evening?' she suggested as if this was a sudden thought.

'Certainly not!' said Jane, shaking her head.

'Mama, you should go,' said Margaret, resting an arm on her stepmother's chair. 'He was kind to us and so were the rest of the troupe, especially Tabitha. They don't have much money and you could give them some for their performance.'

Jane looked surprised. 'So you like this Tabitha?'

'She takes care of the troupe, washing, cooking, sewing,' said Rebecca, glad that her niece by marriage had brought up the subject. 'But now that winter will soon be here, a wagon is hardly the best place for a baby; besides, there will be less work for the troupe. I was wondering...' She paused and bit her lip.

Jane stared at her. 'You wondered whether I would hire her in place of Maud?'

Rebecca smiled. 'How clever of you to read my mind. I'm certain you would find her more than satisfactory. She's good with children and you know how they tire you out at the moment.'

'That might be so, Rebecca, but why should I have need of someone to look after the children when I have you living here? I thought you enjoyed their company.'

Rebecca knew that she shouldn't feel annoyed by that comment. After all, she had a roof over her head and food in her belly and it wasn't costing her a penny to live here. But she worked hard for that privilege and although she was thanked for what she did and received several gifts a year, there were times when she felt put upon and wanted to kick over the traces. Regardless of these feelings, she knew that she had to be careful how she worded her response to Jane's question if she were to help Tabitha. 'I was thinking that Tabitha could step into my shoes if I wanted to spend some time with my brother. Giles was truly dear to both of us, I know, so I am sure you understand my need to see Davy now and then.'

Jane's brown eyes filled with tears again and she reached out and touched Rebecca's arm. 'Of course, I understand. I suppose the least I can do is to go and take a look at these players and Tabitha. But how will I recognise which one is Master Hurst when I have never met him?'

'I could go with you,' said Elizabeth eagerly.

Jane glanced at Rebecca. 'Well, what do you say to that?'

'It is not a play for children.'

'I see. Then you'd have to come with me and as there is no one to care for the children in your absence, it seems that is out of the question.'

Rebecca so wanted to see Phillip in the play again that she said swiftly, 'I shall go and fetch Maud and I will pay her myself if necessary with the money that is over from that which Simon gave me.' She did not wait for Jane to agree, but hurried from the house.

When Rebecca returned, she told Jane that Maud would be with them within the hour. 'Just enough time to allow me to change out of my travelling clothes and wash away the dust of the journey,' she said.

'I can see you're determined to have your way!' Jane pushed herself up from the table. 'You will have to carry a stool for me to sit upon, Becky,' she warned. 'And we will come away if there is aught of which I disapprove.'

'Of course,' said Rebecca, smiling warmly.

'I would not expect you to stand about in your condition. But I swear, Jane, that you will enjoy the performance and you will like Tabitha and approve of what I have done.' With a whisk of her skirts she hurried from the room and upstairs to her bedchamber. Despite her aches and pains and her impatience with her sister-in-law, her weariness had evaporated and she could not wait to see Phillip perform again.

A motley crowd had gathered on the open space where the wagon was parked and there was an excited buzz at the sound of a loud drumbeat and then another and another. The people hushed and the next moment a figure, unrecognisable as Phillip, stepped into the arena. Rebecca felt her pulse quicken as he began to speak.

As with most tales, this one had a moral and Rebecca, who had been too distracted last evening to consider fully what the play was about, now had time to think about its meaning as the story unfolded. She could not take her eyes from Phillip, who not only had the title role, but the difficult task of playing more than one part. He had to magically change himself from an old hag into a fair young woman with lightning speed.

The play came to an end and the cast took a bow to thunderous applause. Tabitha went round with the hat and beamed at Rebecca, who introduced her to Jane. Tabitha bobbed a curtsy as if she were a real lady. 'It's an honour to meet you, Mistress Caldwell.'

'At least you have pretty manners,' said Jane, her expression thawing. 'Tell me, how long will you be staying in Oxford?'

'That depends, mistress,' replied Tabitha earnestly. 'Master Hurst thinks we should stay for at least a sennight, I reckon. I have been told he has no need of me for that time.'

Jane gave her a nod and said no more and Tabitha continued taking round the hat. 'No doubt her husband will also appreciate some work,' said Jane, looking thoughtful as she stood up. 'Maybe I could use him in the garden. Tell me, Rebecca, which one of the players was Master Hurst?'

'I thought you would have asked before now,' said Rebecca, picking up the stool on which her sister-in-law had been seated. 'But I could see that you, too, were enraptured by the play. He had the title role, as well as that of the hag and the fair maiden.'

Jane's jaw dropped. 'Well, you do surprise me, Becky! It's a mystery to me how he managed those changes so swiftly. Beneath that paint no doubt he is as handsome as my stepdaughter thinks.' She took in a breath. 'Still, what is of more importance is the moral of the story. How interesting that it should be *don't judge by outer appearances, beauty is to be found within.* I'm sure you agree with me?'

'I think you'll find that the tale has several strands,' said a voice from behind them.

Rebecca whirled round to see Phillip standing there. He had changed out of his costume and removed the paint from his face and he did look as Margaret and Elizabeth had described him, handsome as a Greek god. 'May I introduce my sister-in-law, Jane Caldwell, Phillip. Jane, this is Master Phillip Hurst.'

Phillip inclined his flaxen head. 'It's a pleasure to meet you, Mistress Caldwell.'

Jane offered him her hand and he brushed it with his lips. She seemed a little flustered and cleared her throat before speaking. 'You played your parts well, Master Hurst. You have a definite talent for such tomfoolery but can you really make a living from it?'

'I have not yet starved and life is never dull,' said Phillip, smiling into her eyes.

Her colour deepened and she touched the crucifix about her throat and then clasped her hands tightly together. 'We were not put on this earth, Master Hurst, purely for our own pleasure.'

'I do so agree,' said Phillip, continuing to smile at her. 'But that doesn't mean that life cannot be interesting and amusing even when it might prove uncomfortable and dangerous.'

'I like my life to be comfortable and secure, Master Hurst, as I am sure does Rebecca,' said Jane, meeting his gaze squarely.

Phillip glanced at Rebecca. 'Yet she enjoys reading of my brother's adventures.'

'I certainly see nothing wrong with that,' said Rebecca, deciding it was time she took part in the conversation. 'A woman would not be allowed to live such a life, alas, so I have to live it vicariously.'

'*Alas,* Becky?' said Phillip, raising an eyebrow. 'You would have such adventures if you could?'

'God forbid that she should ever do so,' said Jane swiftly. 'I think it is time we were going.' She slipped her hand through Rebecca's arm. 'I enjoyed your play, Master Hurst, and wish you well. May the saints preserve you.'

Phillip thanked her for her kind words, but instead of moving away, he took the stool from Rebecca, saying, 'Let me carry this for you and escort you home. There will be cutpurses and other rogues on the streets this even, no doubt, and you might have need of a protector.'

'That is kind of you, Master Hurst,' said Jane.

He nodded briefly and without a word, he set off through the throng. Rebecca would have had no difficulty in keeping up with him if it had not been for Jane, who could not in any way match either pace. Soon they fell behind.

'Well, I have never met a man like him,' said Jane, clinging to Rebecca's arm. 'Charming, but he is now proving a disappointment. What is he thinking of going so far ahead of us when he is supposed to be guarding us?'

'It is odd, isn't it? I wouldn't have expected it of him,' said Rebecca, disappointed herself. She watched as Phillip paused on the corner of the street. He was looking their way, so she waved to him. He responded by jerking a thumb and disappearing from her sight.

'Now where has he gone?' asked Jane, her flushed face exasperated. 'I hope you aren't smitten like the girls by his handsome face, because I am certain dear Giles would not have approved of him.'

Rebecca was tempted to say that *dear Giles was dead* but was much too sensible to do so. Instead she followed in what she hoped was Phillip's wake. They turned the corner into High Street where she had last seen him.

'I assume he knows our destination,' panted

Jane. 'Please do not rush me, Becky. A fall at this stage in my pregnancy could prove serious.'

'There he is now!' cried Rebecca, recognising the back of Phillip's head and the spread of his shoulders beneath the russet-coloured woollen doublet. She was more than a little vexed with him herself, and puzzled. Why was he in such a rush? He was now approaching the Mitre Inn and fortunately he had slowed down. She watched what he did and pointed him out to Jane. 'He has put down your stool and is going into the inn!'

'Why is he doing that? My stool could be stolen. You make haste and get it, Rebecca,' said Jane, giving her a push.

Rebecca ran the few yards to the inn and picked up the stool. She deduced from the noise coming from within that there was a rowdy crowd inside. What should she do? Go in and find Phillip or simply wait here for Jane? Her sister-in-law made the decision for her by coming up and seizing her cloak. 'We shall not hang around here outside a common inn, Rebecca. It isn't seemly! We shall carry on home and if anyone should attempt to attack us, we have the stool to use in our defence. I am disappointed in Master Hurst. He looks fair, but his manners are foul. Obviously he likes to keep low company and is fond of strong drink.'

Rebecca did not believe that was the reason for Phillip entering the inn for one moment, but she was not going to argue with Jane in her condition. She must see her safely home before deciding what to do next. She was still annoyed with Phillip and hoped he had a good reason for his behaviour. She hoisted the stool high against her chest and set off with Jane in tow. It was with some relief that they arrived back at the house without mishap. Annoyingly there were no lights in the house and no sign of Maud.

'Where is that girl?' said Jane, collapsing in a chair.

'Perhaps she is upstairs with the children,' suggested Rebecca.

'If she is not, I will have a bone to pick with her. There should be a lantern lit down here at the very least,' said Jane, removing her gloves and peering at Rebecca through the gloom. 'What if the house had caught fire and no one here to save the children?'

Rebecca lit a candle from the embers of the fire and hurried towards the stairs. Jane rose to her feet and followed her. 'I will come with you.'

The children were sleeping, but there was no sign of Maud. Both women concluded that once they had fallen asleep, the unreliable Maud had decided to skip off home. 'That girl,' said Jane wrathfully. 'It will be the last time I employ her. Now let us to bed. It's been a long evening.'

Rebecca did not argue with her, but left Jane undressing. Instead of going into her own bedchamber, she crept downstairs, took a stout stick from the corner by the door and went outside. There was still some light in the sky, but soon night would descend like a black curtain. If she was going to find out why Phillip had gone into the tavern, then she would have to make haste. She had not gone far when she saw him coming towards her. He appeared to be slightly unsteady on his feet. Had he, after all, been drinking?

'Becky, there you are! You're safe,' he called hoarsely.

'No thanks to you,' she said coolly, stopping and waiting for him to reach her.

He came to a halt a few inches from her and his eyes were like narrow slits in his shadowy face. 'I can understand why you're angry with me...but I had to follow him and...the next moment I was jumped upon and had to fight my way out.' His words were slurred.

She frowned. 'Are you all right? You don't sound like yourself.'

'I—I'll be all right now I know you're safe.' His hand tightened on her arm and he swayed towards her. His thigh brushed her hip and a tremor went through her.

'Are you hurt?' she asked.

'I took a blow to the head.'

Rebecca reached up with gentle fingers. The breath hissed between his teeth as her searching hand found the injury. 'You're bleeding!' she cried.

'Aye, it hurts like hell!' muttered Phillip.

'Who did this to you?'

'I do not know.' He stared at her from beneath drooping eyelids. 'Fortunately there was little money in my purse. I suppose I should be grateful that it was no worse, but I lost *him*.'

She glanced behind Phillip, but could see little, for the mist was coming down over the river and spreading. 'Let's get away from here. You might have been followed.'

He gripped her shoulder and staggered forwards, forcing her along with him. She hung on to him, struggling to keep them both upright, concerned about the effects from the blow to his head. 'Who is this *man* you mentioned? Is he the reason you suddenly disappeared into the Mitre?'

'Is that the name of the inn? I followed him inside, but then I lost sight of him. I thought he might have left by the rear entrance, so I went that way, but there was no sign of our ghost. He had disappeared,' muttered Phillip. 'I went up the alley to the rear and it was then I was attacked.'

'Our ghost?' she asked, her heart thudding as she remembered what he had told her earlier that day. 'You're not saying that you saw my father again?'

Phillip stopped abruptly and she tripped over his foot. This time it was he who pulled her upright. 'If it wasn't your father's ghost, then it was someone extremely like him. I spotted him just as we set off after the play finished. He had your father's walk and then I caught a glimpse of his profile and I was certain it was him. I determined to catch up with him and confront him.'

'You're sure you weren't mistaken?'

'There's nothing wrong with my eyesight,' he said crossly.

'Then my father must have a brother or a cousin, but if that is so why has he never been mentioned?'

Phillip freed a sharp laugh and forced himself to move on again. 'That's easy. Every family has its secrets.'

'I don't doubt it, but an apparition?' She sighed. 'Perhaps it's best if we drop this matter for now. As soon as I get you indoors, I will see to your wound.'

Phillip squinted at her. 'I don't want to be a

bother to you. Frederick can attend it when I get back to the wagon.'

'Don't be a fool!' she said fiercely. 'You'll never find the way in the dark. Besides, we're nearly at the house.' Her tone brooked no argument.

'I wager your sister-in-law won't be pleased to see me.'

Rebecca gave a ghost of a smile. 'She's decided that you're a drunkard and not to be trusted. Fortunately you won't have to face her because she's gone to bed and the children are asleep. She thinks I'm in bed, too, but I couldn't rest. I was annoyed with you, but I was determined to discover why you had deserted us. I couldn't believe that you'd behave the way you did without a good reason.'

'I'm touched by your faith in me,' muttered Phillip. 'But next time I'd prefer it if you didn't leave the house on your own and come looking for me at this time of night.'

'You're not my keeper, Phillip. I did what I thought best and it's a good job I did.' She waved her stick with difficulty. 'If I hadn't found you, then you might have collapsed and spent the night in the open, in a freezing mist. You could have been dead by morning, so at least act as if you are grateful.'

'I am grateful and let's not have an argument. I'm that tired, I could go to sleep here on this spot,' he muttered.

'Don't you dare,' warned Rebecca, 'or you'll regret it.' Her heart was thudding heavily against her ribcage. She was conscious of his weight, just as she had been earlier, and was concerned that the damage to his head could be more serious than she had first thought. Hopefully, he could hang on just a little longer. Another few steps and they should arrive at the front door.

'Is that you, Rebecca?'

She almost jumped out of her skin as her sister-in-law appeared in the doorway carrying a lantern. 'J-Jane, w-what are you doing up?'

'More to the point, what are you doing out here and with Master Hurst to all appearances!' Jane's voice was sharp with disapproval. 'Is he drunk?' She drew closer, holding the lantern so that its light shone on Phillip's face.

'No, he is not drunk,' said Rebecca, attempting to hoist Phillip higher. 'He was attacked, but managed to escape and came to see if we'd arrived home safely.'

'A bit late for that,' murmured Jane.

'Please, Jane, don't continue in that vein,' pleaded Rebecca. 'I don't expect you to help me with him in your condition but, please, get out of the way so I can get him inside.'

'I'm all right!' muttered Phillip. With a great strength of will he straightened up, pushed Rebecca away and stood erect.

'Well, that's a relief,' said Jane, smiling. 'You'll be able to return to your troupe.'

'Aye, I will,' said Phillip, swaying slightly and putting a hand out to the door jamb.

'Don't be so ridiculous, both of you!' cried Rebecca. 'You're in no fit state, Phillip, to walk all the way there. Jane, please, get out of the way and let us inside. Otherwise, I will saddle up the horse and take him back to his friends myself if you won't let him in.'

'How are you going to see your way?' said Jane, a wobble in her voice. 'I'm only thinking what's best for you, Rebecca. This behaviour on his part might be an act to worm his way into this house and seduce you.'

Rebecca almost exploded. 'Don't be ridiculous! He's in no state to even make the effort.'

'This is turning into a farce,' said Phillip with dignity. He raised an arm and bid them both goodnight, squared his shoulders and weaved his way down the path.

'Now, see what you've made him do!' cried Rebecca.

'He made his own decision like a sensible man,' said Jane, grabbing Rebecca's arm and attempting to drag her indoors. 'Come inside, Rebecca. We're going to catch a chill standing out here.'

Rebecca removed Jane's hand and stepped away from her. 'I can't just let him go like that. What if he lost consciousness and fell in the river and drowned?'

With a whirl of skirts, Rebecca turned and followed Phillip. Fortunately she did not have to go far before blundering into him slumped against a tree a few yards from the gate. She thrust the stick that she still carried into her girdle and fumbled for his arm, dragging it about her neck before slipping her arm around his waist. She was conscious all the time of the latent strength of the man. It seemed odd for him to be so defenceless and it upset her.

'What do you think you're doing?' muttered Phillip.

'What does it feel like I'm doing?' she retorted, her voice quivering. 'And don't waste your strength talking. I'm taking you round to the stable. I'll see to your wound and then we can decide what to do next. It makes more sense than you toppling into the river and drowning.'

'What an imagination you have! What does your sister-in-law think of your latest plan?'

'I haven't asked her,' said Rebecca, almost tempted to add that it did not matter what Jane thought because she, herself, had made up her mind on what action to take.

After that neither of them spoke, but went up the path and round the side of the house to the stable. With a sigh of relief she helped him lower himself on to a heap of straw before collapsing beside him.

Chapter Four

As she lay there, getting her breath back, Rebecca found it amazing that so much had happened to her and Phillip in one day. Was his life always so eventful? She rolled over and gazed down at him and although she could barely make out his features, she feared that he might have swooned. What if he fell into a deep sleep and did not wake up? What if he were to die just as Giles had done? She shook him. 'Phillip, Phillip!'

'What is it?' he murmured.

She felt positively lightheaded with relief and smoothed back his dark gold hair from his forehead, where strands were sticking to the wound. 'I thought for a moment you might be dead.'

''Course I'm not dead, woman!' He seized

her hand in a surprisingly strong grip and said, 'What's happened to your wedding ring?'

Rebecca had not expected him to notice its absence. 'I gave it to Tabitha as I no longer had need of it.'

'That's extremely generous of you,' he said, an odd note in his voice. 'Does this mean you've ended your period of mourning?'

'Aye, although I suppose I'll always feel a little sad that Giles should have died so young,' said Rebecca, freeing her hand and rising to her feet.

'Still, to give his ring away…' he muttered.

She flushed. 'Are you thinking I was wrong to do so? It was only because I wanted to help Tabitha. I just hope that Ned won't insist on her returning it to me. Now, no more talking; rest, and if your headache keeps you awake that is to the good.'

'That sounds a bit harsh,' said Phillip, attempting to rise, only to groan and flop back against the straw.

Rebecca frowned. 'I do hope you're going to be sensible as I must return to the house, but I will be back shortly.'

There was a rustle of straw as he shifted uneasily, as if it weren't only his head that ached, but his body as well. 'Will you bring me a drink? Despite what your sister-in-law thinks of me, not one drop of intoxicating liquor has passed my lips since the performance. A cup of ale is what I need.'

'I'll see what's available. Perhaps you can pass the time thinking about *our ghost* and whether the men who attacked you were in his employ and how we can trace them.'

Fortunately the kitchen door was unlocked and a lantern burned on the table. All was quiet. Rebecca collected what she needed: salve, a clean rag, bindings, a blanket, some food, wine as there was no ale, a small bowl and two cups—for she was thirsty, too. Then, carrying the lantern in one hand and with the blanket and a basket over her arm, she left the house, praying that Phillip's condition had not worsened in her absence.

'Your husband…' Phillip's voice came out of the shadows.

Her heart seemed to jerk against her ribs. 'Why are you so interested in Giles? I have no wish to discuss him. How is your head?'

'Bearable.'

She hung the lantern on a hook and placed the other items close by. She could see the wound clearly now and winced. The skin across his cheekbone had been ripped, as had part of his forehead. The blood had clotted, but the jagged wound appeared deep. She felt slightly nauseous, but Phillip's was not the first wound she had tended—so, despite her inner feelings, she presented a calm exterior.

She poured a little of the wine into the bowl and soaked the clean rag in the liquid. She squeezed out the surplus, aware that Phillip was watching her every move. After the briefest of hesitations, she took hold of his clean-shaven jaw and gently eased the dried blood away. Her upper body brushed his chest and she was aware of a sudden tension within him. 'Am I hurting you?' she asked.

'Aye, but don't let it bother you.' His normal voice was that of a light tenor, which he could use to good effect when a song was called for as it had been earlier that evening, but now it sounded rough and his breathing was rapid. 'Although I may add that your hair is tickling my neck.'

'Oh, I beg pardon.' She reached up and caught hold of a strand of her hair that had come loose from her headdress and tried to tuck it out of the way.

'You have lovely hair,' he muttered.

She reached for the jar of goose-grass salve and began to spread it on the wound. 'You don't have to flatter me, you know. I know I'm no beauty. I always wanted to have fair hair and blue eyes, but my father used to get quite cross when I said that and I think it must have been because I have grey eyes the same as he did.'

Phillip stretched up a hand to the dangling tendril of brown hair and twisted it round his finger. 'Your eyes aren't the same colour as your father's. Yours are dove grey and his were the colour of a louring cloud with the promise of thunder to come.'

Her lips twitched. How right he was! 'Now my brother likened mine to the colour of slate,' she murmured.

'He's wrong. Yours are lighter than slate. In truth, they can appear almost silver in a certain light.'

Her fingers trembled as she began to bind up his head. 'You certainly have a way with words, *Master Hurst,*' she said.

'I'd make a dreadful storyteller if I did not,' he responded. 'And why the sudden formality, Becky? Is it that you feel a need to put me at a distance?'

'That would be difficult in our present situation,' she said, tying up the ends of the bandage. 'How does that feel?'

'Comfortable. You make a good nurse.' His tone was as warm and gentle as a caress.

'I see you are intent on making me feel better about myself.' Her voice was uneven. 'I only hope the bandage doesn't work loose during the night. Your wound could turn putrid if straw were to stick to it. Shall we move on? I couldn't find any ale so I brought wine. Is that acceptable to you?'

He sat up, taking her by surprise, and they bumped noses. She gasped with pain and fell back on her heels and rubbed her nose. 'Are you all right?' he asked, reaching out with both hands and easing her upright.

'You've made my eyes water, that's all,' said Rebecca, blinking up at him.

'I beg pardon.' Leaning forwards, Phillip planted a light kiss on both her eyelids.

'What was that for?' she asked in a breathy voice.

'When I hurt myself when I was small my mother used to kiss where it hurt better.' He released her and leaned back against the wooden wall of the stall and feigned sleep.

Tears clogged her throat and she so wished her mother could have been different. What was it about her that her mother had felt no remorse about leaving her behind when she ran off with her lover? Had she really been such an unattractive child? She gazed at Phillip from blurry eyes, intensely aware still of the feel of his lips on her eyelids. How would he react if she bent over him and kissed him? She imagined doing so, remembering another time, another place. Then she told herself that she was being foolish, for a dalliance with him was out of the question. She would only get hurt. There was no room for a wife in his life. With a sigh she reached out for the basket and took out the bread and cheese and poured wine into cups.

'Phillip!' She shook his shoulder.

He opened his eyes and stared at her. 'I've been thinking we need to talk to your brother,' he murmured, which was not exactly true. Primarily his mind had been filled with thoughts of tasting her mouth again and running his hands over the contours of her body, before removing her clothes and seeing her naked and then allowing his lips to follow the path taken by his fingers.

'We? You're prepared to help me get a message to Davy?' Her voice lit up.

'Aye, let's talk about it now by all means,' he said, taking one of the cups from her. 'Unless you're exhausted after what's been a long day and would prefer to retire to your bedchamber?'

'No, I'm not tired,' she lied. 'Bread and cheese?'

He thanked her, draining the cup before biting into the bread and cheese. He did not speak until he had swallowed. 'So were your husband and Davy good friends?'

She darted him a look. 'What is it about my husband that so interests you? I thought we were to discuss the best way to find out what we need to know about *the ghost* from my brother.'

'My interest is purely that of a writer and actor,' said Phillip, taking another bite of the bread and cheese. 'I have never met a young widow before and—'

'I do not wish to become part of some bawdy play that has sprung to life in your mind,' she said tartly.

'Bawdy!' He looked hurt. 'Is that all you think I'm capable of writing? Just because I played a comical and slightly vulgar role amongst others this evening, do not think that is all I can do. I do write serious plays and perform in them, you know.'

'Similar to Greek tragedies, no doubt,' she muttered, biting into her own food. What had made her bite his head off like that? Was it because she wanted him to see her other than purely as a character to write about in one of his plays and then toss her aside when he'd finished with her?

'I don't have any sons falling in love with their mothers and marrying them after killing their fathers,' said Phillip, breaking into her thoughts.

She was taken aback. 'Seriously, is there such a Greek play?'

'*Oedipus Rex.* He doesn't know she's his mother, of course.'

'Obviously, otherwise I don't suppose he would have married her.'

Phillip nodded, winced and reached for her wine and gulped a mouthful before handing the cup to her. Immediately she poured a little wine into his cup. 'You mustn't have too much wine,' she said. 'Tell me more about the Greek plays.'

'There was a woman whose suitors all tried to convince her that she was a widow. Her name was Penelope. They were desperate to marry her.'

'Was she rich and beautiful?'

He smiled. 'What do you think? She had a son and her husband had a faithful dog which he'd left behind. Neither was in favour of any of her suitors. Just like Penelope, they wanted Odysseus to come home.'

'Was he an explorer?'

Phillip frowned and then winced. 'You mean like Nicholas? No, Odysseus had been away to war, but somehow he became involved in other adventures and ended up being away for ten years or more.'

'I don't think I'd have waited ten years.' Rebecca shook her head. 'She must have loved him. You state an exact time,' she murmured, 'that means he eventually returned?'

'He did and he soon rid her of her suitors.'

'And I suppose they lived happily ever after?' teased Rebecca, her dimples peeping out.

'What do you think?' Phillip so wanted her in that moment that he had a real struggle not to reach out and ravish her. 'I think I'd best be going. I'll borrow your horse and see that he's returned in the morning.' He thrust the cup into her hand and made to rise.

His actions were so unexpected that she reacted without thinking. She dropped the cup and placed a hand against his chest and pushed him back against the wall of the stall. 'Certainly not! You must stay here and rest until morning.'

He removed her hand from his chest and said frostily, 'I don't see why that is necessary. If I can talk to you sensibly, then there really is no need for me to keep you from your comfortable bed.'

'Who are you to say whether my bed is comfortable or not? My mattress is stuffed with horsehair, not duck's down,' she countered. 'I would just as well spend the night here to make certain you don't do anything foolish. Besides, we were discussing how to get word to Davy before you began to talk of Greek plays.'

'Then you mentioned Nicholas!'

She scowled. 'I did not. It was you who did that. I only asked if Odysseus was an explorer and from there we arrived at happy endings.'

He shrugged. 'You're near enough right. Anyway, who's to say whether Odysseus and Penelope really existed?'

'Just like Robin and Marion,' she muttered.

For a while they were both silent, busy with their thoughts.

'I did once have a comfortable bed,' said Rebecca, holding herself stiffly, making certain there were several inches between them. 'Unfortunately, when Giles died in an accident, he left a heap of debts and I had to sell everything to pay them off.'

Phillip could have kicked himself. 'Damn it! I had no idea. Probably best I do leave now,' he said on a bitter note.

'I cannot prevent you doing so, but I think you'd be making a mistake.' She glanced at his profile and felt a peculiar catch at her heart. 'Please stay. We haven't finished our talk and I have an idea,' she said impulsively.

'A sensible idea?'

She raised her eyebrows. 'Not in the least. My idea is that you change your plans and instead of going to Greenwich from here, you and your troupe accompany me to Ludlow.' Phillip opened his mouth to speak, but she added rapidly, 'Think! You'll be able to put on performances at the various towns we go through and make more money. I know you're eager to find out whether there is any news of Nicholas, but if you do what I suggest then it shouldn't interrupt your schedule by more than a sennight.' She took a breath, 'And if the Princess Mary also requests that you put on a play, then she might give you a hefty purse and that would make it even more worth your while!'

'By the saints, Becky, when did you plan all this?' He shook his head and winced. 'Damn it, I must remember not to do that.'

'Aye, you must, and I thought of my plan just now,' she said proudly. And without thinking she placed a hand on his thigh. 'So what is your answer?'

'Out of the question,' he said, removing her hand from his thigh and placing it in her lap.

She felt the blood rise in her cheeks. Obviously, he thought her quite mad and he was telling her that even her touch was now unwelcome, but she was not about to give up. ‘So you think it is a crazy idea. Is that because I told you once that I disapproved of travelling players?’

‘Partly, if I’m honest,’ he lied, thinking if only she knew the truth.

‘You believe I’m using you and the troupe just for my own ends?’

‘Aren’t you?’ Phillip leaned back and closed his eyes.

She stared at him, frustrated. ‘It would only be for a short while.’

‘Time is relative to how one spends it. Anyway, I can’t imagine your sister-in-law approving of your travelling anywhere in my company.’

‘That’s why I suggested bringing your troupe along.’

‘They might not approve the idea; besides you might find I’d drive *you* mad if you were in my company for any length of time.’ There was a hint of irony in his voice.

‘Maybe you will,’ she said, sensing he was weakening. ‘On the other hand, I might learn from you and enjoy the experience. You can while away the journey by telling me more of your stories.’ There was a hint of mischief in her voice and daringly she huddled closer to him and slid her hand through his arm.

This time he left her hand where it was because it was growing colder in the stable. Besides, tightly tucked in his arm, her hand was out of harm's way. 'What about your sister-in-law? If she speaks against such a scheme, will you go against her?'

She said triumphantly, 'I have already mentioned to Jane that I would like to visit Davy, so she is half-prepared for my leaving. If I am adamant and she agrees to hire Tabitha whilst the rest of us travel to Ludlow, then I think she will see the sense in my travelling with the troupe.'

Phillip was silent for so long that Rebecca was convinced that he would not, after all, agree to her plan. Then he turned his head and stared her straight in the eye. 'I have misgivings about this idea of yours. If I agree to it, then it would mean that you will have to take over all that Tabitha does for the troupe. Are you willing to do that?'

Relief flooded her. 'Of course, I am. After all, my position here involves taking care of the needs of others, so I see little difference.'

'You'll have to sleep on a pallet and there'll be little privacy,' warned Phillip.

'It will only be for a short period, so I deem I can manage that.' She sighed happily and dropped her head on his shoulder. 'It is so long since I've heard from Davy that I can't wait to see him. You must know how I feel, because surely it is the same with you and Nicholas?'

Gingerly Phillip rested the undamaged side of his head on hers. 'It's not the least bit the same. An elder brother treats a younger sister very differently from a younger brother. I doubt you've ever felt that you had to struggle to match up to your brother.'

'Are you saying that you have always felt inferior to Nicholas?'

'I don't know if I should reply to that, but if I am honest I have to admit that is so.'

'But you are still fond of him?'

'Of course!' He sighed. 'At least you know where Davy is—I don't even know if Nicholas is alive or dead.'

'Let us pray that he is alive—for your family's sake,' she added swiftly. 'I worried when I discovered Davy was going to Ludlow. After all, the king's brother died there and one wonders if Ludlow Castle is cursed. It was sad that Prince Arthur and Katherine of Aragon were only married for a short time. Davy told me that the Queen insists that the marriage was not consummated. How different her life would have been if they had coupled and had a son whilst there.'

'It happened so long ago. I see no need to

think when we arrive there we'll be met by gloomy faces,' said Phillip.

Rebecca yawned. 'Anyway, it is your duty as an entertainer to brighten people's lives.'

Phillip threw back his head and laughed.

His laughter was so infectious that she laughed herself. 'What is so amusing? Is it not true?'

'Oh, it's true all right, but even with the best of intentions, I don't always please folk.'

'You've brightened my life since you've come back into it,' said Rebecca without thinking.

Phillip stilled. 'Have I?'

She chuckled. 'Of course you have. My life has been so dull whilst yours has been full of excitement and happenings.'

'I think I've made it sound more exciting than it is,' said Phillip. 'Tell me, are you cold?'

'Not as cold as I was before,' said Rebecca, blinking at him sleepily and drawing her cloak more tightly about her, but it made little difference as the garment was well worn and thin. Then she remembered the blanket she had brought and patted around the ground in search of it.

'What are you doing?' asked Phillip, raising his head.

'I brought a blanket.' Her hand touched wool and she drew the blanket towards her.

Phillip imagined them being warm and snug beneath the blanket and felt himself harden. *This will not do!* 'It is cold! You must go back to the house,' he said firmly. 'What good does it do, you staying here?'

'I need to make certain you stay awake.'

'Then I'm best remaining cold,' he said roughly. 'You go!'

Rebecca felt hurt by his rejection. She reached for the lantern, but as she did so the wick spluttered and went out. Panic seized her. 'Oh, Holy Mary, Mother of God! I can't see! Where are you?'

Hearing the panic in her voice, Phillip reached out and touched her. 'I'm here!'

She fumbled for his hand and gripped it. 'I hate the dark!'

'There are other things that I fear more,' he said, aware that she was shaking and thinking she needed warming. 'Where's this blanket you mentioned?'

'On—on the ground next to me!'

'Can you pass it over?'

'I—I'll try,' she said, fumbling for the blanket.

He was aware of her fingernails biting into his skin. 'Can you find it?'

'Aye, I have it!' She managed to heave the heavy wool in his direction.

Phillip grabbed hold of it and spread it over them both. 'How is that? Do you feel warmer now?'

She nodded. 'But d-don't leave me, Pip!'

He was touched by her need of him and that she had called him by his nickname. 'I'm not going anywhere. Would you like to tell me why you're so terrified of the dark? Not that you're alone in being so. One of my nephews suffers the same fear, nor can he bear being in enclosed spaces.'

'Wh-when I was very small, if I displeased the w-woman my father hired to keep an eye on me, she would lock me in a windowless chamber without a candle,' said Rebecca. 'My imagination would people that place with all kinds of imps and demons.'

'It never fails to amaze me how cruel and unimaginative some people can be,' said Phillip, angry at the thought of that little girl being terrified in that dark place. He drew her closer and kept hold of her hand. The other she placed against his neck and rested her head on his shoulder. 'This hand is like ice,' he muttered, stuffing it inside his doublet. 'Is that better?'

A soft breath escaped her. 'Aye.' They were

quiet for a few moments and then she said, 'I don't suppose you'd admit to your fears.'

He hesitated, then murmured, 'Heights. Or should I say straight drops from a height. I try to avoid them at all costs. I remember my mother saying that sooner or later everyone has to face their fears and that running away from them only makes them grow. I am not as certain of that as she was.'

'Me neither,' said Rebecca, pleased that they were in accord. She marvelled that he should share his fear with her.

'How did you cope with the darkness and not go mad?' he asked.

'I sang,' said Rebecca, and began to softly sing a country air.

Despite his aching head, he began to sing along with her. If this was a story or play, how would he write this scene? he wondered. Perhaps they would make passionate love and then he would have to put an obstacle in the way of their remaining together. He considered star-crossed lovers: Tristan and Isolde, Pyramus and Thisbe, Lancelot and Guinevere. No happy endings for any of them.

Suddenly he realised that Rebecca had stopped singing, but she could not have fallen asleep because he was aware of her hand worming its way inside the opening in his shirt. Her fingers were toying with the hairs on his chest. What if her hand were to slip a foot or so? No, he would not dwell on such thoughts. Instead, he would attempt to plot the play he must present before the king during Epiphany, but that proved impossible. He could not ignore those tantalising fingers, neither could he bring himself to ask her to remove her hand. Instead he gave in to temptation and turned her head and kissed her. He had half-expected her to freeze and pull away from him, but she didn't. Instead her lips parted and the tip of her tongue weaved about his. Almost of its own volition, his hand slid inside her bodice and curled about her breast. It was several minutes before his lips travelled the same path and he felt her gasp as he nuzzled her nipple. For a moment he stilled, thinking that perhaps he had reached the boundary of allowable behaviour from her and would have hastily retreated, but it seemed he need not do so because she curled an arm about his neck and held him there. That gesture was enough to answer the question that had plagued him since yesterday and his desire for her was such that he cast restraint aside along with his hose and did what he had been longing to do since that kiss.

Rebecca responded with a passion to equal

Phillip's. How often when in the marriage bed had she pretended, after seeing Phillip at court, that it was he in her bed when Giles made love to her? Now it really was his hands and lips that were caressing every inch of her. Even places that Giles had never explored. Afterwards she had been racked with guilt, wondering if by using such a pretext she was committing adultery, but what was taking place now was far beyond anything she had experienced and she cried out as pleasure flooded her whole being. Yet even as she clung to Phillip and held him inside her, he was struggling to be free of her.

Afterwards she lay on her back, barely aware of the straw scratching her shoulder, feeling ashamed and desolate. 'I don't know what to say,' she said in a low voice. 'You must consider my behaviour wanton.'

'No.' Phillip covered her with the blanket and then he sat, holding his head, struggling with the conviction that if his brother did not return, then he would have no rival for Becky. If his brother was dead… The thought horrified him. That he should think such, because of his lust for this woman, meant that he must stay away from her. 'There will be no going to Ludlow,' he added in a muffled voice.

'What!' She pushed herself up. 'You won't

take me, because of what's happened between us just now?'

'For what other reason?' he snapped.

She blinked back tears. 'You are disgusted with me, especially after my accusing you of having Tabitha as your mistress.'

He lifted his head. 'God's blood, no! Did I say that?'

'It's the only reason I can think of for your changing your mind. I behaved shamefully just because I was in need of even a little tenderness—'

'Tenderness!' He made a noise in his throat. 'You think I was tender?'

'You weren't rough and you did not rush it like a horse taking a fence. Only then you—'

'What?' He stared in the direction of her voice.

'I think you know.' She sighed.

He was silent for a moment and then said, 'I needed to spill my seed outside your body. What kind of man do you think I am? If you were my wife, it would be different.'

'But I'm not your wife and unlikely ever to be so,' said Rebecca, her voice hollow. 'Yet if you don't consider me a whore and we both agree that it must not happen again, I see no reason why we shouldn't go to Ludlow.'

'You're not being realistic,' he said vehemently, suddenly having a vision of them making love in the wagon whilst his brother's body floated in the sea. It must not happen. Nicholas had always shown such strength, intelligence and determination, even as a youth. Their father had boasted of his prowess, whilst Phillip—how could he ever forget his father calling him a pretty boy, adding that he would never be able to match up to his older brothers in manual skill and brainpower?

Rebecca touched his arm tentatively. 'I am! What is it you are scared of? It—it's not as if we'll be travelling alone. Please, Pip, do this for me?'

Phillip felt himself weaken, touched by her plea. The image of his brother's body suddenly evaporated and he told himself it was the blow on the head that had been the cause of the vision. He had to prove to her that he was strong enough to do this for her. He reached up to the bandage, which had come loose and was slipping over his eyes. 'Of course, if we see *the ghost* in Oxford again, there will be no need to go to Ludlow,' he said firmly, beginning to dress.

'I would say there is more need,' said Rebecca, not wanting to be parted from him. She searched for her clothes in the dark and pulled on her gown before leaning back against the wooden partition and huddling inside the blanket. 'If he is no ghost, but kin to me and Davy, then my brother needs to know of his existence.'

'All right!' said Phillip, running a hand over his chin. 'But before I go anywhere, I must inspect the premises that Gawain Raventon mentioned to me; also Frederick plans to visit a friend at his old college. Whilst I do that, you mustn't wander the streets in search of our *ghost* in case he intends you harm.'

'Why should he? He might not even know of my existence. Anyway, it's not easy to find people, however hard you search for them. He might not even know that I am a widow and could be looking for Rebecca Mortimer.' She hoped she wasn't babbling. It felt so odd talking about such matters in the dark, after having shared such passion, but suddenly she desperately wanted to get away from Oxford and to experience Phillip's life as a player.

'If so, he could have trouble finding you.'

She agreed. They fell silent and did not speak again for the remainder of the night.

Rebecca stirred. Something was scratching her cheek and for a moment she thought it was one of the children. 'Go away,' she muttered, waving an arm about.

There came no giggle or chatter or scampering feet and suddenly she was fully awake. Her heart raced as she sat up in the straw and gazed about the stable, but there was no sign of Phillip. She groaned and buried her head on her arms. How was she to face him after what had happened between them last night? She pushed down the blanket and got to her feet and made her way over to the door and peered out. Daylight had come and, doubting he would have gone into the house, she decided he must have returned to the wagon to explain his absence. She hoped his head felt much better.

She collected the blanket and basket and hurried to the house. The kitchen was deserted and the fire almost out. She tended to the latter first until she had a good blaze going because it was a frosty day. Then she went up to her bedchamber and washed and tidied herself and collected a warmer cloak and put on a hat. She was on her way downstairs when she heard the door of Jane's bedchamber open, but not wanting to be delayed, she simply called up, 'We've no bread or ale, Jane, and little else to eat, so I'm going shopping. I shall be as quick as I can. I still have some money that Simon gave me.'

'Wait!' shrieked Jane. 'What happened to Master Hurst?'

'That I am going to find out. I will see you soon,' replied Rebecca, unbolting the front door and hurrying out. She ran towards the gate and in no time at all was making her way into the town centre, glancing about her as she did so at people going about their business, searching not only for Phillip, but a man who looked like her father. The sooner she saw Phillip the sooner she would know if matters stood all right between them and she could trust him to keep his word. There was a cold wind blowing and the air felt as if it was taking bites out of her cheeks. She thought of Tabitha and the baby and hoped that the wagon was still in the same place.

She need not have worried; it was there on the waste ground. A camp fire had been lit and Phillip was eating whilst he stood warming himself, obviously listening to what Ned was saying. Had he already told the troupe of his intentions and was Tabitha's husband criticising them? Neither man had noticed her presence and she was almost upon them before Phillip looked up and saw her. He was wearing a hat and she could see the bandage slanting beneath its brim. There was an expression in his eyes that caused her heart to sink.

Nevertheless she managed to infuse warmth into her voice. 'How is your head?'

'Frederick's not too pleased with me,' replied Phillip, grimacing.

She was dismayed. 'You mean because of my plan to go to Ludlow?'

'No, although I doubt he'll come with us. Think about it, Becky. This bandage doesn't do much for my appearance, does it? What parts have I been playing recently?'

She groaned. 'I never thought of that. What will you do?'

'He'll either have to pick another play or write a new one,' said Ned, glancing at them both. 'Although Jack's a lot better now, he's got an irritating cough. Besides, he's a bit young and inexperienced for some of the female roles. We could do with enlisting another player for next year. Either way it means more work for us if we are to go to Ludlow in the coming days.'

She said hesitantly, 'But you are not against the idea?'

Ned rubbed his jaw. 'As long as you can sort matters out with Mistress Caldwell to hire Tabitha as a live-in servant, then I'm prepared to fit in with your plan. I'm grateful for your gift to Tabitha and I'm glad of an opportunity to help you.'

Rebecca was quite overcome and impulsively she reached up and kissed Ned's cheek. 'Thank you, Ned! I am most grateful.' He reddened and mumbled indistinctly before climbing inside the wagon. Rebecca turned and met Phillip's stare and her colour rose. 'I am grateful to him and yourself.' She hesitated. 'Last night—'

'Shall we draw a veil over last night?' he said roughly, putting down the bowl. 'Neither of us was ourselves.'

She cleared her throat, knowing she would never forget last night. 'I agree. When do we leave for Ludlow?'

'Give it a day or two. I want to try to find our *ghost.* Besides, I still have to inspect the property in Broad Street for the Raventons and you need to arrange matters with Mistress Caldwell about Tabitha and the baby.'

'Of course!' She moistened her lips nervously.

Phillip scowled, wishing she hadn't drawn his attention to her lips by licking them. He hoped he could find the *ghost.* There was no doubt in his mind the journey to Ludlow was going to be fraught with difficulties. He must have been crazy to agree to it.

Chapter Five

Rebecca wondered whether, in the circumstances, she should give up the idea of going to Ludlow altogether, although she was desperate to see her brother in the flesh. Not only to reassure herself of his well-being, but she also felt that by talking to him, she was bound to learn more about her father's past. Even so, if Phillip really didn't want to go—

'Listen, Phillip,' she said urgently. 'Perhaps we should forget Ludlow after all. If it's going to cause you more work, then—'

'Forget it! After all the fuss you made and all because you've got cold feet?' Contrarily, now he could escape spending a sennight or more in her company, he was determined to make her adhere to her original plan. He wanted her to have first-hand experience of what it was like being a strolling player—if they should ever decide there could be a future for them together, she needed to know what she was in for. His blue eyes glinted. 'You made such a good case for why the troupe should go. If fortune is with us, we could earn some decent money on the journey and a fine purse from the princess when we arrive there.'

'All right! We will go,' said Rebecca, her spirits lifting. 'Now where's Tabitha?'

'She's gone shopping. Maybe you'll see her on your way home. I'll be in touch and let you know my plans.'

He turned away, considering his other occupation as spy for Cardinal Wolsey. It was Sir Gawain Raventon who had suggested Phillip offer his services to the chancellor. As a travelling player Phillip could feed back to him information about any unrest in the places he travelled through. He had realised only that morning that he had a perfect excuse to visit the court of Princess Mary, whose guardian was an enemy of Wolsey. He was bound to welcome any information about her and would pay well for it. But Rebecca must remain unaware of his role of spy as it could prove dangerous.

* * *

As Rebecca entered the house, she was greeted by an impatient Jane. 'You seem to have been an age. No doubt you've been with Master Hurst.'

'Not for very long as he had a commission to execute for the Raventons,' said Rebecca, emptying her basket on to the kitchen table. 'They're planning to open a bookshop and print room on Broad Street.'

'It should do well for them with so many learned men living in the city,' said Jane, taking up a knife and reaching for the loaf which Rebecca had purchased. 'I suppose Master Hurst's interest is due to his brother having had a book published?'

'It's more than that,' said Rebecca. 'Nicholas has shares in the business and Phillip has the authority to deal with any matters arising in his absence.'

'His brother must have a lot of faith in him,' said Jane, cutting several slices of bread. 'But wouldn't it be more sensible for him to give up his wanderings and dedicate himself to his business affairs?'

'Perhaps he will, once he returns home, but Phillip and his eldest brother have had no word from Nicholas for a while.'

'That is worrying. How long has he been away?' asked Jane, spreading butter on the bread.

'For several years, I think,' said Rebecca, filling two cups with small ale. 'Where are the children?'

'I've set them to gathering up the windfalls in the garden.' Jane sat down and took a drink from one of the cups. 'I presume Master Nicholas Hurst doesn't have a wife?'

Rebecca shook her head.

'Well, at least he has enough sense not to make some poor woman miserable by his being away so long. Now Master Phillip Hurst obviously must have recovered from the attack on his person if he is able to inspect this property?'

'Aye, but the damage to his face is noticeable, which means that he won't be able to act a woman's part as he did last evening.'

'So what are his plans now?' asked Jane.

Rebecca hesitated, pondering on how much she should tell her sister-in-law. 'Most likely he will stay in Oxford for another day or so in the hope of finding the so-called *ghost.* Phillip is convinced he saw a man who looked like my father in Oxford last evening. That is the reason he was in such haste and left us behind.'

Jane's eyes widened. 'Are you telling me the truth?'

'Of course!' Rebecca frowned. 'Unfortunately he lost sight of him so we still don't know who it was. If he doesn't find him in the next day or so, I've decided to travel to Ludlow. Hopefully Davy will be able to tell us whether Father had a cousin or even a brother, although why he hasn't mentioned either to me is a mystery.'

For several moments Jane did not speak and then she said stiffly, 'You say *us*.'

'Master Hurst and his troupe will accompany me,' replied Rebecca, lowering her gaze to conceal her blush and breaking off a bit of bread crust and popping it in her mouth.

'The troupe! By all the saints, Rebecca, do you know what you're doing?'

Rebecca's head shot up. 'Of course I do. I'm not a fool! And I must speak to Davy.'

'But why do you have to go so soon and with the players?' asked Jane.

Rebecca thought about the question. 'I cannot be away when you have the baby. Besides winter will be here before we know it and the roads could become impassable. This way, I'll have someone to protect me on the journey and Phillip is planning to put on a play wherever we break our journey for the night.'

'I thought you said he was unable to perform due to his injury?'

'He will write a new play and I suppose he'll be able to take on a different role where the injury does not matter. As for me, I will take Tabitha's place.'

'Hmm!' Jane bit into a slice of bread and butter. 'I really don't think it is appropriate that you should travel with them as the only woman in the party, for I suspect you have it in mind that Tabitha and her child will remain here with me.'

Rebecca gazed at her steadily. 'That's the general idea.'

'You could take Maud in her stead.'

A startled Rebecca shook her head. 'No, thank you! In any case, there wouldn't be enough room in the wagon.'

'You mean you'll be sleeping in the wagon with the men?' gasped Jane.

Rebecca could only think afterwards that it was guilt that caused her to react angrily. 'God's blood, Jane! I'm not a child, I'm a widow of twenty-four and I see no reason why I shouldn't trust Phillip and the troupe. My sleeping quarter will be curtained off, I am sure. I have known Phillip since I was eight years old and the others are decent men.'

'All right, there's no need for such a display of temper,' protested Jane, her hands fluttering on the table.

'I beg pardon,' said Rebecca, instantly regretting her outburst. 'Tabitha will be calling here later today to see if you are willing to hire her. She does not expect the position to be a permanent arrangement, but it should suit both of you until I return.'

Jane rose to her feet and leaned on the table. 'You seem to have it all worked out, so I suppose I must accept you are set on this course. At least I know now that my husband is not losing his wits by claiming to have seen a ghost. Perhaps this man will make himself known to you before you leave Oxford and the journey will prove unnecessary.'

Rebecca didn't respond to this, but was relieved to realise that her sister-in-law appeared to be accepting her scheme. She hugged Jane and then went to call the children to come and eat. She wondered how long it would be before Phillip came to tell her that they must leave. Could he really pull a veil over last night so easily? She supposed only time would tell.

Phillip had finished his tour of the premises intended for the printing room and shop, and now decided to visit the Mitre Inn on High Street. He wondered if he should be searching for a man by the name of Mortimer or if their *ghost* went by a different name. Did the men who had attacked him have any connection with him or were they just common footpads? Of course, there was always the possibility that someone had suspected him of spying and wanted to be rid of him. It was an uncomfortable thought and caused him to glance over his shoulder several times on the way to the inn.

The Mitre was crowded and he had difficulty not only in ordering a cup of ale, but scanning the customers' faces to see if there was any he recognised. Drawing a blank, he asked the innkeeper whether he had a guest staying by the name of Mortimer, but his question was greeted with a shake of the head, so Phillip drank up and left.

After a walk around the city, he returned to the wagon where he found Frederick gathering his possessions together.

'So you are leaving us?' said Phillip, regret in his voice.

The old man nodded his head. 'I'm sorry, lad, but at this time of year my rheumatics are chronic. I need a warm berth. Perhaps when winter is over, then I'll be able to travel with you again. I'll be sharing my old friend's lodgings and helping him with his students.'

Phillip shook his mentor's hand. 'I'm going to miss you.'

'I'll miss you, too, lad.' There were tears in Frederick's rheumy eyes as he patted Phillip's shoulder. 'I hope all goes well and you find what you're looking for. Hopefully I'll see you in Oxford again before long.'

The two men parted.

It was over the midday meal that Phillip discussed his plans at length with the rest of the troupe and gave Tabitha a message for Rebecca. Soon after, Ned and Tabitha left with the baby to visit Jane Caldwell's home, whilst Jack went off on business of his own, leaving Phillip to make a start on the script of the play the three men hoped to perform en route to Ludlow. He had changed his mind about staying in Oxford another day and intended leaving in the morning if Rebecca was in agreement. Only for a moment did he question again the wisdom of living in close proximity with Rebecca for a week or more. Then he told himself that the circumstances would be very different from last night.

Early the following day, Rebecca opened the front door and felt a rush of desire and excitement as she gazed at Phillip. The bandage emphasised the warm colour of his skin and did not detract in any way from the perfect symmetry of his face. Really, she was playing with fire travelling to Ludlow with him. The night they had spent together had only served to strengthen her desire for him.

'Are you ready?' he asked in a voice that lacked emotion.

'Aye, almost,' she replied coolly. 'Have you finished writing your new play? Ned said that if you had then we would leave today.'

'Near enough,' he said, wanting to sweep her off her feet and swing her up in the air before allowing her to slide slowly against the length of his body to the ground and kissing her. 'Fortunately there is more action than words in this play and we should be able to perfect it with practice before we reach Ludlow,' he added.

'You must have worked hard.'

'Through most of the night.'

His answer caused her to recall to mind again how they had spent the night before and her smile faded. 'Surely you should rest. Your head, does it not hurt?'

'Aye, but no matter!' He rested his shoulder against the doorjamb.

'Is there a role for you in your play?'

He smiled slightly. 'Aye, but my face will be hidden by a mask.'

'A mask!' She frowned. 'Is that wise?'

Phillip's smile faded. 'I want no scold from you. I have made my decision and will stick to it.' He straightened up. 'Have you packed all you need? I would like to be in Banbury by late afternoon.'

She was surprised. 'Is it not seven leagues or more?'

'Aye, and the wagon will slow us down and that is why we must leave as soon as possible.' He seized her by the shoulders and turned her round. 'Go, fetch your baggage! I have bid Ned and Jack to travel on ahead. It should not take us long to catch up with them.'

She hurried indoors, calling over her shoulder, 'Where is Tabitha and the baby? I have had my baggage ready since she and Ned left yesterday afternoon.'

'She's keeping an eye on the horse.'

Rebecca glanced at him. 'So you rode here. Were you expecting me to ride my horse?'

'That is your decision.'

She hesitated. 'I say my horse, but it is not really mine. It belonged to Giles and after his death I was reluctant to sell it, despite needing the money. In the end Simon bought it from me. I would hate it to get stolen.'

'Then leave it behind. I am prepared for you to ride pillion with me; when we catch up with the others, you can decide whether you wish, instead, to travel in the wagon.'

Rebecca wasted no time discussing the matter further, but hurried into the parlour. Jane and the children looked up as she entered the room. 'Master Hurst is here and we are to leave immediately,' she said.

Jane struggled to rise as Phillip followed Rebecca into the room. He indicated that she sit down. 'Please, do not disturb yourself, Mistress Caldwell. I only came in to reassure you that I will protect Becky with my life if necessary.'

'I expected no less,' Jane surprised him by saying. 'Rebecca tells me that you are trustworthy and, as she is normally a woman of good sense, I have decided to accept her word for it. Tell me, how is your head?'

'Much better, thank you.' He flashed her a smile of infinite charm that brought colour to her cheeks. 'I appreciate your concern. Tabitha is without. I'll send her in to you, shall I?'

She nodded and clasped her hands on her belly. 'Then all that remains is for me to wish you both a safe journey. I pray that Davy is able to help you solve the mystery of the mysterious figure, so akin to Rebecca's father.'

He thanked her again.

Rebecca kissed the children and Jane, picked up the canvas bag containing a change of garments, toiletries and other necessary items before turning to Phillip with a serious expression on her face. He wondered if Becky had told Jane that he was trustworthy purely to reassure her—or did she honestly believe it? He hoped it was a mixture of both. After all, he certainly would not have made love to her if she had not encouraged him.

He took the bag from her and, with a last farewell, they left the room. Tabitha was standing at the gate and hurried to meet them. They exchanged a few words before parting. Rebecca paused to look back at the house, wondering, with a sudden sense of foreboding, if she would ever see it again. She pondered a moment on Phillip's vowing that he would give his life for her protection. Had he meant what he said?

Her thoughts were interrupted by a summons from Phillip and she walked swiftly to where he was tying her bag to the saddle of his horse. She noticed that he had a proper pillion seat and wondered whether she would prefer to ride with him all the way to Ludlow. Wagons could be uncomfortable vehicles in which to travel, bouncing and rocking on uneven roads. She felt a tap on her shoulder and then was taken by surprise as strong arms slid round her waist from behind and lifted her off her feet and up into the pillion seat. She was aware of an inner trembling as she looked down at Phillip and their gazes locked. 'So—so this is the start of my adventure,' she said.

'Aye, and hopefully by the time we reach Ludlow you'll have more insight into my life and will have changed your opinion about whether it is preferable to that of working in my brother's shipyard.' He relaxed his hold on her and swung up into the saddle and gathered the reins into one hand.

They were both silent as they rode through Oxford, gazing about them still for any sign of their *ghost.* They passed through the North Gate and soon left the town behind. It was not long before they came upon the wagon. Phillip and Ned exchanged a low-voiced conversation before Phillip turned to Rebecca and said, 'I've decided to ride on ahead to get permission for us to perform in the market square close to Banbury's High Cross. What do you wish to do? Come with me or ride in the wagon?' He let the words hang in the air.

'I'll come with you,' she said. 'There is still much we have to discuss.'

Phillip raised an eyebrow, unfastening her canvas bag and handing it to Jack. Having already arranged what procedure to take if the wagon should suffer a mishap on the way and not arrive in Banbury at the expected time, the men had no more to say.

Phillip urged his horse on and they soon left the wagon behind. There was little traffic on the road and due to a lack of rain the going was good underfoot. He wondered what it was Rebecca wished to discuss with him. Unless she had only said that so the other two would think that was her reason for choosing to ride with him.

Then out of the blue she surprised him by saying, 'Do you know if the Raventons have given any thought to whom they will put in charge of the new premises on Broad Street?'

He glanced over his shoulder at her. 'They did not discuss it with me. Why do you ask?'

'I wondered if they had Nicholas in mind when he returns if he were to decide to settle down. After all, he does have shares in the company and he could be planning to turn his latest experiences into another book.'

Phillip's heart sank. If that was the Raventons' intention it could throw Nicholas and Becky together, presuming his brother was still alive. 'It might prove too unexciting for Nicholas. Besides, if he does return safely and decides to stop travelling, Christopher will want his help to run the business. You might not have realised it when you came to the yard as a girl, but my family not only build ships to order, we also build some vessels to hire out.'

'I didn't know that,' said Rebecca. 'Is it profitable?'

'There's always the risk of a ship going down in a storm, but my father and now Christopher would not have persisted with that line of business if it didn't pay.' Phillip decided to change the subject. 'What else do you wish to discuss with me?' he asked.

'I want to hear about the play you plan to perform this evening and describe the mask you will wear.'

He allowed himself to believe that she was truly interested in his work. 'I am reluctant to describe the mask as it will lessen the impact when you see it in place.'

'You've roused my curiosity.' She tapped him lightly in the back. 'I deem you are a tease, Pip

Hurst. Why must you be so secretive? What is this play?'

He grinned. 'It concerns a battle.'

'An historic battle?'

'Aye, although it has and it hasn't taken place yet.'

She leaned towards him. 'You talk in riddles.'

He could feel her breath on his skin and could not resist reaching up a hand and placing the back of it against her cheek. 'Are you warm enough?'

A quivering breath passed through her as she remembered his taking her cold hand in his own and placing it inside his doublet. If he hadn't, then most likely they would never have made love. 'Aye, but then your body is protecting me from the wind. Are you warm enough?'

'I'm not cold.' He removed his hand and she eased back on the pillion seat, worrying that he might deem her too close.

'Can you hear what I'm saying?' she asked.

'Well enough. Are you comfortable in such a position?'

'I am not uncomfortable. Of course, if you were to urge your horse into a gallop—'

'I would give you fair warning.'

'Good! So this battle?' asked Rebecca, sitting up straight.

'I will give you a clue. It is full of imagery and is supposed to echo a battle that took place a long time ago.'

'Are you a seer and have kept it secret all this time?' she asked in a mocking voice.

'I thought you were clever, Becky. I will say no more, rather I will let you carry on guessing.'

'And will there be a reward if I give you the right answer?'

'Maybe.'

She sensed he smiled and blew lightly on the back of his neck to attract his attention again. 'Is it a battle between the forces of good and evil?'

'Clever lass! But I'll want more information than that if you are to be rewarded.'

She wondered what her reward would be and felt a curl of excitement in her belly. 'It is a battle that is to take place at the end of the world and has been described in such a manner that you have some idea what garb to wear. There will be a dragon representing Satan himself and a fierce princely angel with a shining sword. His name is Michael and his feast day is on the twenty-ninth day of this month. Is that what gave you the idea?'

'You will have your reward,' said Phillip, smiling. 'But right now we'll need to put on some speed if we are to arrive in Banbury before Ned and Jack.'

Rebecca whooped and then felt ashamed for giving way in such an exuberant manner. Just because she had guessed aright and they appeared to be on reasonably easy terms again, she must not take anything for granted where he was concerned. For the moment she would rest easy as she had left her responsibilities behind in Oxford, and until they arrived in Ludlow, she was free to be herself to relax and enjoy the rest of the journey by Phillip's side.

'So this is the mask you are going to wear tonight?' Rebecca turned the item carefully between her hands. They had arrived in Banbury halfway through the afternoon; by the time the wagon had joined them two hours later, Phillip had arranged most that was needful for the play. Rebecca had shopped for food, so they could have a meal before the performance. Jack had then been sent out with a drum to attract attention and inform the townspeople of the entertainment that evening.

Phillip turned away from his survey of the market square and the castle that loomed above the town and stretched out a hand for his mask which she handed over to him. It was one he had used in another performance and made of fabric stiffened with layers of thick paper glued together and painted black and red. It had horns and eye slits, as well as nostrils with holes that enabled the wearer to breathe the easier.

'What a pity that you can't play the hero,' said Rebecca, watching him. 'Although I suppose you have played the part of St George in the past?'

'I have played the saint, the dragon and the damsel he rescues,' said Phillip, holding the mask to his face.

Rebecca caught the glitter of his eyes through the slits and when he spat out a couple of his lines, she received something of a shock, for his voice was unrecognisable. 'You don't sound like yourself at all!'

He lowered the mask and his eyes flashed blue fire. 'I should hope not when I'm playing the prince of darkness.' His voice was deep and harsh.

'When you speak like that you send a shiver down my spine,' said Rebecca. 'Put the mask aside whilst I change your bandage.'

'As long as I make the audience shiver, too.' Phillip set the mask, which was shaped more like a helmet than a simple face mask, on top of the hamper that contained the costumes and props. He sat down and began to remove the bandage.

'They'll hiss and boo you,' she said.

'And enjoy doing so,' said Phillip, 'and then they'll cheer when Ned casts me down to hell.'

Rebecca was only half-listening as she stared at the ugly cut. 'It will be some time before this heals completely and you could be left with a scar,' she murmured.

Ned, who was already dressed for his part as the archangel, in a breastplate and white robe with large wings and a helmet circled by a crown, nodded. 'You were fortunate, Phillip; an inch closer and the swine could have taken your eye out.'

'As long as you don't do so with that sword,' warned Phillip, smiling. 'At least you look the part.'

Ned rubbed his jaw. 'I only hope I remember my lines.'

'Jack will prompt you if you forget,' said Phillip.

Rebecca, taking a bandage and salve from the box she had brought with her, felt nervous and said the first thing that came into her head. 'I remember having dealt with a splinter that caused a putrid wound and the youth died within a sennight.'

'On that cheerful note I will excuse myself,' said Ned, grimacing. He went to the back of the wagon with the script, drawing the curtain behind him.

Phillip glanced at Rebecca and she guessed by his expression that she had definitely said the wrong thing. 'I beg pardon. I wasn't thinking. Do you think I've upset Ned?' She watched Phillip reach for the bottom half of his dragon garb and pull it on as she unrolled the bandage.

'I am glad you are aware of such dangers, although when you first spoke I was concerned because Ned must forget it is me behind this disguise.' He reached for the top half of the dragon costume. 'But then I thought about Satan being a fallen angel, so once he would have been like a brother to Michael. That means this battle could be painful to the latter because he remembers what Satan once was. Yet he knows how the battle must end. So perhaps it is good that Ned uses his almost brotherly feelings towards me in this role.'

'I have never thought of it like that,' she murmured. 'One could almost feel sorry for Satan.'

Phillip raised an eyebrow. 'He chose the path he took. Anyhow, let's hope that Jack doesn't allow his mind to stray if Ned does forget his lines.' He summoned her forwards. 'Now the bandage.'

Rebecca stepped over a pair of shoes and stood

over him, determinedly controlling her nerves. The wound appeared clean enough, so she applied more salve before fixing the clean dressing into place, careful to keep a little distance between them. She wanted nothing more than that all would go well with the performance and they would be rewarded with a goodly sum. By doing so, surely they would feel the journey worth all the effort. Her job done, she wished him well before making herself scarce and leaving the wagon.

Phillip's eyes followed her, but then he squared his shoulders and of necessity put her out of his mind. He opened his mouth wide, exercising his jaw, allowing the story to play over in his thoughts. He and Ned had briefly rehearsed the moves he had written into the play, based partly on those they had used in *St George and the Dragon.* He expected their performance this evening would be far from perfect, but if they were to make any money, then at the very least it had to be good. He must stop toying with the idea that Rebecca could become part of this life he had worked so hard to build for himself and remind himself that it was an insecure and sometimes dangerous world he inhabited. Soon they would part, he for Greenwich, whilst she returned to Oxford with her brother.

* * *

The play was finished and Satan lay vanquished, happily with the mask still in place and the undamaged side of his head against the ground. The applause was thunderous and Rebecca sent thankful prayers winging heavenwards as she set a jug and three cups, as well as a plate of bread and salted pork and apples, on the folding table in the wagon. Part of her had not wanted to watch the performance in case something went wrong. If it had been an utter failure and the crowd had booed the actors and thrown rotten cabbages and turnips and windfalls at them in way of reward, she would have been utterly dejected. As it was, she need not have worried because it had been a battle royal of a performance that evening. If it went as well during the rest of their journey, she felt certain there would be smiling faces from the men. Now she was going to leave them to discuss their performances and retire for the night. She had already unrolled her pallet in the small space behind the curtain and wasted no time slipping behind it.

The following morning Rebecca had awoken before the men and had had to step carefully over them to go outside. The sun was already above the horizon and by the time she returned with freshly baked bread, she knew she would have to wake them if they were still asleep, so as to make certain they would arrive at their next destination in plenty of time.

She was only a short distance from the wagon when Phillip emerged from behind the canvas flap. His mop of flaxen hair was in disarray and the bandage had slipped. He pushed it back into place and stretched. Then he caught sight of her and smiled.

'It went well last night,' said Rebecca, returning his smile.

'Better than I deemed it would.' He placed a hand on the side of the wagon and vaulted to the ground. 'There wasn't a sound from you, so I presumed you were asleep when we came in last night.'

'I slept well considering how apprehensive I felt before the performance. You really do have cause to congratulate yourself, you know,' she said seriously.

His smile widened. 'You enjoyed it?'

'I was surprised just how believable was your transformation from angel to monster.'

'That was my intention.' His blue eyes glinted wickedly. 'But in the light of day I'm not so frightening, am I?'

'Hmm! I'm not so sure,' she teased, gazing

up at him. Then her smile faded as she noticed blood on the binding. 'The wound's bleeding again. Most likely it's because you move your head about so much within the mask during the performance. Is there any way the mask could be altered so it doesn't slide against your head?' She reached up to inspect the bandage more closely.

'Couldn't you fasten it more tightly?' asked Phillip.

'I'll replace the one you're wearing now and see if I can do that,' she murmured. 'Perhaps I should make the bandage thicker.'

'You do that,' said Phillip, frowning. 'But be quick about it because we must be on our way soon. As for the mask, I'll speak to Ned about it.'

'Ned and Jack are awake?'

'Aye, it is all right for you to enter the wagon.' He helped her up, his hand warm and firm about hers.

'Where is our next destination?' asked Rebecca, hoping that he had not noticed her hand trembling in his grasp.

'Warwick,' he replied, freeing her hand.

'Another town, another castle,' she murmured, reminding herself that they need must keep their distance.

Phillip thought about how Warwick's last lord had been beheaded by the king shortly after he had ascended to the throne. Since then Henry had strengthened the castle's defences and had yet to hand it over to its rightful owner, the present Earl of Warwick. Obviously he was not prepared to trust him despite to all appearances he was one of the king's faithful subjects. Phillip would watch and listen whilst in the town and gauge the temper of its citizens and report back to Wolsey, still the king's closest advisor. He thought that the problem with being involved in such matters was that one had to take sides. There could be no sticking to the middle road. By choosing to work for Wolsey, his enemies became Phillip's, too. If they were ever to discover he was working for the cardinal, then his life could be forfeit. Such danger was another reason why he had not taken a wife.

'And where after Warwick?' asked Rebecca, after bidding Ned and Jack a good morning.

'Hopefully Kidderminster and then Ludlow,' said Phillip, turning away. 'I'll be back shortly,' he called over his shoulder.

'He makes it sound close when he says it like that,' said Ned, relieving Rebecca of the basket. 'Well, if the next couple of evenings go as well as yesterday, then I'll have no complaints.'

'And if, when we reach Ludlow, we are invited

to perform before the princess, that will be even better,' said Jack happily.

Rebecca thought of her brother and wondered what he would make of her travelling with the troupe. Hopefully he would understand. After all, it was not as if Phillip was a stranger to him. More important, perhaps, would be his response to what they had to tell Davy about the *ghost* who looked so like their father.

Chapter Six

'Phillip, stop!' cried Rebecca.

He brought the wagon to a halt in Ludlow market square, several yards from the great stone edifice of the castle gatehouse. Beyond the outer bailey's protective walls could be seen the towering battlements of the keep. His horse had thrown a shoe earlier that afternoon and so they had travelled the rest of the way in the wagon. 'What is it?' he asked.

'I would swear we just passed Davy, only he vanished into the crowd before I could be absolutely certain and call out to him!' Her bright eyes met Phillip's.

He smiled. 'Which way did he go?' She gripped the corner of the seat and twisted her body, trying to spot him, but it proved difficult. Phillip placed an arm about her waist, fearing she might lose her balance. 'Be careful!' he warned.

She darted him a look and thought how they both seemed to have managed to do as he suggested and drawn a veil over that night in the stable. Their relationship on the journey had felt to her almost as that of a brother and sister, frustrating in its way, but far more sensible and useful in the circumstances. It was only when she slept that she relived that night in her dreams. She gripped his shoulder, gazing back the way they had come along the High Street. 'If it were Davy, then perhaps he was heading for the church,' she called. 'I'll get down and see if he is inside, shall I?'

'I'll come with you,' said Phillip, passing the reins over to Jack. 'Wait here! If anyone asks what you're doing, tell them we intend to get permission to put on a play here this evening. Ned, if you could take my horse to the blacksmith, I'd appreciate his replacing that shoe as swiftly as possible.'

He took out a coin and tossed it to Ned before climbing down. He reached up for Rebecca and swung her down, releasing her as soon as her feet touched the ground. They headed in the direction of the church, despite the fact that there was now no sign of Davy. For a moment they paused outside St Laurence's and became aware that someone was playing the organ within its walls. 'Shall we go and see if that's Davy?' asked Rebecca.

Phillip opened the door and ushered her inside. She gazed about her but it took several moments for her eyes to adjust to the gloomy interior before she caught sight of her brother. He was not alone, but with a young man whose voice soared magnificently to the rafters.

Rebecca and Phillip exchanged glances. 'I hate to interrupt them,' he murmured.

'Aye, he has the voice of an angel, although he does not look as I would imagine an angel to look,' she whispered, for the young man had jet-black hair and his clothing was of a sombre hue.

There came a pause in the proceedings and so she walked towards her brother. The young man caught sight of her and brought his dark head down closer to Davy's. He turned and stared in his sister's direction. 'Rebecca, by all that is holy, what are you doing here?'

'I've come to see you, of course,' she replied, unable to tell, from the sound of his voice, if he was glad to see her. He had always been a little offhand when caught up in his music.

As it was, her brother rose to his feet and came towards her with arms outstretched. 'It's an unexpected pleasure to see you. It's been so long!'

They hugged each other and then he held her off from him and looked down at her. 'You look tired,' he said, sounding concerned.

Rebecca shrugged. 'I've been travelling for days. As for you, brother, you look so fine in the princess's livery of blue and green, although I fear that you still do not eat enough.'

His austere features broke into an even wider smile. 'Still the same old Rebecca, wanting to stuff me up with food. I eat enough for my needs,' he said firmly. 'Tell me, little sister, what brings you here besides familial affection?'

She linked her arm through that of her brother. 'I have questions to which I hope you can provide the answers. But I must ask you to forgive me for interrupting your work.'

'You've no need to worry. We can resume our work later.' Davy turned to the young man and spoke softly before saying to his sister, 'This is Tomas and he's Spanish. He accompanied his father on a visit to the queen, but when she heard Tomas sing, she decided to send him here, knowing her daughter would have great pleasure in hearing him.'

Overhearing those words, Phillip wondered if there was another reason why the queen should have sent the young Spaniard here. A secret message from her nephew, the King of Spain, perhaps.

Rebecca inclined her head in Tomas's direction and he bowed to her. Then he said something to Davy in Latin. He nodded and Tomas walked over to the line of heavily carved misericords nearby and pulled down one of the seats and sat on it.

'Perhaps we should sit down, too,' suggested Rebecca. 'This might take some time.'

'You said *us* earlier,' said her brother, making no move to join the young man. 'Who have you travelled with?'

Phillip moved out of the shadows of a soaring pillar into the light and came forwards with his hand outstretched. 'Davy, it's good to see you.'

'God's teeth, if it isn't Pip Hurst!' exclaimed Davy, taking his hand and shaking it. 'I never expected to see you two here together! What is this about?'

Phillip glanced at Rebecca and smiled. 'Your sister needed a protector on the road and, as I happened to be in Oxford, I volunteered my services.'

'I presume the pair of you did not travel alone,' said Davy, wrapping his gown of blue and green tightly about him and looking slightly disapproving.

'Of course not,' said Rebecca. 'We are here with Phillip's troupe of players and they hope to put on a play later today.'

'Your sister has been of great help to us,' said Phillip smoothly.

'I never thought my sister had such an appetite for adventure,' said Davy.

'I'm beginning to understand the fascination of such a life,' said Rebecca lightly.

'Is that why you've come to see me?' he said abruptly. 'You seek my approval. Is it that you've tired of living with the Caldwells? I believe Pip is quite popular with the ladies and so I hope you've been behaving yourselves. I have my reputation at court to consider.'

His words stunned Rebecca and her cheeks burned with embarrassment. 'May I remind you, brother, that I am a widow and do not need your approval. I tell you now that I am no man's mistress.' She made to walk away, but Phillip caught hold of her arm and brought her against his side.

'You have an odd notion of the etiquette in such matters, Davy,' he said, aware that the Spaniard was staring at him. 'Maybe that comes from listening to court gossip. Whilst I am no angel, nor am I a satyr either. If you spent more time with your only sister, then you'd know her better than to judge her in such a way. If you wish to know the truth about our relationship, it is that of old acquaintances. There are occasions when we disagree and argue and others when we are very much in accord. She considers my brother, Nicholas, the more worthy man than myself.'

Rebecca protested, 'You are as good as he.'

Davy looked uncomfortable and said stiffly, 'I apologise. I have little contact with the fairer sex and our mother was…'

'Was what?' cried Rebecca, increasingly annoyed with her brother. 'What has she to do with anything? I am not the least like her. And I'll thank you not to pass such judgement on me again.'

There was an uncomfortable silence.

'Very well—again, I apologise,' said Davy, two spots of colour high on his cheekbones.

'I accept your apology. Now will you please listen while I explain what brings me here?' Rebecca could contain her impatience no longer. She paused slightly for effect. 'Simon Caldwell believes he saw Father's ghost.'

Davy paled and took a step back. 'Where did he see this apparition?'

Rebecca blinked at him. 'You believe in ghosts, brother dear?' she asked, surprised.

'Why not? I'm certain Father had plenty

of unfinished business to deal with on earth. Continue!'

'Simon confided in Phillip as he knew he would be likely to recognise our father if he saw him and Phillip did see a man in Oxford whom he swore was the image of our father, so I began to wonder if Father had a brother or a cousin.'

'I wish you hadn't asked me that,' said Davy, sitting down abruptly.

Rebecca clutched Phillip's arm. 'Why?'

Davy rubbed his face with his hands. 'Father had a twin brother! Identical in looks, but so different in their ways.'

'Wha-what happened?' asked Rebecca, flabbergasted.

'He ran away with our mother.'

Rebecca was so shocked that she could only stare at him. Phillip placed his arm around her and led her over to the misericord and sat her down. 'Now that we did not expect,' he murmured.

Her head was in a whirl. 'How could they betray Father? He must have been so hurt. No wonder he was bitter and used to get so angry with me.'

'Father hated Uncle Anthony, even before he ran away with our mother,' said Davy heavily.

'But why didn't you tell me any of this?' cried

Rebecca, reaching out a hand to him and then letting it fall. 'It explains so much. He was frightened of being hurt all over again, that is why he would not show me affection.'

Davy surprised her by kneeling in front of her and taking her hand. 'Please, don't get upset. Father threatened that if I ever spoke of either one of them, he would beat me black and blue. I was scared of him and dared not risk disobeying him. Be glad that you were too young to remember those days.'

'But surely you could have told me all this after Father died?' said Rebecca, disagreeing with him.

Davy shrugged. 'What good would it have done?'

'It would have helped me to understand Father better, so I could forgive him,' she said reasonably. 'And we wouldn't have had to come all this way to see you.'

He hesitated. 'Perhaps I should have done so because I have wondered since if Mama might have come to see us if she knew Father was dead. I am certain she did care about us.'

'Whatever she felt, it could not have been love,' said Rebecca sharply. 'Otherwise she would never have deserted us.'

Warring emotions crossed Davy's face. 'You

didn't know her like I did,' he said eventually. 'I had a lot of difficulty believing that she could have behaved the way she did. Unless—'

'Unless what?' demanded Rebecca.

'It doesn't matter,' said Davy gloomily.

Exasperated, Rebecca looked at Phillip, wondering what he made of it all. He raised an eyebrow but remained silent. 'What am I to do?' she asked. 'It can't be anyone else but my uncle, can it?'

'No. It could be that he has heard of your father's death and that's why he's come looking for you,' said Phillip. 'The question is—for what purpose?'

She sighed. 'It's not as if there was money in the family.'

'But there probably is,' said Davy, staring at the pair of them. 'But it's Uncle Anthony who has it. He was the elder twin, so he inherited.'

'But inherited what?' cried Rebecca, getting to her feet and pacing the floor. 'A thriving business, land, what?'

'The manor of Minster Draymore,' said Davy hoarsely. 'Our grandmother was a Draymore. I vaguely remember her, but our grandfather, a Mortimer, died at the Battle of Bosworth, so well before I was born. I told you, didn't I, that I thought we could be descended from the

Mortimer who once owned Ludlow Castle? We are, but not so it matters.'

'Oh, dear God!' said Rebecca, wrapping her arms about herself. 'Why did this uncle have to come back into our lives?'

Phillip said, 'It must be your uncle who's hired Master Caldwell to do the rebuilding on the manor house! It was where the so-called ghost was first seen, after all.'

Rebecca lifted her head. 'But surely Simon would have recognised his name when he was mentioned as the owner?'

'If you remember, he said that he'd never met the man who'd employed him. As for the name, it's possible your uncle used another name, as well as an agent to deal with the matter for him,' said Phillip, holding her gaze.

For a moment she could only stare at him, wondering what difference this news might make to her life. She wondered if he was thinking the same. Then Davy, his face alight, said, 'Perhaps Mother sent him to find us! She could have regretted her actions and, having heard about Father's death, wanted to make amends.'

Rebecca shook her head. 'I can well understand why you should want to believe it so, but why did she not simply accompany him to Oxford?'

'Perhaps she feared we might reject her,' said Davy.

'It seems to me, Brother, that you've set your mind on forgiving her.' Rebecca's voice was stony.

'It's what Christ told us to do,' said Davy.

Rebecca flinched. 'Brother, I believe I have a good reason why I should find it difficult to forgive her.'

Phillip intervened. 'This debate isn't getting either of you anywhere. You need to make a decision. Do you try to make contact with your uncle or not? After all, it could be that your mother is dead.'

'If she is, then it will make no difference to me,' said Rebecca, firming her chin. 'She's been dead to me for most of my life and I would prefer it to remain that way. You might consider that harsh, Phillip,' she added, catching his eye, 'but you didn't grow up without a mother's love.'

'I wouldn't deny it, Becky,' said Phillip, going over to her and taking her hand. 'But we both know your father wasn't the easiest of men and she might have had a good reason to run from him.'

She snatched back her hand and her lips quivered. 'B-but she didn't have to run away with Father's twin. They—they both betrayed him and because of that Father became a different person. Most likely he would have treated me more kindly if they hadn't behaved the way they did!'

'Possibly, but could it be that you are making excuses for your father now?'

His words puzzled her. 'Why should I make excuses for him?'

Phillip hesitated.

'Say what you think!' said Rebecca, her eyes as hard as pebbles. 'After all, you didn't hesitate to say what you thought earlier about my feelings for your brother.'

'I was confident that what I said was true.'

'Have you ever thought you could be mistaken, Phillip?' she snapped.

'Enough, Rebecca,' said Davy, sounding weary. 'You're normally a sensible person, but you make mistakes, too. Let's forget about Father. He's dead. We need to come to a decision about Uncle Anthony. I suggest that we try to make contact with him.'

'We? You mean you,' said Rebecca tartly, 'for I will have nothing to do with him!'

The two men exchanged looks that angered her further. She knew what those looks meant. That she was a woman and allowing her emotions to rule her. So what if that was true? Tears of rage and disappointment pricked her eyes. *I've had enough of men! Why can't they be more like women?* As her tears spilled over, she turned and ran out of the church.

She stood outside, wiping her eyes with her sleeve, wishing that she had not come to Ludlow. She would have been happier not knowing the truth. And how could her brother have embarrassed her so by saying what he did about her to Phillip? As for the latter, when was he going to realise that she preferred him to his brother, otherwise she would not have welcomed him into her body? Perhaps she had given Phillip reason to believe in the past that she had once been in love with his brother and considered him a real hero, but surely after the night they had spent together, he should know better?

'So what do you plan to do next?'

Rebecca jumped at the sound of Phillip's voice. She turned to face him and wished she could say what was in her heart. Instead she muttered, 'I cannot think at the moment. Besides, I thought you and Davy had already decided upon the best course of action.'

Phillip hesitated, then he put his hand beneath her chin and tilted it. 'Perhaps,' he said lightly. 'But doubtless by the time we return to Oxford, you will have hatched a plan of your own.'

'I will not meet my father's twin,' she said,

a tremor in her voice, as she gazed up into his eyes. *So blue that they rivalled a cloudless sky.*

'That is your decision,' said Phillip, resisting the urge to plant a kiss on her mouth for saying earlier that he was as good as his brother.

'But you think I should meet him, don't you?'

'You must do what you deem is right.'

'I will,' she said firmly. 'Will you be returning to Oxford?'

'That was my original plan. Why do you ask?'

'I—I thought you'd go straight to the court at Greenwich after all that's been said.'

His expression altered and he dropped his hand. 'I do not spend much time at court. The king likes variety and it is his Master of Revels, Sir Henry Guildford, who organises matters for His Grace's entertainment. Of course, Henry often requests certain people to perform before him and I am generally only expected to put on a play for special occasions, such as a feast day, although there are times when he summons my troupe unexpectedly. So I will not be going directly to Greenwich Palace, even if the king has changed his plans and moved his court there before the latter half of December. I will be travelling to Christopher's house and staying there for a while. So you don't want to believe all your brother says about the ladies or even your own eyes.'

'I accept some of what you say, but why shouldn't I believe in your powers of attraction?' said Rebecca in a slightly breathless voice. 'You're a handsome man. You might hide yourself behind a mask or cosmetics and wig, but there is no question that there must be plenty of women who would swoon at your feet and warm your bed.'

Phillip's brows snapped together and his eyes darkened with anger. 'So you have chosen to believe your brother's gossip and decided that you were just one in a line of women whom I've made love to! Well, it is not true! The king might be unfaithful to the queen and have an illegitimate son, but I have no intention of apeing him by taking a mistress and doing likewise. I know I should not have made love to you that night in the stable, but we both have a fair idea why it happened. Still, when I eventually marry I will remain faithful to my wife. At the moment my situation is unsuited to matrimony—I need peace and quiet to write and women are too much of a distraction.'

'Then I will take myself off if I am such a distraction to you,' she said, tossing her head.

'Don't be a fool, Becky. You are behaving like

a child rather than a grown woman. I hold you in too much esteem to treat you ill.'

Did he really mean that? Her uncertain grey eyes met his guileless blue ones and both held fast. 'I deem that you are trying to make me feel better about myself,' said Rebecca in a whisper.

He cocked an eyebrow. 'And what were you doing when you told me that you find me handsome? I remember you hinted that as a younger brother I might feel cast in the shade by Nicholas. Of course, that was well before you told me that I was as good as he.'

'And so you are, but it is true that sometimes a younger sibling suffers from a lack of confidence,' said Rebecca. 'Perhaps that is why you enjoy the art of disguising so much. It means you can pretend to be someone other than yourself.'

A ghost of a smile lifted the corners of his mouth and he drawled, 'How well you know me, Becky. Perhaps if you were to come to court during the twelve days of Christmas, then you could pretend to be my wife to keep the other women at bay. I would then not have to bother with a real one.'

'You're teasing me. I'm sure you'd want a woman altogether different from me to fill that role,' she said.

'I'm not so sure as you of that,' he found himself saying as his gaze washed over her. 'Perhaps we should act out such roles some time.'

Her heart began to thud. 'I don't know why we are having such a conversation when we both have more important matters to think about,' she said breathlessly.

Phillip nodded. 'I would not deny that,' he rasped. 'I have a play to put on and Davy has taken up my idea that he speak to Lady Salisbury, the princess's governess, about our performing inside the castle.'

Rebecca's mood instantly changed. 'This evening?'

'The performance will have to be this evening if it is to take place. Davy has told me that Princess Mary and her entourage leave for Worcestershire in the morning. As it is, there is no guarantee she will grant him permission to return to Oxford with us.'

'He said that?' Rebecca nibbled her lower lip. 'Surely if he explains—'

'Would you want to explain the situation to an eleven-year-old girl whose father has cast doubt on her legitimacy for having married his brother's widow and now wants that marriage annulled?'

She was shocked. 'You believe the princess is aware of that?'

'Mary is no fool,' said Phillip.

'Poor little princess,' said Rebecca softly.

'Aye, much better not to be too close to the throne,' said Phillip, smiling grimly. 'As for Davy, he does not want to lose his position at her court, but he does want to make contact with your uncle.'

Rebecca nodded. 'I can see another reason why that might be. If our uncle is rich and he were to make Davy his heir, then he would not have to worry so much about losing the favour of the princess.'

Phillip agreed and slung an arm about her shoulders. 'Come, Becky, let's return to the others. You will see your brother later, after he has spoken to Lady Salisbury. Although after the way he insulted us both, I don't know why we should wish to be friends with him at all.'

'You know why,' said Rebecca, allowing her head to rest on Phillip's shoulder a moment. She was confused as to what his real feelings were towards her because so much of his life was a pretence.

'One forgives one's family much,' said Phillip. 'Although will the princess, even though she shares her mother's religious fervour, be able to forgive her father?'

Rebecca considered his words. 'What are

you trying to suggest? That I should forgive my mother for leaving me? Well, I am not so religious that I am ready to do that!' Without another word, she ducked beneath his arm and walked away.

Rebecca watched the two men as they took another bow in Princess Mary's direction. Her Highness signalled to Phillip to step forwards and dropped a purse into his hand, thanking him for his performance. She added that there was supper for them in the kitchen. Her youthful face was animated so that she looked much prettier than she had done earlier, when her small mouth was set hard as she had watched a white-robed Ned send the red-and-black evil-looking dragon crashing to the earth with a hefty whack of the sword. She had taken it all so seriously, thought Rebecca. As had the young Spanish singer, Tomas, and his uncle, whom Davy had pointed out to her.

Earlier, her brother had told her and Phillip that word had reached them that Henry had elevated his bastard son to Duke of Richmond and Somerset, as well as making him the Earl of Nottingham. To what purpose? Surely the princess must be wondering what the boy's elevation would mean for her future? Fortunately she still appeared to be all that a princess and heir to the throne of England should be. Gems sparkled in her headdress and at her throat and the blue-silk gown she wore glistened with tiny crystals.

What wouldn't I give to wear such a gown, even for just an evening! thought Rebecca. Yet she knew that she would not change positions with the young princess for all the jewels in England, and she was ready to leave for home. Happily the princess had consented to Davy returning with Rebecca to Oxford after consulting with Lady Salisbury but she had added a condition. In a sennight he must report to her at Tickenhall Manor, refurbished at great expense by the king as a bolthole from the plague and much closer to London.

Rebecca was thinking about that as she left the hall in the wake of the men. The wagon had been brought into the inner courtyard and there the men changed into their everyday garb before they made their way across to the kitchen, which was in a separate building to that of the great hall. The food was good and filling and with the performance over and having been applauded and rewarded, the men relaxed, but Rebecca could not.

As she ate a slice of roasted chicken, she could not take her eyes from Phillip as he talked to one of the chefs and serving men before turning to Ned. Was he explaining the situation about her brother and their uncle to the other player? Had her uncle returned to the area purely because he now intended living in the manor house at Minster Draymore? And where had he and her mother been all this time? Sensing her eyes upon him, Phillip looked up and met her gaze with a questioning look. Her pulses began to race and she felt as if she could not breathe and knew she had to get some fresh air.

Outside in the courtyard the atmosphere was only marginally fresher, for the smell of cooking food and wood smoke hung in the air, but she took deep breaths and walked away from the building. At least there was a moon and myriads of stars. Then she heard a door open behind her; she turned and saw Phillip, although she could barely make out his features beneath the brim of his hat.

'Why have you come out here?' he asked. 'You have no cloak and you could catch a chill.'

'I needed fresh air and wanted to be alone for a while.'

'Is that a hint for me to go away?'

'You're entitled to take the air as much as I am, not that it's much fresher out here,' she said in a low voice. 'It's as if the walls have captured the fumes and are holding them prisoner.'

'The air will be much fresher higher up,' said Phillip, glancing up at the battlements. 'Not that I'm suggesting we go up there, even though Davy was saying there is an excellent view of the countryside.'

'Even so it's a good idea,' said Rebecca, wasting no time picking up her skirts and running over to one of the towers.

'Don't be a fool!' shouted Phillip. 'It could be dangerous.'

'You don't have to come with me,' she called over her shoulder.

'It'll be dark on the stairway and you might slip.'

She hesitated, but then decided it wouldn't be pitch black because there were openings in the tower walls. 'I'll be careful,' she shouted, entering one of the circular towers where she remembered glimpsing the foot of a spiral stairway.

By the time Phillip reached the tower she was out of sight. Worried about her safety, he barely hesitated before seizing hold of the rope that served as a handrail and beginning to climb. Fortunately moonlight slanted through the opening close to every turn, but the way was extremely narrow. Once he heard her stumble somewhere above him out of sight and he swore savagely and made haste.

Rebecca emerged on to a narrow walkway. Her heart was pounding with exertion and she felt slightly sick instead of excited. She rested against the wall to catch her breath and gazed out at the countryside. Silver and black in the moonlight, it stretched for miles to the distant hills, which bordered Wales. Her knees began to shake and she moved back, turned and retraced her steps. It was much more frightening descending and she had to go slowly. Then she saw a dark shape below her and heard breathing, and felt relief as the next moment she collided with Phillip.

He seized her by the shoulders and rammed her against the wall. 'I hope it was worth it, you lackwit! What were you trying to prove?'

'I—I wasn't trying t-to prove anything!' she stammered. 'I j-just wanted to see the view, only w-when I got up there I knew it would be more sensible not to linger.'

'At least you have some sense,' he growled. 'Was the view worth it?'

'It was beautiful, but now let us go down,' she said.

'I should wring your neck.'

'Just for climbing a tower?' She forced a laugh. 'Don't you think that's a mite excessive as a punishment? Now let me pass.'

'I should keep you here all night,' he said, his wine-scented breath on her face.

A pleasurable thrill surged through her as his body crushed hers against the hard stone wall. 'That would be foolish. It's cold here.' Her foot slipped on the uneven stone step and she clung to him. 'And dangerous, as you warned me,' she whispered.

He loosened his grip and seized her hand, placing it on the rope. 'Now get going!'

She had no choice but to obey him and carefully descended the steps, conscious of his presence close behind her. It was a relief to emerge into the courtyard and she did not wait for Phillip to catch up with her, but ran over to the wagon. She expected him to follow her and wasted no time retiring behind the curtain. She did not undress, but curled up on her pallet in the darkness and drew her blanket over her, shivering with a mixture of excitement and nerves. Perhaps he still wanted to punish her, but maybe he would make love to her? He had been physically roused there on the stairs, despite the danger. Why had she felt a need to provoke Phillip to anger, knowing that by doing so she was putting both their lives at risk? Perhaps it was because discovering that her mother had run off with her father's brother had filled her with not only fury, but shame that her own mother could behave in such a way. She hated her for what she had done and knowing that Phillip was not on her side in this had been so hurtful.

After a while, when he did not enter the wagon after her, she began to feel forlorn. Why had he not followed her? She had begun to believe that he cared for her. After all, he had risked his life climbing those steps, despite his having a fear of heights. He had called her a lackwit, so perhaps his anger with her was greater than his desire for her? She continued to hope he might yet come, but none of the men came and eventually she remembered that they were sleeping in the castle and drifted into sleep.

She woke the following morning to find herself alone still. She decided to get up and make her way to the kitchen. Hopefully there she would find warmth and food and at least one member of the troupe.

As Rebecca crossed the courtyard, she realised that she was not alone in rising early. There were several people out and about and when she entered the kitchen it was to discover all was hustle and bustle. Only then did she recall that the princess and her entourage were leaving for Worcestershire that morning. She caught sight of Phillip talking to someone and hesitated before making her way towards him. He caught sight of her before she reached him and broke off his conversation. His expression was unsmiling and she guessed he was vexed with her.

'So when do we leave?' asked Rebecca without preamble.

'You're not travelling with me,' said Phillip shortly, hoisting a saddlebag over his shoulder. 'Your brother is borrowing a horse for you; he decided that the pair of you will reach Oxford the swifter without the wagon.'

Her eyes searched his handsome face for any sign of regret. 'So what are your feelings about that?'

Phillip raised his eyebrows. 'Did you expect me to disagree with him? He is your brother after all. Besides, I've come to the conclusion that I've used up enough time coming here and will make my way to Greenwich alone.' Naturally, he kept quiet about visiting Cardinal Wolsey with information about the princess's Spanish visitors. 'Perhaps I'll see you again in the not-too-distant future.' He raised a hand in farewell and strode out of the kitchen, leaving her feeling rejected and close to tears.

Chapter Seven

It had been the most tedious of journeys. Almost at the last minute Davy had informed her that the Spaniard, Tomas, was to accompany them. So instead of having her brother all to herself, she felt sidelined as he and Tomas talked to each other in Latin. She could not help but compare the return journey to that of the one to Ludlow which had been full of interest and excitement. She was relieved beyond measure when she saw the spires of Oxford appearing through the autumnal mist as if they belonged to some heavenly city. She had missed Phillip more than she had thought possible. At least she would soon be seeing Jane and the children. The time away had made her realise how fond of them she was, so it had been worth the journey for that reason alone.

It proved that they had also missed her and welcomed her warmly. The children were a little shy with Davy and Tomas, but Jane appeared pleased to see them both. When Davy asked after her husband and whether there had been any sign of the so-called *ghost,* she shook her head. 'I have seen no one answering to your description. Perhaps you should visit my husband and see if he has any news.'

So Davy set out for Minister Draymore whilst Tomas asked to be excused as he wished to visit one of the colleges. Rebecca, also, remained behind as she had much to tell Tabitha and Jane about her travels. Whilst Tabitha wanted to hear all about the play and how it had been received, Jane was more interested in the princess and Lady Salisbury and their clothes and jewels. Rebecca, who had taken mental note of these, was able to describe them in detail, much to Jane's satisfaction. Of Phillip's decision to go on ahead to Greenwich, she said little, but Tabitha was anxious to know what his absence might mean for her and Ned.

'You mustn't worry,' said Rebecca. 'I'm certain Ned will have good news for you on his return. In the meantime, you will remain here.'

'Ned and I have never been apart since we first met and I can't wait to see him,' murmured Tabitha, patting the baby's back after feeding him.

'He told me that he missed you, too,' said Rebecca, experiencing a yearning to be back with Phillip and the troupe despite the discomfort.

'I'm glad,' said Tabitha, beaming. 'Ned's not one to show his feelings.'

'That's men for you,' said Jane, smiling at the baby.

'But I wonder when next we'll see Master Phillip,' said Tabitha.

'I wonder,' murmured Rebecca. 'He does have a play to write to perform before the king and because he does not wish to be distracted, no doubt he will shut himself away at his brother's house. He told me that he also needs to get in touch with the Raventons. Which means it could be some time before we see him again.'

Phillip put down his quill and moved from the chair to the bed and lay down. He closed his eyes and thought over what he had written. Then his mind wandered to thoughts of Rebecca and he regretted, not for the first time, the cold manner in which he had taken his leave of her. But he had been unable to say what was really on his mind and ask why had she run from him to the wagon. At the time he had thought he had frightened her with his talk of wringing her neck. He had wanted to follow her to reassure her that he would never harm her, but he had been in a state of arousal and knew that temptation awaited him in the wagon. Knowing that Ned and Jack would be sleeping in the castle, he had forced himself to walk away. He sighed and ran a hand through his hair. Maybe right now she, too, was regretting the way they had parted? He needed to find out.

The sound of the door opening alerted him to his eldest brother's presence and he opened his eyes. 'I didn't realise you were back until my goodwife told me,' grumbled Christopher, closing the door behind him. 'I never know when you're going to turn up. You really should give up that wandering life of yours and settle down.'

Phillip groaned. 'You should say that to Nicholas, not me.'

'I will when I see him again.'

When, not if! noted Phillip and immediately sat up and stared at his brother's stocky figure. 'You've heard from him?'

'Not from him but of him,' said Christopher, sitting at the foot of the bed. 'I've received a message from our kin in Bruges. It's not all good.'

'He's not rotting in some foreign prison, is he?'

'Begad, no! Apparently Nicholas fell in love with some woman, not knowing she was betrothed to a Spanish sea captain. This captain had been away for nine months or more and so she indulged in a passionate affair with our brother.'

Phillip experienced a flood of relief. 'Are they to wed?'

'No, unfortunately the Spaniard returned and discovered them together. A fight ensued. It was something of a bloody affair, so I'm informed, but both survived and Nicholas is licking his wounds at a secret location. God permitting, we can expect him in England within the month.'

Phillip's grin faded and he rasped his unshaven jaw with a fingernail. 'A secret location? Does that mean Nicholas believes himself to be in danger?'

'You've hit the nail on the head! He deems it possible that the sea captain could still want him dead.' Christopher sighed and rubbed his face with his hands.

Phillip was aware of conflicting emotions, wondering how this might affect him and Becky. He reached for the cup at his elbow and downed its contents. 'He's obviously no longer in love with Beth Raventon, but does he love this woman or was he driven purely by lust?'

'Whatever his feelings for her, let's hope he comes safely home and finds himself a sensible English woman and settles down. If you're not prepared to stay here permanently and help train my boys, then he must take over some of the organisation so I can spend more time seeing to their training,' said Christopher firmly. 'Can I depend on your being here until Nicholas returns? I have an order to complete.'

'That was my plan. I can write here as well as anywhere else. As long as I have the evenings to myself, I'll put most of the daylight hours at your disposal,' said Phillip absently. 'Which reminds me. That favour I asked of your goodwife—?'

Christopher's chin slumped on to his collar bone and he blinked at his brother. 'Aye, they can come here. I just hope they can do what's necessary.'

Phillip stifled a yawn. 'Would I foist them on you if they weren't likely to be of use to you? Tabitha is a hard worker and Ned's strong—his father was a carpenter. Ned might not have finished his apprenticeship, but he's the best you can get considering there's a shortage of experienced ship's carpenters.'

'That's why I need you,' said Christopher.

'What of the younger one? What's his name? Jack.'

'He's a quick learner and can help out in any way you see fit. I'll be back to keep him in line within the week, but come the latter half of December I'll be engaged at court.'

Christopher nodded. 'All right. But you do realise if you ever decide to marry and have a family, you're going to have to rent or build a house of your own one day.'

'I'm not a fool, brother,' drawled Phillip, pouring more wine. 'Now after all you've just said, I think it would be best if I left for Oxford in the morning in order to tell the troupe they're needed here.'

'I suppose the sooner you're gone, the sooner you'll return,' said Christopher, glancing out of the window towards the river. 'Although it looks like there could be a storm brewing.'

As Rebecca darned the heel of a pair of hose, she had to admit that without Phillip on the scene, she was finding life almost as dull as the journey back from Ludlow. How long would it be before she saw him again? She wouldn't be feeling so irritable if he was here and they were friends once more. She had matters to discuss with him and wanted to know his thoughts. Her uncle—

not that she wanted to meet him—had not been seen again at Minster Draymore or in Oxford and, although her brother had asked Jane's husband to get in touch with the agent who had employed him, nothing had been heard from him so far. Davy and Tomas had stayed in Oxford only a couple of days more before leaving to rejoin Princess Mary's household, so the search for their father's twin was no further forwards. What would Phillip suggest she should do?

Feeling restless, she put down her darning and went over to the window and gazed out. The wind had whipped most of the leaves from the trees and it was howling around the house. Despite it only being halfway through the afternoon it was already getting dark. She prayed it would not rain, otherwise Jane and the children would be soaked. Her sister-in-law had insisted on going out, saying that this would be her last opportunity to visit an old friend and her family before she was confined to the house for the last few weeks of her pregnancy.

Suddenly Rebecca heard an almighty crash and the whole house shook. She started with fright, wondering what had happened. Due to the noise of the wind, she was unsure where the sound had come from, but decided most likely it was from outside. With her heart in her mouth, she reached for her cloak and hurried to the front door. As she opened it, the wind caught it and if she had not clung on to it, she feared the door would have been torn off its hinges. She managed to manoeuvre herself around the door and pull it shut. Then, struggling against the wind, she set off around the house in search of the cause of the noise. She had not gone far when she discovered that a tree had been uprooted and crashed on to the roof.

She was aghast and for several moments could do no more than stare at it. Then, knowing she could do no good standing there, she turned and, with the wind at her back, scurried towards the front of the house. A figure loomed up in front of her, but she couldn't do anything to stop herself from being blown against him.

'God's blood, Becky, what are you doing out here?' shouted Phillip, gripping her by the arms. 'When are you going to use your common sense, woman?'

'Don't call me woman!' Her first reaction on seeing him was delight, then he opened his mouth and what he said filled her with indignation. 'I heard a noise and I had to come and see what caused it,' she said, a sparkle in her eyes. 'I thought that was sensible, but you obviously don't agree. That aside, I have to say that I'm pleased to see you because I need your help. A tree has blown over and fallen on the house and something has to be done.'

'Talk sense, Becky! What can we do in this wind? No, let's get inside.' He hustled her to the front door as the first heavy drops of rain landed on their heads and shoulders.

'Are you sure it's safe?' she asked, clinging to his arm, glad of his strength.

'Has the tree come through the ceiling downstairs?'

'It hadn't when I left the house.'

'Then hopefully it is safe,' said Phillip, smoothing back a strand of wet hair from her face with a hand that quivered before forcing open the front door.

Once inside and with the door closed, they collapsed against it. 'I haven't known a gale like this for an age,' gasped Rebecca, wiping her wet face with her sleeve.

'Me neither,' said Phillip, smiling across at her.

Rebecca blinked at him and returned his smile. 'When did you get here?'

'Two hours ago. I decided to make the journey before the weather worsened.'

'I'm glad you did,' said Rebecca. *Obviously he was no longer angry with her and that made her feel good.* 'I'm all alone in the house and I doubt this storm is going to blow itself out in a hurry. Shall we move away from here? There's a freezing draught coming under the door and we'll be warmer by the fire. That's if the tree hasn't crushed the chimney stack and extinguished the fire since I've been out.'

They went into the parlour. Phillip's eyes swept the room. 'Nothing much wrong here, although, it looks as if some debris has been dislodged from above.'

Rebecca removed her wet cloak and sank on to the settle in front of the fire and warmed her hands. 'Have you come for Ned, Tabitha and Jack?'

Phillip removed his cloak and hat and draped them over a stool. He thought it was typical of her to be concerned about others before herself. 'Aye, I've come to take them all to Greenwich. Tabitha can help in my brother's house, as you suggested, and the men can labour in my brother's shipyard while there is an order to finish. There will be little work during the winter, so I will need to rethink matters after that.' He flopped down on the settle beside her and glanced at her. 'But obviously, if I'm here with you, that isn't my only reason for coming to Oxford. I had to see you, Becky.'

She let out a soft 'Oh!' and turned her head and stared directly at him.

For several moments Phillip could only return her stare. Amongst other things he had come to tell her that he had news of Nicholas, but the sound of that 'oh' and the expression in her eyes caused him to hesitate about mentioning him. 'I wasn't kind to you,' he said, sitting beside her and taking her hand.

Her fingers quivered in his grasp. 'I behaved badly. I set out deliberately to annoy you by climbing the tower. I was hurt because you thought I was an unforgiving daughter. I know you didn't use those exact words, but they hurt all the same.'

'I didn't mean to upset you.'

'No.' Her voice was warm. 'You knew and loved your mother, so naturally you find it difficult putting yourself in my shoes. I wish I'd been your mother's daughter.'

'No, don't say that! It really would make you my sister and I don't feel the least brotherly to you.'

She stared at him with a blush on her cheeks. 'I'm tempted to ask you what you do feel, but I deem that wouldn't be sensible.'

'Not the least bit sensible. If I were to kiss you—'

'It would be an enjoyable experience but as we both know not wise with us all alone in the house.' She tried to turn their conversation to matters less fraught with emotion, although her heart beat fast at the thought. 'We must check the upstairs chambers; there must be a hole in the roof and the rain will be ruining the bed-chambers. It wouldn't surprise me, either, if the kitchen fire has gone out. I'm hungry and would like a hot drink and no doubt so would you. I should go and see.'

Phillip kissed her hand before releasing it. 'I suppose I should thank the saints that most of the time you're such a sensible woman,' he said drily.

'But you're not thanking them, are you?' said Rebecca, flashing him a saucy look as she rose to her feet.

He stood and gave in to temptation, catching hold of her and bringing her against him to kiss her long and hard. Then he released her without a word. She led the way to the kitchen, thinking that as long as they were sensible, what harm could there be in a few kisses? Especially when that one made her smile and want to carry on smiling.

'There's a hellish mess in here,' said Phillip, looking over her shoulder as she gazed in dismay at the kitchen. A large amount of soot and debris had come down the chimney and not only put out the fire, but spread over the hearth, floor, table and shelves. Specks still floated in the air.

'I can see Jane bursting into tears when she sees this,' said Rebecca grimly.

Phillip stood with his hands on his hips, looking up at the ceiling. 'See the cracks. If it's this bad down here, then—'

'—how bad is it upstairs?' muttered Rebecca, doing an about-turn and making for the stairs.

'Wait!' Phillip hurried after her and seized a handful of skirt and dragged her down the stairs and into his arms. 'I'll go first.'

Rebecca decided not to argue with him. She liked a strong man and there were times when she was glad to be told what to do. 'I just hope Jane and the children aren't out in this weather,' she said, following him upstairs.

'Where are they?'

'Visiting a friend of hers, the other side of Oxford.'

'If your sister-in-law has any sense, she'll stay put,' said Phillip, pausing in a doorway. 'There's a hellish mess in here, too. Whose bedchamber is this?' He went over and put a hand where branch and trunk joined to test how firmly it was wedged.

Rebecca sidled into the room and stared in horror at the branch on top of her bed. A lump of plaster from the ceiling fell and she thought if it had happened in the night she would have been crushed to death. 'Mine!' she said starkly.

He glanced at her. 'Sweet Jesu! You've had a lucky escape!'

She saw that he had lost some of his colour. 'Do—do you think there is any danger of the whole place collapsing?'

'No! We're not in any danger,' he replied swiftly. 'Although the tree might shift with the wind and send masonry crashing down. I doubt if it would cause any damage downstairs inside the house.'

'Then perhaps we'd better go downstairs,' she responded in a shaky voice. 'Simon is going to have to know about this.'

Phillip's expression was grim. 'As soon as the gale abates, I'll go to Minster Draymore and tell him what's happened.' He put an arm around her in way of comfort.

Rebecca allowed herself to lean into him for a moment. 'Thank you. In Jane's condition she's going to need him. She might be accustomed to coping without him when he's away so often, but this situation is different.'

'Of course it is. I don't know anyone who's had a tree fall on their house. Now stop worrying. You go downstairs whilst I check the other bedchambers.'

'I'll come with you,' she said hastily, clinging to his arm.

He smiled down at her. 'There's no need. I'll just open the doors and look inside.'

'Even so I'm coming with you,' she said, much happier if they stayed together.

They found only the adjacent room damaged slightly and went downstairs. Phillip placed some wood on the parlour fire whilst Rebecca filled two cups with ale. Then he stood, gazing down at the smouldering logs, knowing that if Jane and the children did not return that night, then he would have to stay here. He still felt shaken by how close Rebecca had come to death and knew that he couldn't leave her alone. Would he be able to resist temptation and keep his distance?

'Do sit down,' said Rebecca, touching his sleeve.

He sat beside her and took the cup she offered him. As he drank the ale he was conscious of her staring into the flames and thought she looked sad. He wanted to make her smile as she had done earlier. 'It's not the end of the world,' he said lightly.

She turned and smiled at him. 'No. Our situation could be a lot worse. You will stay, won't you? At least until Jane and the children return.'

He frowned. 'You think I would leave you alone?'

'Of course not,' she said hastily. 'I just don't know what you had planned.'

'I'm doing what I planned to do, so unless you've changed your mind and want to be rid of me…'

'No, but this can't be exactly what you intended,' she said, gazing into her ale.

'I didn't think I'd get you alone,' said Phillip. 'I deemed I'd be safe from temptation.'

'And instead…' Her voice trailed off.

'It wouldn't be right to take advantage of us being alone.'

Why not? she thought rebelliously. Before he had allowed himself to be tempted to kiss her. Could he be thinking of what she had said about being no man's mistress? A matter of honour. Hopefully it was not the thought of his brother that was restraining him. Presumably there was no news of him, otherwise surely he would have mentioned him? They drank their ale in a silence that seemed to stretch and stretch as it grew darker outside and the flames on the hearth sent shadows dancing about the walls.

'If there was a saw or axe we could try and

get rid of some of the branches and use them for firewood,' said Rebecca, breaking the silence.

'They would need to dry out before burning, but if there's an axe here we could trim off some of the foliage, which would make getting rid of the tree easier when the time comes,' said Phillip, sounding as if glad of an excuse to be active.

'Of course! And I've just remembered that Father's old carpentry tools are in Simon's work-room. There'll be saws and an axe amongst them. Simon bought them from Davy. He was thinking that if he had another son, then he could become a carpenter. James is destined to be a stonema-son if all goes well.'

'It's not always a good idea to plan your child's future for him,' mused Phillip.

'You're thinking of your own situation,' said Rebecca. 'Who was it who encouraged you to tell stories and then to act them out?'

Phillip thought there was nothing he would have liked more than to act out his favourite love story right now. Instead he said, 'Mother was a great one for telling stories about the family and she'd embellish her tales in such a way that Nicholas and I would double up with laughter. She was an excellent mimic and would take us to see mystery plays and, during the Twelve Days of Christmas, we would don a disguise when the mummers came to the house and act out parts,' Phillip's voice was soft with remembrance.

Rebecca envied him. 'You were fortunate. Our Christmastide was always a sober affair. I confess that I preferred summers at your father's boatyard.' She slid off the settle and sat back on her heels on the floor, watching the light from the fire cast shadows in the slight hollows beneath his cheekbones. 'I enjoyed watching you work and even as a youth you were developing a skill to equal my father's, however much you might deny it.'

Phillip's brow knitted. 'I'm not denying it. I might have baulked at having to bend to my father's will and that of yours, but I did find pleasure in working with wood and seeing a ship grow beneath my hands. When I return to Greenwich in a few days' time, I'll be working in my brother's shipyard to help him fulfil an order for a galleon and I'll enjoy doing that.' He paused. 'And what about you? No news of your uncle?'

Rebecca shook her head. 'If there was a trail that might have led us to him, it's gone cold. He's vanished just like the ghost Simon believed him to be.' She gazed towards the window as the wind flung the rain against the glass and shivered. 'What terrible weather to be out in.'

'Are you cold?'

'No. It's just this talk of the past and ghosts.'

'You don't talk much about your husband.'

She glanced at Phillip. 'I see little point in doing so. He was a good, thoughtful man, whom I liked and respected, but I wasn't in love with him. Have you ever been in love?'

'I have imagined myself in love several times.' He leaned forwards and picked up a log and threw it on the fire. 'But love that lasts—' He brushed the sawdust from his hands. 'Would you like to remarry?'

'That would depend on the man who asked me,' said Rebecca, her pulses quickening. She rose to her feet and picked up the empty jug.

'Nicholas is alive,' said Phillip, watching for her reaction.

She almost dropped the jug; as it was she spilt the dregs of ale. Why had he chosen that moment to tell her? She could not help but notice that he gave her the news after asking whether she would ever remarry. Why? After the reassurance she had given him that he was his brother's equal in her eyes, he surely did not still think she wanted Nicholas for a husband? The difficulty was how to dissuade him of that without having to say it point blank.

'I'm so glad for *you. You* must be so pleased,' she said emphatically.

'Of course I'm relieved that my brother is alive. I can't wait to see him and hear of his adventures from his own lips. I know you admire him,' added Phillip, choosing his words carefully.

'Admire his writing, aye,' she replied. 'Where is he?'

'I don't know. He has gone into hiding.'

'Oh!' She felt compelled to be blunt. 'You have roused my curiosity. Although your brother is not a man I would choose to marry, I am fascinated by his adventurous life.'

Phillip felt his heartbeat quicken. 'Fascination, admiration—is that all you feel for him?'

'Aye,' she said simply.

She might not realise it, but Becky had given him the answer he needed. He considered the terms of the wager he had made with Nicholas, more than a little annoyed with his brother for complicating matters by falling in love with a woman who was already betrothed. Why could he not have chosen someone who was free to marry him? Phillip knew that if he himself were to marry Becky, he was going to need all the money he could get his hands on and one could buy a lot with two gold pieces. He pulled himself up short. Perhaps he was getting ahead of himself. Just because she did not wish to marry Nicholas, it did not say she wanted to take him as a husband for better, for worse! This needed some thought. Becky might have survived a few days travelling with the wagon, but she'd had a hard life and he wanted to be able to offer her something more than a wagon or temporary lodgings in which to make a home for them.

'Perhaps we should talk some more whilst we eat,' he said easily. 'If that isn't asking too much, considering the state of the kitchen.'

'I'll see what I can do.' Rebecca beamed at him and lit a candle from the fire and left the parlour. She expected him to follow her, but he didn't.

Phillip was busy thinking some more. How deep did her feelings for him go? They had discovered passion together when they had coupled but was that due to lust or could it have been love? He wanted for both of them a love that would last a lifetime. Still deep in thought, he rose and lit a candle and went upstairs to see if the tree had shifted at all. Through the hole in the roof he could see a patch of sky and clouds scudding by. A scattering of raindrops fell on his face; stepping back, he attempted to move the largest of the branches, but it did not shift.

He decided it was unlikely to move and cause any more damage at the moment. He went back downstairs and into the kitchen but Rebecca was not there and so he strolled back to the parlour where he found her, nibbling on a fingernail whilst staring into the fire.

She dropped her hand and looked up at him, frowning. 'Where did you go?'

'Upstairs to check if there was any change in the tree's position.'

'Oh!' Her expression relaxed.

He sat beside her, noticing bread and cheese and ham on a platter on the table. 'Cooking is out of the question, of course,' he said.

She smiled. 'Aye. Help yourself.'

He did so and also sliced enough bread for her to eat. Once they had satisfied their hunger, she gazed at Phillip with a question in her eyes. 'So are you going to tell me about Nicholas?'

Phillip hesitated, uncertain how much to tell her. 'He was involved in a fight with a Spaniard and sustained an injury. Hopefully he'll return once the weather improves. Then he will be able to recuperate and get his strength back.'

'Do you think he'll decide to settle down at last?'

'Any man of sense would do so,' said Phillip, brushing crumbs from his doublet.

'You do not consider your brother a man of sense? Now that I find surprising coming from you,' she said in a mocking voice.

'I don't risk my life to the extent he has done. He can't see when it's time for him to stop,' said Phillip, exasperated. 'Nicholas needs to accept that he's been fortunate in surviving so many dangers over the years.'

She agreed. 'Makes for exciting reading, though. I can't imagine him living a mundane life here in England.'

'It doesn't have to be mundane,' he frowned, suffering a sudden recurrence of inferiority. 'Did you find our journey to Ludlow dull?'

'No, uncomfortable at times, but interesting with plenty to occupy my mind,' she said warmly. 'And this afternoon has turned out to be quite exciting with only a hint of danger.' She patted his hand and his fingers curled around hers.

'So you like living in Oxford and travelling?' He toyed with her fingers, raising them to his mouth and nibbling them.

Rebecca chuckled. 'You're tickling. It'll be even more interesting when the Raventons open their business here. Do you know that I once worked for them at their premises in London?'

Phillip was instantly alert and dropped her hand. 'No!'

She raised her eyebrows. 'There is no need to sound so shocked. It was only for a short time after Beth had her baby. She showed me how to set type and work the printing press when the men weren't there, as well as allowing me to help in the shop.'

Phillip mused, 'You could be a real help to Nicholas if he ended up managing the business here in Oxford. He needs a sensible woman on the scene.'

She felt so exasperated by those words that she could have wept. She had expected different from him after their early exchanges. 'I hope you still aren't matchmaking.'

'No, but if you don't marry him, you could be foolish enough to end up marrying a knave like me,' said Phillip lightly.

Her pulses fluttered. Of course he was jesting because he had already stressed that he had no room in his life for a wife. 'Obviously a fate worse than death,' she muttered.

'I wouldn't go as far as that,' said Phillip. 'But people can often marry the wrong people. You know, my brother has a habit of falling in love with the wrong women.'

Rebecca rolled her eyes. 'Nuns?'

The parlour was so dark now that if they hadn't been so close to the fire he wouldn't have been able to make out if she was teasing him or not. 'Don't be frivolous,' he said.

'I beg your pardon,' she said meekly. 'Do you mean married women?'

'Aye, one is a good friend of yours. She suggested that I marry her and I was willing but the idea didn't meet with her guardian's approval so the plan was scuttled.'

She sat up straight and caught the amused gleam in his eye. 'You're teasing me.'

He grinned. 'It's the truth. Ask Beth.'

'Beth asked you to marry her?' squeaked Rebecca. 'Is that why you took to roaming because you couldn't have her?'

Phillip smiled and could not resist brushing her lips with his in a way that was entirely enticing. She struggled against the feeling of having molten honey in her veins and tore her mouth from his and held him off with one hand against his chest. She would not have him toy with her emotions. 'But you're still roaming and say you have no room for a wife in your life. Is that because of your feelings for Beth? If so you should not use me as a substitute.'

'You misinterpret my actions.' Phillip frowned. 'As a direct result of her offer of marriage, I attained my heart's desire, so you could say that I have every reason to love her, only…' He paused.

Rebecca felt as if a sliver of ice was making its way down her spine. Never had she imagined that Phillip could be in love Beth. 'Does—does Gawain know of your feelings for her?'

'Beth loves him. He knows I'm no threat to their happiness,' said Phillip.

'And you're content with just friendship from her?' asked Rebecca huskily.

A sudden gust of wind rattled the windows, drowning out his answer. Then there came a banging at the door and voices shouting to be let in. Feeling frustrated, Rebecca wanted to ask him to repeat what he had said, but knew she couldn't keep those at the door waiting and she hurried to let the family in out of the storm.

Chapter Eight

Rebecca ushered the girls into the house and took James from Jane, who was breathing as if she had been running a race. 'I know what you're going to say,' panted the latter, to all appearances looking as if she had fallen in the River Cherwell.

'No, I'm not going to insult you, love,' said Rebecca. 'But why didn't you stay put until the storm blew itself out?'

'There was nowhere to stay!' cried Jane, collapsing on the chest by the door. 'A tree came down and smashed through the roof.'

'I don't believe it!' A flabbergasted Rebecca perched on the edge of the chest with James on her knee.

'Here, give him to me!' ordered Phillip, appearing suddenly. 'His teeth are chattering. The sooner he's in front of the fire the better.'

Rebecca handed her nephew to him with thanks before turning to Jane, who was staring at Phillip as if he was an apparition. 'Where did he come from?' she gasped.

'Greenwich. He came to tell me that the family had had news of Nicholas,' replied Rebecca, taking Jane's hands and removing her sodden gloves and chafing her fingers. 'More to the point, we've had our own disaster here—but you mustn't worry,' she added hastily. 'Phillip is going to fetch Simon as soon as the storm abates.'

'Why—why? What's happened?' asked Jane.

'A tree's uprooted and crashed into the roof,' she said cautiously. 'Now you'll understand why I said "I don't believe it" about your friend's disaster. But you mustn't fret. Do you think you can walk to the parlour? You can lean on me.'

'Give me a few moments,' muttered Jane, gripping Rebecca's hand tightly. 'You say Master Hurst is going to fetch Simon?'

'Aye, he suggested it himself.'

'How kind of him,' said Jane, her expression lightening. 'Although I don't think we need to worry about the baby. I only carried James the last few yards. Margaret and Elizabeth ran with him most of the way. We were blown here, but the naughty boy was soaked through with splashing in puddles and I became quite cross with him.' She placed a hand on Rebecca's arm and rose to her feet. 'I think I can walk to the parlour now. What is the state of the kitchen?'

'We'll sort it out in the morning,' was Rebecca's reply.

Jane sighed heavily. 'Well, I suppose what is important is that you're unhurt and the children and I arrived home all in one piece. Fortunately my friend fed us well before the tree fell.'

Within the hour wet garments were exchanged for dry ones and the decision made that they would all spend the night in the parlour. Between them Phillip, Rebecca and the girls carried down mattresses and bedding. As Rebecca settled on a mattress in front of the fire with the two girls, she thought it doubtful that she and Phillip would have the opportunity to resume their conversation. She could not help wondering how the night would have turned out if the family had not come home. If only she had an answer to her question about Beth.

The following morning Rebecca woke, after a series of disturbing dreams during which Gawain and Phillip fought with wooden swords whilst she and Beth stood watching aghast and attempting to drag them apart, to find a message from Phillip on the table, saying that he had already left for Minster Draymore and hoped to return that evening. She tapped the paper against her teeth, thinking about her dream and how ridiculous dreams could be. She could only pray that he would not meet with trouble on the road. At least he hadn't wasted any time setting out and no doubt that would please Jane and improve his standing in her eyes.

Fortunately the storm had abated somewhat by the time Phillip reached Minster Draymore, although it had left its mark on the countryside. Most of the deciduous trees had been stripped of their leaves and a number had been uprooted, although he was able to skirt the one that blocked the road without too much difficulty. Simon was not at the cottage and so Phillip left his horse tethered to a post around the back of the house, cropping the grass, and set out to walk to Draymore manor house.

As he had hoped, he found Simon there. He was not alone, but with several other men and they were gazing down at what appeared to be a pile of rubble. Phillip hailed him and he turned and came hurrying over to Phillip.

'You want me?' he said, looking pale.

'Aye, Master Caldwell. You're needed at home.'

He looked anxious. 'Is it the baby?'

Phillip reassured him that all was well with his wife before adding, 'But the storm has uprooted a tree and it's fallen on the house.'

Simon swore and ran a hand over his weather-beaten face and looked distraught. 'Why did this have to happen now? We've trouble here, too. A wall that the men had partially rebuilt collapsed during the storm and it brought down an older wall with it and we've unearthed a skeleton.' He scratched the back of his neck. 'But my family must take priority. I must leave this in Ralph's hands. I'll come with you now. Just allow me a moment to speak to the men.'

Phillip wondered whose skeleton it could be. Perhaps a child whose parents could not bear to be parted from it. He thought of Rebecca's mother and uncle and whether they might know something about it. He could understand how annoying the setback must be to Simon Caldwell and hoped that Ralph was dependable. It could be some time before the master mason could return here.

'I'm ready, Master Hurst!' Simon tapped him on the shoulder and Phillip turned and went with him.

On the journey they discussed the situation facing Simon back at the house. Knowing nothing could be done that day, he had arranged for some of the men to bring some necessary equipment the following morning.

It was evening by the time they arrived in Oxford. The wind had dropped and the sky was full of stars. The master of the house was welcomed warmly with hugs and kisses and not a few tears. As for Phillip, travel stained and weary, Rebecca only had time to exchange a few words with him as he drew her aside at the front door.

'I was thinking about your not being able to use your bedchamber,' he said, gazing into her shadowy face. 'There are rooms above the premises in Broad Street and I'm certain Gawain and Beth would suggest you make use of them at such a time. It wouldn't surprise me if they visited Oxford in the weeks to come. I'll get in touch with them and explain the situation.' He took a key from his pocket. 'Here, take this. The rooms are unfurnished, by the way, so you'll need to take a pallet or mattress to sleep on.'

Rebecca hesitated only a moment before accepting the key, knowing that now was not the time to speak of what was on her mind. 'I suppose I shall not see you for some time now.'

'That depends on several factors, but I'll let you know when Nicholas is safely home.'

'That is good of you,' she said in a listless voice. 'I hope you have a safe journey and that all goes well with your shipbuilding and playwriting.' She held out her hand.

Phillip ignored it and kissed her on the lips before vanishing into the night.

Rebecca sighed, wondering what she was to make of that kiss, and went inside the house. She told Jane and Simon about Phillip's suggestion. Jane was in favour of the idea and suggested that the girls keep her company whilst the worst of the mess was cleared away.

So, the following morning, after a couple of men arrived from Draymore Manor with some necessary building equipment, all that Rebecca and the girls needed was loaded on to the wagon. They rode with it and it was not long before the three of them were inspecting not only the rooms upstairs, but in Rebecca's case those on the ground floor.

She could so easily picture where the printing presses would go and benches for setting type and bookbinding in the back room, while the front would be used as a stationers and book-shop. How she would enjoy being part of such a business herself. But, of course, if Nicholas was put in charge she would rather not be in-volved. Besides, once Jane's baby arrived, she would have even more need of her.

To be living in the middle of the town proved to be much more interesting than at the house on the outskirts. From the front window over-looking the street one could not only watch the townspeople going about their business, but the students and their masters and those visitors to Oxford staying at the inns. The girls soon tired of such entertainment and on the fourth day re-turned home to see how the builders were get-ting on with the repairs. To her astonishment it was later that day that Rebecca spotted two fa-miliar faces reining in their horses below in the street. She had put aside her sewing and wasted no time hurrying downstairs. Before Sir Gawain could even produce a key, she had the door open and was welcoming him and Beth Raventon to Oxford.

Sir Gawain was dark haired and had penetrating blue eyes in a strong-boned face. He looked surprised to see her, but recovered quickly and shook her hand before helping his wife to dismount. Beth voiced her astonishment, unlike her husband. 'Rebecca, what are you doing here? I intended calling on you as soon as possible, but to see you here now is a delightful surprise.' She kissed Rebecca's cheek.

'It was Phillip Hurst's suggestion that I stay here,' replied Rebecca, returning Beth's kiss. 'I was alone in the house when he arrived out of the blue. There was a violent storm that brought down a tree in the garden and wrecked my bedchamber. He has since returned to his brother's house, but he said that he would be in touch with you.'

'Obviously we missed each other,' said Beth, patting Rebecca's shoulder. 'But how distressing for you! Are the rest of your family safe?'

'Aye, and Jane's husband has deserted his labours at Draymore Manor to oversee the repairs to the house,' said Rebecca. 'Of course, I will move out now you are here.'

'Nonsense!' exclaimed Beth, her expression lively. 'We made no plans to stay here because we knew it wasn't furnished. We shall be spending the next few nights at the Blackfriars' lodging house where our man Sam has already taken our baggage. Phillip was right to say you could make use of the apartment.' She glanced at her husband. 'Don't you agree, Gawain?'

'I certainly wouldn't argue with his decision. I wonder if he's had any news of Nicholas?' said Gawain, taking the horses' reins.

'I can reassure you somewhat on that score,' said a relieved Rebecca. 'Although you might wish to stable your horses before I tell you what I know.'

'I'll see to them,' said Gawain, squeezing his wife's shoulder affectionately. 'You go inside with Rebecca, sweeting. It's too cold out here to stand gossiping.'

Beth wasted no time following Rebecca inside the building, pausing downstairs for several moments to gaze about her before climbing the stairs to the upper storey. Rebecca took her cloak and ushered her to a seat near the fire. She gazed at her in admiration. 'I do like your headdress and gown. What a beautiful shade of green and the style of the bodice; it is different from the one you were wearing last time I saw you.'

'Ah, that is due to the lady Anne Boleyn,' said Beth, glancing down at her gown. 'She returned to England not so long ago after being in the service of the Queen of France. Some are saying that her father wanted her home because King Henry has tired of his other daughter, Mary, as his mistress. Fearing Cardinal Wolsey will use his influence to get rid of him, he is hoping Anne will deal the Cardinal's plans a blow.'

'What is she like?' asked Rebecca, wondering if Phillip had met this Anne Boleyn.

Beth gave a wry smile. 'I agree with Gawain that this daughter is a very different proposition from the other one. Clever, cultured, musical and an excellent dancer.' She trailed a hand down her bodice. 'This is in the French style and Anne Boleyn has introduced the French hood, that I am wearing now, to the king's court.'

Rebecca inspected the headdress more closely. It was made of green velvet and studded with tiny crystals on a band that followed the curve of the upper face and was attached to a veil that fell down the back of the head. 'It is very different from the gable style everyone was wearing not so long ago.'

'Aye, the queen still wears it. She does not care for the changes in fashion.' Beth sighed. 'It is a terrible thing for a woman to be cast aside when her childbearing years are over. Most of the time, Katherine lives a very secluded life, seeing only the occasional visitor from Spain. She is seemingly unaware of the threat this new Boleyn girl might present.'

'My brother Davy, as you know, is a member of the Princess Mary's court,' said Rebecca. 'He speaks of the king deliberately separating mother and daughter.'

Beth sighed. 'It is true, I fear. What has also saddened the queen is that her nephew, Charles V, the Holy Roman Emperor and King of Spain, has broken off his engagement to Mary and married a Portuguese princess. Not that I was ever in favour of such a match! He is so much older than Mary. But it does mean that the king and Wolsey will have to look around for another suitor for her.' She grimaced. 'Enough gossip.'

Rebecca smiled. 'Tell me, how was your journey? I presume from what you said earlier that you did not have the time to visit the Hursts' at Greenwich.'

Beth nodded. 'Gawain wanted to leave me behind in Kent with the children, but I insisted on coming.' She warmed her hands by the fire. 'The king has requested his company for part of November; as we both believe the children need me with them once winter sets in, I determined to spend this time alone with my husband. Gawain's aunt is taking care of the children.'

'I have met her and know how much she cares for them,' said Rebecca.

'Aye, and she sent her greeting to you,' said Beth, smiling. 'I told her that I hoped to see you. What do you think of our new venture here in Oxford?'

Rebecca's eyes sparkled. 'I deem it an excellent notion. Phillip told me that you might be considering asking his brother to take charge here.'

Beth's smile faded. 'Ahh, Nicholas. You said that you had news of him? He has been found?'

'I believe so, although Phillip told me he did not know of his whereabouts. He was injured in a fight with a Spaniard, according to whoever sent Christopher the news.' She frowned. 'These Spaniards seem to get everywhere.'

'How terrible for all the family,' said Beth, shaking her head. 'Nicholas will be fretting to get home, but no doubt his Flemish kin are spoiling him.'

'His Flemish kin? How is it that the Hursts have kin in Flanders?' She rose and began to prepare hot drinks for her friends.

Beth's brow creased in thought. 'I don't know all the ins and outs of it, but I believe one of their grandmothers was Flemish and that the Hurst grandfather accompanied the king's grandfather into exile during the wars between the Houses of Lancaster and York during the last century.'

'You mean the old queen's father, King Edward?' Rebecca glanced at her.

'The fourth. That's right.'

'Do you mind my asking how you became acquainted with the Hursts?' asked Rebecca casually.

'Not at all.' Beth's eyes danced. 'The first time I saw Phillip was when he brought Nicholas's journal to me at Raventon Manor. This was when Gawain was my guardian. Phillip is a little younger than me, but he was so charming and handsome that I was greatly impressed by him.'

'He told me that you asked him to marry you,' said Rebecca, glancing up from her task of mulling wine.

Beth laughed. 'A ridiculous notion, but all mine, although he was prepared to agree to it due to his frustration.'

'Frustration? You—you mean he—he lusted after you?'

'God's blood, no! Although he was so desperate that he was prepared to marry me. His frustration was to do with his love of storytelling and he was ripe for adventure. He wanted to leave the shipyard behind and go travelling with a troupe of players. Of course, Gawain, as my guardian, wouldn't countenance such a match and quite cheerfully Phillip and I both agreed to give up the notion.'

'I see.' Rebecca's heart was lighter but there was another question she wanted answered. 'He is fond of you—would you say there is a special bond between you?'

Beth cocked her head on one side. 'Without our input Nicholas's journal would never have become the successful book it did. We are both proud of the work we put into it, so that links us together. I cannot see us working together on Nicholas's next book.'

'I see,' murmured Rebecca.

Beth's eyes twinkled. 'You seem very interested in him.'

Rebecca flushed. 'I hadn't spoken to him for an age and then purely by chance I met him in Witney where he and his troupe were performing at the feast.'

Beth looked interested. 'Was he good? I know that Gawain spoke to his brother, Christopher, about his being allowed a leave of absence from the shipyard. Christopher hoped it would rid Phillip of what he believed was an excuse to escape what he called real man's work.'

'It is what I used to think,' murmured Rebecca, grating nutmeg into the wine in the pan. 'I'm glad you've made matters clear to me. I had thought he might have been in love with you.'

Beth laughed. 'He didn't tell you that, did he?'

'No.' Rebecca placed the remains of the nutmeg on the table and then sliced apples into the brew.

'He didn't hint that Nicholas had also believed himself in love with me, did he?'

'He only mentioned that his brother had been in love with a friend of mine,' said Rebecca, her eyes gleaming. 'So it really was you?'

Beth shrugged. 'I think Nicholas was just looking for a wife and he'd heard that I was in the market for a husband. I'm certain that if I'd had no hand in making his book a success he might not have bothered making my acquaintance. As it is, I deem he was glad to return to doing what he loves best, exploring strange and exciting places.'

'Perhaps he would have settled down then if you'd agreed to marry him,' said Rebecca. 'Phillip now seems to hold the opinion that Nicholas is in need of a sensible wife and should give up his wanderings. For a while he was of the opinion that I was in love with his brother and would suit, but I have dissuaded him on that score. As for himself, he says he has no room in his life for a wife and I cannot imagine his giving up the wandering life of a player.' Rebecca sat back on her heels and sighed. 'Just like your younger self, I find Phillip charming, interesting and comely, although there are times when he exasperates me so that I want to shake him up by doing something quite shocking.'

Beth smiled. 'You're a sensible woman and I wouldn't presume to give you advice. But I can understand why you find yourself viewing a Hurst brother as husband material. You have been married before and must find it frustrating not having a man to care for and your own household to organise.'

Rebecca said gloomily, 'But I'm not always sensible and I would have appreciated your advice.'

'I will not take the responsibility. What if I advised you and you married the wrong brother? Now, that brew…' Beth breathed in the heady fragrance '…how long before it's ready?'

'Soon,' murmured Rebecca, frowning. 'I wonder if my mother ever felt this indecision.'

'Your mother?'

Rebecca hesitated and thought *why not have Beth's thoughts on this at least?* She cleared her throat. 'Phillip says that every family has its secrets. Mine was that my mother deserted us when I was only a small child. It's only recently that I've discovered that she ran off with my father's twin brother.' She got up from her knees and went and fetched two cups. 'It came as a terrible shock as I didn't know my father had a brother.'

Beth looked at her with concern. She took the cups from Rebecca and placed them on the table before putting her arms around her and hugging her. 'What a difficult time you've been having lately.'

Rebecca felt tears well in her eyes. 'He's been seen,' she blurted out.

'Who? Your father's twin?'

'Aye! We think the news must have reached him that Father is dead. Davy came to Oxford hoping to find him, so he could speak to him, but he appears to have vanished again. I admit that I don't want to talk to either him or my mother, but Phillip thinks I should if it were possible,' said Rebecca, her voice trembling. 'What do you think I should do?'

Beth patted her back and then held Rebecca at arm's length and stared at her intently. 'On this I will speak my mind. I understand your not wanting to have anything to do with either of them, but if it were me and they came looking for me after all this time, then I would want to know the reason why.'

Rebecca sighed and wiped her eyes with the back of her hand. 'You are like Phillip. But then you're both people who believe in seizing every opportunity and gaining more experiences in life.'

Beth smiled. 'You and Phillip seemed to have had a lot to say to each other.'

'He's not the strong, silent type of man. Perhaps it is because he has a love of words and is interested in what makes people do what they do.'

Beth smiled. 'You've seen him in a play. Do you think he becomes the character he's playing?'

'Aye!' Rebecca gazed into space, a faraway look in her eyes. 'I went with his troupe to visit my brother in Ludlow. I didn't suffer from tedium once.'

'What about discomfort?'

'Oh, that! Of course, it wasn't always comfortable, but it was different from my life here in Oxford,' she said, her enthusiasm spilling over, 'and interesting! Phillip is so good at what he does and cares about the rest of the troupe.'

'You admire him.'

Rebecca stared at her. 'I suppose I do,' she said slowly.

'And you obviously like him?'

Rebecca lowered her head and suddenly remembered the wine mulling on the fire. She reached for a cloth and removed the pan from the heat. 'He puts me to the blush. Me, a widow woman! And he considers me unforgiving because he had a mother who loved him and I had no experience of such. If we hadn't known each other when we were younger and spent that time travelling together and then him arriving in the middle of the storm and being so helpful, then I don't suppose I'd miss him at all.'

'You're obviously regretting his absence for reasons that you don't care to admit,' said Beth softly.

Rebecca poured the wine into the cups. 'He plays hot and cold with my emotions. He's made it plain he has no intention of settling down and taking a wife, but then he kisses me in a manner that is—' She stopped abruptly.

'Deliciously arousing?'

Their eyes met in understanding. 'Inappropriate,' said Rebecca fiercely.

'Unless—' murmured Beth.

But Rebecca was not to learn what that *unless* was because the door opened and Gawain entered the room. 'That mulled wine smells good,' he said.

For an instant Rebecca wanted to shout at him

Get out! She needed to know what Beth would have said next, but already her friend was handing her steaming cup to her husband. Then she crossed the room to where there was an empty cup and placed it on the small table. Rebecca filled it and then forced a smile at husband and wife. 'We should have a toast.'

Gawain smiled and raised his cup. 'To our new venture here in Oxford.'

The two women echoed his words. As they drank the rest of the wine, the Raventons spoke to Rebecca of their plans, which to her amazement included her.

'I've never forgotten, Rebecca, how you helped us capture a murderer and hence saved the girls' lives and mine,' said Beth.

'I will never forget how you rewarded me by teaching me to read and write,' said Rebecca.

'You were such a willing and clever pupil,' said Beth seriously. 'It has always stuck in my mind how speedily you learnt not only to read and write, but all that I shared with you about printing and books in our London business. Due to your being a widow and living in Oxford, naturally my thoughts turned to you when we decided on this venture.'

'Of course, we do not expect you to give all your time to it, but we thought that perhaps you would enjoy spending a couple of half-days in the shop,' said Gawain, smiling down at her. 'We understand that your main priority is helping your husband's sister with her children.'

Rebecca was deeply touched that they should consider her in such a way. 'I'm exceedingly grateful for your kind thoughts,' she said unsteadily, putting down her empty cup. 'And I accept your offer, although I imagine it will be some time before I am needed.'

'We are hoping it will be no more than a month before all is ready,' said Beth. 'Much depends on the weather remaining dry, for we have arranged for the equipment to be transported from London. Our master printer served his apprenticeship in the city and is looking forward to the challenge that this new position presents to him.'

'Does he know that you intend to employ a woman to assist in the shop?'

'Of course, and he had no choice but to agree,' said Gawain, 'after all, Beth helped her father in the shop before he left his business to her. The man is married and will be bringing his wife and children with him. They will make their home in these rooms.'

'What about Nicholas Hurst?' asked Rebecca, tentatively.

Gawain glanced at his wife who immediately said, 'Nicholas's alive, but not yet in England as far as we know.'

'Then, of course, we'll consult with Nicholas as soon as the opportunity arises,' said Gawain.

Rebecca had no choice but to be satisfied with that answer. The other two made ready to go downstairs and she said, 'I would offer you a meal only I have little food here and I must also visit Jane and see how she fares.'

'Do not worry yourself,' said Beth, patting her arm. 'We will be supping at the lodging house. Tell me, how is Jane? Is she in good health? When is the babe due?'

'November,' replied Rebecca. 'She keeps well, but it'll be a relief to all of us when she has been safely delivered. Hopefully, by then the repairs to the house will be completed.'

'Then let us not keep you if you are to visit your family,' said Gawain.

Without more ado, Rebecca took her leave of them and left the building. She crossed to the other side of the street and stood, gazing at the premises she had just left, thinking over all that she and Beth had discussed. Had she said too much? What conclusions had Beth drawn from what she had told her? Perhaps that her feelings for Phillip went far deeper than she was prepared to admit. She wasted no more time lingering in the street, but hurried home.

Rebecca had decided not to tell Jane and Simon her news about working in Broad Street just yet. After all, who was to say that everything would go according to plan? It was best to leave it nearer the time. Besides, it was obvious to her that the majority of their attention was in getting the household back to normality as soon as possible.

Fortunately that now appeared to be later that week; already some of the men had returned to Draymore Manor House. She had seen Beth only twice more whilst she was in Oxford and that was never alone, so there had been no opportunity to discuss Phillip with her. But her friend did present her with a gift of two of her gowns.

'I thought they might be of some use to you, Rebecca,' said Beth warmly. 'They no longer fit me and the material still has plenty of wear in it; they should suit you well.'

Rebecca was appreciative of the kind thought behind the gesture. It was obvious to her that the gowns had hardly been worn. She thanked her and wished there was a favour she could do for Beth in return. Rebecca had always found it difficult to accept a gift and have nothing to offer in return.

On the same day that the Raventons left the city, Rebecca moved back into her old bedchamber with mixed feelings. She had become accustomed to having more time to herself, but, of course, that had meant she had much too much time to dwell on her relationship with Phillip. There was a constant dull ache inside her and she longed to see him again.

Her life resumed its old pattern, but at least she now had something to look forward to in the coming months. She could only hope that Jane's baby would be born before the print room and shop opened on Broad Street. Simon had ceased work on Draymore Manor House, saying that he had decided the weather was much too inclement to labour outdoors and as there had been no correspondence between him and the owner's agent, he was staying at home. With the birth of Jane's baby imminent, he wanted to be at hand. So he began work on the interior alterations to the university church of St Mary the Virgin. Rebecca wondered what Phillip would think of there being no more sightings or news of her uncle. She had received no word from Phillip, so could only assume that his brother was still out of the country.

Chapter Nine

Phillip was smiling as he strode along the path towards Christopher's house. The wind was sharp, but the sun was bright in a hard blue sky. His work at the shipyard was finished and he and his troupe had recently been summoned by the king's Master of the Revels to entertain Henry and certain visitors from abroad just for one evening. They had been well paid for their efforts and it had been interesting meeting the King's new fool, Will Somers. His ability to prattle merrily in a manner that amused the King must have made him the envy of many players, but it was one that Phillip did not share. Being so popular with the King meant he was seldom absent from his presence, but if he were to fall from favour, he had more to lose than most.

Suddenly Phillip heard his name being called and his blue eyes brightened as he recognised that voice. 'Nicholas!' he cried in delight, bounding towards the tall rangy figure heading his way. 'There was a time when I feared I might never see you in this world again!' He was about to hug his brother when he noticed that Nicholas's right arm was in a sling. 'Is this the result of the attack in Bruges?' he demanded.

'I'll tell you in a moment,' said Nicholas, shoving the stick he carried beneath his arm and clasping his brother's hand.

Phillip returned his brother's regard with a sense of shock. There was a familiarity about his features that owed naught to the relationship between them. Rather it was because with age Nicholas had grown more like the king than ever. Was Nicholas, himself, aware of the similarity? It was there in the narrow nose and the colour of the eyes, not to mention the hint of auburn in his abundant flaxen hair. And the beard! What had possessed him to allow his beard to grow? At least his mouth lacked the petulance of the king's and his figure was finer.

'You've altered since last I saw you, Pip,' said Nicholas, patting his brother's shoulder. 'The merry youth I left behind when I first set sail has matured into a fine man. I only half-believed our brother when he told me you'd begun to take life much more seriously, but I can see that it is true. No doubt now you have reached twenty-four summers you have decided to return to that occupation more fitting to a man and find yourself a wife.'

Phillip's eyes narrowed. 'I have not forgotten our wager, Brother, and I have some way to go before catching up with you in years. In a sennight you'll be thirty. It is you who need to find a wife first.'

'I need no reminding, but I tell you that I have resigned myself to a solitary life, a celibate life,' said Nicholas firmly.

Phillip's heart seemed to turn a somersault. 'Celibate! You? After all your adventures abroad and the women you've had! I can't believe it!'

'Believe it or not, I need to repent of such a life—all I require now is peace and solitude.'

Phillip blinked and rubbed his jaw. 'I fear the injuries you sustained have addled your wits. I have heard a little of your story from Christopher about the fair maid in Flanders. Is that what this decision is really about?'

'You could say that. Women might be alluring, but they are also deceitful.'

'You can't really believe that about all women,' said Phillip.

'This, dear Brother, is not a matter for discussion at the present time,' said Nicholas, his expression determined. 'I've other matters requiring my attention. I've a ship to catch.'

'Where are you off to now?' asked Phillip, startled. 'And what of your broken arm?'

Nicholas's lips tightened. 'You're going to find this difficult to believe, but after travelling thousands of miles without coming to any real harm but for that fracas in Flanders, I was attacked whilst in London.'

'By the devil, you were!' exclaimed Phillip, his eyes widening. 'Were they footpads?'

'It was dusk, there were three of them and it happened so swiftly that I only caught a glimpse of their faces, but they spoke in Spanish, so it seems that the business in Flanders is not over yet. I believe their intention was to kill me and they might have succeeded if a stranger had not come to my aid.'

'Obviously there is a connection between these attacks,' muttered Phillip, frowning. 'But Christopher told me you went into hiding. Have you any idea how they managed to find you and follow you to England?'

'Obviously my hiding place wasn't as secret as I thought,' said Nicholas. 'What I can't understand is why they waited until I reached London before making an attempt on my life.'

'Lack of opportunity?' Phillip's tawny brows drew together in a frown, reminded of the attack in Oxford, but he was convinced those men had been common footpads because there had been no more attempts on his life. 'It's also possible that only one man followed you and he would not risk attacking you on his own.'

'But there was more than one of them,' insisted Nicholas.

'Aye, but there are Spaniards aplenty over here. The queen still has strong ties with her homeland and there are also merchantmen who have business in London.'

'There's a thought,' said Nicholas, his eyes narrowing. 'Our brother is worried about my safety and that of his family, so I decided to make myself scarce.'

'What is your plan?'

'I am considering becoming an academic and might even take holy orders.'

Phillip's jaw dropped. 'You can't be serious!'

Nicholas's mouth set. 'I am utterly serious, but I haven't time to discuss it with you now. One thing is for certain—I will not visit London again in a hurry. Right now I am on my way to Oxford, so cannot delay.'

'Oxford!' Phillip seized his brother's free arm. 'Have you been in contact with the Raventons? Is that why you're going there?'

Nicholas paused. 'No, I've had no exchange with them for an age. Why do you ask?'

'Because they're opening a business there.'

For a moment Nicholas looked interested, then he shrugged. 'If that's what they want to do, then it is their decision. Most likely I will sell my shares to them and distribute the money to the poor.'

Phillip could scarcely believe what he was hearing. 'A worthy sentiment, Brother, but is this really what you want to do? I cannot believe you would turn your back on the world, but if you really want to sell your shares I will buy them.'

Nicholas's eyes flared; for a moment he just stared at Phillip before saying, 'I didn't know you had any money worth mentioning. If you're thinking that, despite what I've just told you; you can possibly still win our wager of two gold coins, then you're mistaken. I will not marry.'

Phillip's emotions were in turmoil. He made no sign of it, but said lightly, 'I confess I did have hopes of your doing so when I first heard you'd fallen in love again. Just for an instant I believed that you'd found yourself a wife and I rejoiced in your happiness.'

'Sorry to disappoint you,' drawled Nicholas, rubbing his injured arm. 'But I seem to make a habit of falling for women who are already spoken for. If I had known Louise's situation earlier, I would have kept my distance. She has almost broken my heart. You've never seen such eyes and hair, and seemingly so willing to please, so biddable. Just the kind of wife I needed.'

This news definitely did not bode well for his winning their wager, thought Phillip. He tried to make light of the situation. 'I hope you've written it all down in your journal?'

Nicholas sighed. 'Aye, but I don't want you altering it and making all's well that ends well. Your imagination might make you an excellent teller of tales, but I would like my next book to be a more serious work.'

Phillip was disappointed. 'Why must it be serious? Don't you want it to excite the readers of your last book and sell really well?'

Nicholas hesitated. 'Very well. If you can turn it into another success, then you can have half the proceeds. The rest can go to the leper hospice.'

'That sounds fair and the money will come in useful.' Phillip paused and said casually, 'Do you remember Rebecca Mortimer, whose father worked at the shipyard? She married, but has since been widowed. She lives in Oxford and is a friend of the Raventons.'

Nicholas nodded. 'Aye, I remember her—she was responsible for naming a murderer when Beth's life was in danger.'

Phillip's stride faltered. 'I'd forgotten she was involved in that affair.'

Nicholas did not miss a step. 'I remember, at the time, thinking that she would make a good spy for Wolsey. You weren't thinking of match-making, were you? You didn't have her in mind as a wife for me?'

'How did you guess? I had thought she was perfect for you because she always appeared so sensible.'

'Thanks! But you can forget about it. Pity all you learnt from her father went to waste,' he said sardonically. 'I know you've been helping Christopher on and off, but he tells me that you're still travelling with that troupe of players of yours, as well as entertaining the king.'

Phillip rasped a fingernail against his chin. 'I enjoy the life, but I confess I make more money in one evening at Henry's court and spying for Wolsey. You'd find it interesting at Henry's court, but you're best keeping your distance. Besides, you'll find more learned men in Oxford. Court can be a dangerous place, especially if one is close to the throne.' He lowered his voice. 'Shortly after you left on your travels, it reached the king's ears that the Duke of Buckingham had been gossiping about the king's lack of a male heir and of his own prowess on that score. As you know, Buckingham had royal blood in his veins—so maybe it was more than just foolish talk that caused the king to get rid of him.' He drew a finger graphically across his throat.

Nicholas came to a halt and tapped a fingernail against his teeth. 'I see your point, but surely there is no risk of that happening to me? Our family has been building ships for Henry and his father for years and our connection to the royal family via the king's maternal Yorkist grandfather has never been broached.'

Phillip shrugged. 'The King read your book and has asked after you. Recently, I noticed, he is sporting the beginning of a beard.'

Nicholas looked exasperated. 'I see that I should have stayed away.'

Phillip said abruptly, 'I'll go to Oxford with you. I'm sure Christopher would appreciate my keeping an eye on you. You haven't spoken to him of your intention to take holy orders, have you?'

'No, I have not.' Nicholas looked at him suspiciously. 'Do you want to come because you hope to persuade me to change my mind and marry the oh-so-sensible Rebecca, so you can win our wager?'

'I am not that short of money that it is vital I win our wager.'

'So you are a success,' said Nicholas, his eyes scanning his brother's handsome features. 'Then why do you not wed Rebecca?'

'I am considering it. You are somewhat of a hero to her and her family, you know,' he added in a droll voice.

'I'm glad I am a hero to someone.'

'I am certain there are plenty of other women who consider you heroic and I will make you even more heroic when I have your journal in my hands,' said Phillip.

'Am I to believe that she and they do not consider you heroic?'

Phillip's eyes twinkled. 'I act the part. It is not the same.'

'But you also look the part,' said Nicholas, with a shrug. 'You should have been with me in London and together we would have vanquished those rogues who attacked me. Then I could have boasted of your heroic deeds and you could be a real hero to her.'

'It is something I dream about amongst other deeds as she haunts my dreams,' said Phillip softly. 'But really, Nicholas, you shouldn't allow a couple of disappointments in love to put you off all women.'

'It has not put me off women,' snapped Nicholas, flushing. 'I truly loved Louise, but I will not marry another just to please you and Christopher. For he, too, would have me wed and beget a quiver of children. I will test my calling to the Church. I can see myself being happy living the academic life and, if so, I will take holy orders!'

Phillip knew better than to argue with his brother when he was in this mood. 'If that's what you want, Nicholas. At least you'll be safe behind monastery walls.' Some devilment made him add, 'I wager, though, that by Christmas you will have realised that it is not the life for you and will be chasing after a woman again.'

'You are being reckless,' said Nicholas tersely. 'How much will you wager, Brother? Another two gold pieces?'

Phillip hesitated. 'From my knowledge of you, Brother—why not?'

Nicholas laughed. 'A fool and his money are soon parted. You will not win this wager either, Pip. From the way you speak of her, you are finding the fair Rebecca difficult to resist. You will tie the knot before I do.'

Phillip made no answer, but gazed at the craft moored a few yards away. 'Is this your boat?' he asked.

Nicholas nodded. 'Aye, my baggage is already stowed. I suppose you'll manage somehow without a change of garments.' He raised an eyebrow.

'I can always borrow your raiment, just as I did when we were younger,' said Phillip mildly, helping his brother aboard before casting off. 'Will you at least agree to meet Rebecca and her kin? They all know of you and will be eager to hear more of your adventures.'

Nicholas cradled his broken arm against his chest and smiled. 'Aye, I'd like to thank her for winning me four gold coins. Besides, I can see you won't give me a moment's peace until I do.'

Rebecca stood at the foot of an oak tree, flanked by her nieces and nephew. Her hands rested on James's shoulders as they peered up through the bare branches to the mewing kitten that clung to one far out of reach. 'You shouldn't have brought the kitten with you, James,' she rebuked.

'But there was a big rat, Aunt Rebecca,' said Elizabeth. 'It could have gobbled up Puss.'

Having seen a few rats in her time, Rebecca could understand why her niece should fear that happening, but it did not help her to solve the problem of getting the kitten down.

'What are we going to do, Aunt Rebecca?' chimed Margaret.

Before Rebecca could answer, James wriggled free from beneath her restraining hands and lisped, 'Lifth me up and I'll climb to the top of the twee. We mutht get Puss down before he falls and bweaks all his bones on the gwound.'

'You're too small!' said Margaret scornfully, folding her arms and hunching her shoulders, 'and I'm not risking it!'

'But we can't leave Puss up der,' said James, pointing a chubby finger. 'He's only a baby and is fwightened. I must be bwave and climb up,' he gulped, attempting to scramble up the bole of the tree.

'Stop that at once!' ordered Rebecca, seizing him by the waist. 'Your reach is not long enough, love. If one of us is going to climb this tree, then it will have to be me, although why the foolish creature had to go scampering to the very top, I cannot understand.'

'A squiwkle went up and Puss wanted to show that it could climb, too,' said James.

Margaret sniffed. 'You mean a squirrel, and only a baby like you could believe that kittens can think like we can. Now come out of the way whilst Aunt Rebecca climbs the tree. If you stay where you are, she'll squash you if she falls.' She drew her brother towards her despite his struggles.

Rebecca thought, *Thank you, Margaret, for that thought!* She glanced left and right before dragging her back skirts between her legs and tucking the hem into the girdle at her waist. Hopefully no one she knew would come past, because there was no doubt in her mind that her appearance and actions were most unseemly. She stepped back several paces and took a running jump at the lowest branch and experienced a thrill of triumph as she managed to get a grip and lever herself up. After that it did not seem so difficult to swarm up the tree. She arrived at the place where the kitten was perched and made her first tentative move along the branch.

'You're ever so high, Aunt Rebecca,' called Elizabeth. 'How are you going to carry Puss and hold on to the branches at the same time?'

At the sound of her niece's voice, Rebecca glanced down. Instantly her head swam and she stumbled and fell forwards on to the branch. She clutched the bark in fright and swore, closing her eyes tightly and sending up a prayer and counting to ten as well.

'Hell's bells! Becky, what d'you think you're

doing climbing all the way up there?' shouted a voice that so startled her that she almost lost her grip. A scream escaped her. She had to be imagining that was Phillip's voice. 'Becky, are you all right? Can you hear me?'

The muscles of her stomach fluttered and she found the strength to shout, 'Of course I can hear you! I'm not deaf.'

'Do you need help to get down, Mistress Clifton?' enquired a different voice.

Rebecca peered down through the branches to see to whom it belonged, but that made her feel so dizzy she had to close her eyes. 'I—I'll be all right. Ju-just give me a moment.'

A soft paw patted her hand and instantly she remembered why she had risked life and limb by climbing the tree. She opened her eyes and stared at the kitten and made soothing noises to it. Then, after taking several deep breaths, she cautiously removed a hand from the branch and reached out to grab it. The movement sent a last lingering acorn thudding into the leaf litter below and the kitten scampered away. Instinctively her eyes followed its descent and she found herself looking down into a bearded weatherbeaten face. Its owner appeared vaguely familiar, but for a moment she couldn't think who he was and then realisation hit her.

'Master Nicholas Hurst!' she exclaimed.

The corners of his eyes creased in a smile. 'You recognise me even with the beard,' he said, sounding flattered.

Rebecca nodded and the branch shook, and she was reminded of her precarious position. She gulped and tried to take her mind off the danger. It had been a shock to see Phillip's older brother, hero of many an adventure, standing at the foot of this tree. No doubt he would attempt to come to her rescue, but there was no way that she wanted him to swarm up the trunk to attain it. She did not want him to see her with her gown all bunched up, revealing her bare legs and with her hair in disarray where it had caught on twigs.

In her agitation her hand slid from the branch and she almost lost her balance. She screamed and managed to grip the branch with her thighs. 'Oh, Holy Mary and our Blessed Saviour,' she gasped, her heart thudding so loudly she thought that they would hear it below. It felt as if it was about to bounce out of her chest.

The next moment she heard a voice shout, 'Hang on! I'm coming!'

'No, no, please don't bother,' yelled Rebecca, aware of that exposed expanse of bare flesh. She could hear the sound of boots scraping on bark. What was Nicholas going to think of her when he saw her in such a state? A face hovered into view and a mixture of relief, surprise and warmth exploded within her. 'It's you, Phillip!' She half-expected him to make a jest at her expense but instead he gazed at her with a tortured expression and muttered a string of oaths that caused her cheeks to blanch. 'Really, do you have to be so—so uncouth!' she exclaimed.

'D'you have to be such a fool?' he snapped, gripping the branch to which she was clinging. 'You could have broken your pretty little neck if you'd fallen. In fact, we could both still break our necks getting down from here,' he added savagely.

Hurt and anger replaced the pleasure she had felt in seeing him. 'I didn't ask you to climb up here, so why don't you go straight down again?' she said, glaring at him. 'You should have fetched a ladder.'

'Now that's what I call gratitude.' His blue eyes seemed to catch fire from the sparks in her grey ones. 'I didn't risk my life coming all the way up here to go down empty-handed. You should know what it cost me to make such an effort. Anyway, why didn't you fetch a ladder?'

'Because I thought I could do this and it would have meant going all the way to the house and

I'd have had to drag James away and he'd have shouted the place down.'

'I thought you might fall if I wasted time going in search of a ladder. As it is—' he glanced down and then looked up quickly at her '—we should make a move.'

'If you're under such duress, why didn't you leave it to your brother to come to my rescue?' she hissed.

'Because he has a cursed broken arm,' replied Phillip, smiling grimly.

'Oh!' He had quite taken the wind out of her sails. 'How did that happen?'

'I'd rather not be having this conversation right now,' said Phillip through gritted teeth. 'Let go of the branch and give me your hand.'

She noticed that he was clinging on to the tree with both hands. 'Is that one of your jests? How can you possibly take my hand if you don't let go of the tree yourself?'

'I'll let go when you let go!'

Rebecca hesitated. 'How do I know I can trust you to let go?'

'You can't,' he replied with a tight little smile.

It was then she remembered him telling her of his fear of heights and she recalled that evening in Ludlow when she had climbed up the tower and he had followed after her despite his fear.

Now she had to admire him for venturing to her rescue again and the warmth she had felt earlier at the sight of him expanded, so that she felt as if she was glowing. 'I'd prefer it if you just backed down and then I'll follow you,' she said softly.

He raised an eyebrow. 'You have to let go of the tree first. By the way, what happened to the kitten?'

She flushed. 'I'm sure there's no need for you to ask that question.'

'Scampered down the other side of the tree?'

She sighed. 'It's ridiculous us having this conversation as if we were sitting in Jane's parlour. You didn't want to talk before, you wanted to get down.'

'I still do, but the sight of your legs distracted me. Do you know that you have the most shapely calves?'

Her lips quivered. 'If that comment was meant to take my mind off our situation it failed. You should not be staring at my legs, *Master Hurst.*'

'It helps me not to think of the drop, *Mistress Clifton.*' Phillip placed his hand on her leg.

Rebecca started as his touch sent a fiery sensation to her feminine core. 'What are you doing?' she demanded breathlessly.

'Giving in to temptation whilst trying to

fathom out how to make you let go and trust me,' he admitted.

At least he was honest, she thought. 'That is not the way to do it. Of your courtesy, remove your hand, please?' she asked unevenly.

'I beg your pardon,' he said meekly, removing his hand, but continuing to stare at her with an unfathomable expression until she felt so hot and bothered that she closed her eyes in an attempt to shut him out. His arm went round her waist and her eyelids flew open. 'What are you doing now?' she cried.

'I have to get a hold on you to rescue you,' he said reasonably. 'Now put your arms around my neck and lean towards me and I'll ease you down from the branch.' She hesitated. 'You have to trust me, Becky love.' His voice was silky soft and very persuasive.

Love! He had called her love! Suddenly she felt unexpectedly calm and, relaxing her grip on the tree, she put her arms around his neck, one by one.

Phillip eased her from the branch, praying that he would not slip, intensely aware of the feel of her feminine softness in his arms. 'Now one step at a time,' he said.

Rebecca followed his lead. Her boot slithered on the bark and she gasped with fear, thinking she would fall, but he held her safe, although some of the colour had drained from his face. They remained still, pressed against each other for several moments.

If the circumstances were only different, thought Phillip, knowing he must not allow himself to be distracted by lustful thoughts. He moved carefully to the branch below and brought her down with him. Then he searched for the next branch with his boot whilst keeping his eyes on her. He felt her breasts rising and falling agitatedly against his chest and swore as he felt himself go rigid. 'Can't you keep still?' he groaned.

'I am keeping still,' she gasped, aware of his arousal.

Determinedly he let go of her and told her to hold on to the branch above. He had no choice but to glance down to where his brother and the children had stood not so long ago, but they seemed to have disappeared and he was aware of the drop. His legs suddenly seemed to turn to jelly and the next moment he was sliding, jolting and jarring from branch to branch before he slammed to a halt against the trunk.

Shocked by his sudden fall, Rebecca gave no thought to her own safety and followed in his wake, sick with worry, only halting when she caught up with him. He was slumped against the tree with his eyes closed. There were abrasions on his cheeks and nose where twigs had slapped him in the face. 'Are you all right? Have you broken any limbs?' She ran a hand along his arms and down his legs. His thick lashes swept up and he stared at her from dazed eyes. 'Can you move?' she demanded, her voice shaking. Inconsequentially, she thought that his eyes seemed to have turned to a midnight blue and, for a moment, she felt as if she might drown in their depths. Then he grabbed hold of her and kissed her.

A punishing kiss at first, but then it grew gentle and went on far longer than any of their other kisses; she wondered how lips so sensitive could be rousing within her all sorts of sensations. Then abruptly he lifted his mouth. 'I beg your pardon,' he said, a mite breathless. 'But I needed that kiss.'

'*Needed?* What do you mean? That you felt a need to punish me?'

His eyes gleamed wickedly. 'That, too! Anyway, don't I deserve a kiss for coming to your rescue?'

'I thought you were really hurt,' she cried, pushing him away. 'You tricked me all for the sake of a kiss.'

'I am hurt,' he protested, 'and I've lost my hat.'

'Never mind your hat! I've scratched myself, too, coming down that tree.'

He gazed at her and saw blood oozing from a place on her neck and without thinking Phillip licked the blood away. Rebecca could scarcely believe he had done that and she stared at him, a question in her eyes. Their relationship seemed suddenly to be moving on apace to that physical closeness that they had shared once before and which she had not really expected in light of his brother's arrival. *Nicholas! Where had he and the children gone?* Then she became aware of children's voices and, with a sigh, pushed herself upright and managed to stumble to her feet.

'You really do have shapely legs,' said Phillip, gazing at her from beneath drooping eyelids as she dragged her skirts loose and smoothed them down. He reached for his hat and plonked it on his head.

'You shouldn't be looking at my legs. I—I must look a mess,' she said, attempting to tidy her hair, which had come loose and hung either side of her face and down her back.

'What are you worrying about? My brother isn't here to notice. I'm surprised he and the children went off the way they did, leaving us still up the tree.'

'Me, too. I don't know why you should still think I care what he thinks of me.' She stopped fiddling with her hair. 'My admiration for you is what absorbs me just now. You've displayed amazing bravery for one terrified of heights.'

He grinned and his chest appeared to swell. 'I wouldn't argue with you. Let's agree that you and I both showed amazing courage.'

For a moment they just stared at each other, their faces aglow, only to be roused by the sounds of children screaming, a dog barking and a man shouting. For a moment they both froze and then Phillip seized her hand. 'Come on, that sounds like trouble!'

Rebecca allowed herself to be tugged along the path. Her heart was pounding and she could only pray that the children had come to no harm.

Chapter Ten

As Phillip and Rebecca drew closer to the source of the commotion, they saw a woman hastening towards the group, waving a stick. 'It's Jane!' cried Rebecca in dismay. 'What does she think she's doing, leaving the house and running in her condition!'

By the time they arrived on the scene, the dog had been sent yowling on its way after Nicholas had snatched the stick from Jane and wacked the cur on the nose. Margaret and Elizabeth were clinging to their stepmother, whilst a white-faced James clutched the kitten with one hand and clung on to Nicholas's sleeve with the other.

'What were you thinking of, climbing a tree when I needed you?' Jane flung the words at Rebecca. 'An-and then for th-that dog to attack James!'

Before Rebecca could say a word in her defence, Jane pushed Margaret away and pressed a hand to her side and groaned. Rebecca looked at her anxiously. 'Are you all right? Is it the baby?'

'I deem it is so,' gasped Jane. 'How could you be so foolish as to climb a tree? What if you'd fallen just as I have need of you? But it is not just the baby! I've had dreadful news and had to come looking for you. Fortunately the children and this man heard my shouts.'

Rebecca's heart sank. What could have happened to cause Jane to leave the confines of the house? She placed a reassuring arm around Jane's shoulders. 'You must stay calm. What news do you speak of?'

Jane rested against her, taking several slow deep breaths. Then suddenly she straightened up and said in a stark voice, 'We must not linger! I'll explain once we're back at the house.'

Nicholas shot a glance at Phillip. 'Brother, if I can be of no further use, then I'll return to our lodgings.'

Jane glanced at Nicholas. 'I recognise Master Phillip Hurst, but you I do not know, sir, and I owe you thanks. Despite your broken arm, you made some effort to protect the children from that cur. I see your sleeve is torn and there is blood on your hand. At the very least we should do something about them.'

Rebecca said quickly, 'Jane, this is Master Nicholas Hurst, newly returned from his travels.'

Recognition gleamed in Jane's brown eyes. 'Of course! The explorer!' She took a deep breath. 'Please, come back to the house with us. One of the girls can tend your wound and mend your sleeve and you might yet be of further use to me.'

'What is it you require, Mistress Caldwell?' asked Phillip.

'Aye,' said Rebecca. 'What is this terrible news?'

Jane did not immediately reply, but stood with her eyes closed, breathing deeply as before. After a few moments she opened them again and said, 'Catastrophe! A lad came from the church with a message concerning my husband. He has fallen from the scaffolding and he'll have to be carried home.'

Rebecca was stunned. 'Is he badly hurt?'

'He's unconscious.' Jane's voice trembled. 'He should never have been up the scaffolding at his age, but he would not be told. He still thinks he can do all that a young man can do and leap around like a frog in—in spring.' She glanced at Nicholas and gave a wobbly smile. 'No doubt,

Master Hurst, you are grateful not to be married with a young family in such a situation.'

'What is it you want of me, Mistress Caldwell?' asked Nicholas after the barest hesitation.

'I do not expect you to help fetch my husband, but you—' She turned to Phillip. 'It is the church on High Street. Will you make haste?' she pleaded.

'Aye!' He glanced at Rebecca. 'I'll speak to you later,' he added before hurrying away.

Jane gripped Rebecca's arm. 'He is a good man. Dearest, will you fetch the midwife?'

'Of course! You'll be all right until I return?' she asked anxiously.

Jane flashed a brief smile. 'I'll have to be and at least I'll have the other Master Hurst to assist me.' She turned and seized the hands of the youngest children and lumbered towards the house, calling over her shoulder, 'Come, Master Nicholas! You can help keep the children distracted by telling them a story.'

Rebecca looked at Nicholas, who was obviously struggling to conceal his dismay. 'I know this mustn't be what you want, but I would truly appreciate your help in this,' she said rapidly.

'I am willing to be of assistance, but I fear I will be a disappointment to them. I know no stories suitable for children and nor do I have Pip's gift of mimicry.'

'I am sure you will think of something,' urged Rebecca. 'I must not delay any longer.' She turned and hurried in Phillip's wake.

'Now here's a real to-do,' she said, catching up with him.

Phillip gazed down into her worried face and knew that now was not the time to voice what was in his heart. 'I hope Master Caldwell's accident is not as serious as she fears.'

Rebecca gnawed on her lip. 'I, too, although I confess my fears are for Jane. It is no easy matter giving birth and I can only pray that the midwife is at home when I get there.' She paused. 'Jane is expecting Nicholas to entertain the children.'

Phillip frowned. 'That wouldn't please him. Despite all appearances he does not feel easy around children.'

'But he is a teller of tales of sorts, isn't he?' murmured Rebecca. 'And James already looks up to him because of Nicholas defending him.'

'I would be the first to admit that he showed great courage doing so, especially with a broken arm,' said Phillip.

Rebecca smiled. 'You and he have both proved your worth as men of derring-do this day. You climbing that tree and coming to my rescue…'

'I admit I was almost tempted to leave you up there,' he said straight-faced.

'You are a tease,' she said, chuckling and punching him lightly on his forearm.

Warmed by that sound, he knew definitely he had naught to fear from his brother where she was concerned and seized her hand and drew it through his arm. 'I've had no opportunity to tell you how Nicholas came by his broken arm. He was attacked whilst in London.'

Rebecca gasped. 'But that is both of you to have suffered in such a way.'

'A coincidence. Those who attacked my brother were apparently Spanish, so he believes that it is connected with the fight he had with the Spanish captain in Flanders and the man wants him dead.'

'You mean Nicholas was followed to London?'

'I have wondered whether two of his attackers were already in London and maybe have been watching out for his arrival for some time.' Phillip paused. 'How much further is it to the midwife's house?'

'Not far.' She gazed up into his face. 'To want to kill Nicholas just because of a fight in Flanders seems extreme. Is there something you are not telling me?'

Phillip hesitated. 'As I've said before, we all

have enemies. Maybe Nicholas has made more than most on his travels?'

Rebecca nodded. 'Aye, it has not been an auspicious start to your brother's visit to Oxford. I presume he is here because of the business on Broad Street?'

Phillip shook his head. 'No, he came here because he is considering becoming an academic and taking holy orders.'

'What!' She stared at him in astonishment. 'Does he believe he will be safer behind a monastery wall?'

'My brother is no coward, but is testing a calling.' He paused as they came to an alley that led on to High Street. 'Let's put this aside for now. Jane and her husband and the children must be our first priority. Is it much further to the midwife's house?'

'We are nearly there,' said Rebecca.

They both fell silent and a few moments later she stopped outside a terraced house. She freed her hand and flashed him a smile and knocked on the door. Phillip waited only for it to open and to be assured that the midwife was within before walking away.

He found the church door ajar and went inside. The scene that greeted him was enough for him to understand how Simon Caldwell had come to fall. Part of the scaffolding had come apart and collapsed. He could see no sign of the injured man but noticed two men talking. He strode over to them. They turned to face him as he approached. The younger one looked pale and shaken and the elder looked grave and unexpectedly welcomed him by name.

'Master Hurst, I am glad to see you.'

'We have met before?' asked Phillip, scanning his face.

'Aye, at Draymore Manor, the day after the storm.' Phillip remembered and recalled suddenly the skeleton that had been uncovered and wondered if it had been identified. 'You have come from Mistress Caldwell, I presume?'

'Aye, her travail has started and she could give birth this day. How is Master Caldwell?' asked Phillip, shaking his hand.

The man shook his head. 'I'm afraid I have sad news. Master Caldwell is dead.'

'That is bad news!' Phillip could so easily imagine what this meant to the whole family.

'So what do we do?' asked the younger man, running his hand repeatedly through his chestnut hair. 'It hardly seems right to take his body home whilst his wife is abed giving birth to their child.'

'Where is his body now?' asked Phillip.

'In the vestry, but it cannot remain there. Part of the church is still used for mass and the vestry will be needed.'

Phillip considered what was best to do in the circumstances and came to a decision. 'Master Caldwell has a workshop in his garden, so perhaps we could place his body there until the news can be broken to his wife.'

Both men nodded. 'But how will we transport it there?' asked the younger.

'Surely you know of a horse and cart we can borrow?' said Phillip, wishing he did not have to do this.

'There's the wagon we used for transporting materials, but it doesn't seem right taking Master Caldwell in that,' said the young man dolefully.

'We have no choice,' said the other.

'Then let's do it,' said Phillip with a grim smile, hoping that Rebecca and the midwife were well out of the way by now. He could only pray that Jane would not die in childbirth, leaving the three children orphans. It would be a heavy burden for Rebecca to carry if that were to happen.

Rebecca pushed open the front door and stepped over the threshold. She held the door open so the midwife could enter with her bag. The older woman cocked her head to one side and her eyes met Rebecca's as there came the sound of a baby crying. 'It sounds as if I have come too late,' said the midwife.

'At least the baby is alive!' cried Rebecca, amazed that the whole process of giving birth had happened so fast. 'No doubt Jane will be in desperate need of your assistance,' she added, leading the way to the stairs.

She took them two at a time, only to pause when she reached the top for sitting in front of her was Nicholas Hurst with the two youngest children either side of him. His broken arm hung free of its sling and he was drinking from a pewter cup. His face looked strained and pale beneath his tan and his hand shook as he lowered the cup. 'Thank all the saints, you're here,' he said.

'You looked exhausted,' said Rebecca, placing a hand on his shoulder. 'How is Jane?'

The midwife interrupted, looking down at him in disapproval. 'Allow me to get to the mother,' she said.

Nicholas staggered to his feet and pressed himself against the wall. 'As you can hear, the child is born. I hope I never have to go through such an experience again.' A shudder went through him.

Rebecca felt sorry for him, but even more did she pity Jane. What state would she be in if Nicholas appeared drained of all strength? She hurried after the midwife, followed by James and Elizabeth. 'Mama has had a baby boy,' babbled the girl.

'I've never met a woman like her,' called out Nicholas. 'She has the tongue of a fishwife and as for the rest…' His voice trailed off.

'Children, where is Margaret?' asked Rebecca. 'Perhaps you can find her and the three of you can accompany Master Hurst to the parlour and see that he has more wine and some food.'

'She is with Mama,' said Elizabeth, hanging on to her aunt's skirt. 'We wanted to see the baby, but she wouldn't let us. She told us that we were too young and that we must stay with Master Hurst.'

Surely Margaret had not helped her mother with the birth? thought Rebecca, her heart racing as she imagined the condition Jane might be in. She shooed the two younger children away. 'You can see the baby soon, I promise. Just you take Master Hurst downstairs and see that he has all that he needs.' She did not stay to see if they did as told, but hurried after the midwife.

Jane was propped against the pillows with her babe in her arms and talking rapidly to the midwife. As for Margaret, she was curled up on the bed beside her mother.

Rebecca's face lit up. 'You're all right!'

'We're both well,' said Jane, her face wan. 'Although I hope I never have to depend on a man's help again in such a situation. I think he would have fainted at the critical moment if I had not seized him by the hair and screamed at him.'

Rebecca sank on to the bed. 'You—you mean he was in here during the birth?'

'Under duress! But he gathered his wits together and the pain brought him to his senses,' said Jane defiantly, 'and I did beg his pardon afterwards for the hair I pulled out.' She glanced at the midwife and handed the baby to her. 'If you'll allow me a private moment with my sister-in-law.'

Rebecca suddenly had a strong urge to giggle. 'Oh, my goodness, no wonder he looked so exhausted. At least it was a new experience for him. I cannot begin to imagine how he helped you with his arm in a sling,' she added unsteadily.

Jane sniffed. 'He managed well enough. I asked him about his broken arm and he told me about some woman he had planned to marry in

Flanders, only to discover that she was already spoken for and the man in question had tried to kill him.'

Rebecca was taken aback. 'I knew he'd been attacked, but I didn't know what lay behind it. What else did he tell you?'

Jane's eyelids drooped and she wriggled about as if trying to get comfortable. 'I had to stop him because I knew the birth was imminent. I'll give him his due. On the whole he did exactly what I told him to do, whether he liked it or not.' She sighed. 'Now where's his brother? I thought he would have been here with news of Simon by now. He'll be so delighted that he has another son.'

Rebecca pulled herself together, marvelling at Jane's sanguine attitude. 'You must give him time, Jane. It could be that they'll need to hire a cart to bring Simon home. Let's hope he's gained consciousness.'

'Well, I hope they won't be much longer. We must send for the priest and have the baby baptised. We'll call him Simon Peter after our first baby that died,' she said, yawning. 'And maybe add Nicholas, as well. Despite everything, Master Hurst was a help to me and he is a man to be admired for his courage.'

After what Jane had said about him a few

moments earlier, Rebecca was surprised by her words, but all she said was, 'Of course', and was glad to have another errand to run. 'I'll go and fetch the priest now.'

Jane closed her eyes. Rebecca turned away and went to speak to the midwife. 'You will stay here until I return?'

The midwife nodded.

Rebecca kissed the baby on the cheek and left the bedchamber. She hurried downstairs and found Nicholas in the parlour. She discovered that she was looking at him with new eyes in the light of what Jane had told her. Obviously he was more a man of parts than she had thought and had a vengeful husband on his tail. He was sitting on the settle, talking to the children.

'Master Nicholas, are you hungry? If so, would bread and butter suffice until I can prepare a meal?' she asked. 'Jane would like me to fetch the priest to baptise the baby.'

Nicholas rose to his feet with alacrity. 'I will be having supper with a friend in college this evening, so I deem it makes sense for me to leave now.'

'Of course, if you feel you must go, then I will not detain you,' said Rebecca, offering him her hand. 'I don't know what Jane would have done without you,' she added. 'She is considering Nicholas as one of the baby's baptismal names.'

'I don't know what to say.' Nicholas flushed as he took Rebecca's hand and shook it. 'Except that she is a brave and resourceful woman.' He placed his arm in its sling. 'I hope all is well with her husband. I'll see myself out.'

Despite his words, Rebecca accompanied him to the door and the children trailed after them. 'You will come again, won't you, Master Hurst?' said Elizabeth, smiling shyly up at him.

Nicholas paused in the doorway and Rebecca could sense that the girl's request had taken him by surprise. 'I deem your parents are going to be too occupied to want visitors,' he said abruptly and before Rebecca or the children had the chance to delay him further he hurried away.

'I don't think he likes us,' said James forlornly.

'I'm sure he does,' said Rebecca, ushering the two children back inside. 'Now you must be on your best behaviour whilst I go and fetch the priest.'

It was on her return that Rebecca saw the horse and wagon drawn up outside the house. She picked up her skirts and ran up the garden path and was about to enter the house when

Phillip appeared from the direction of the rear garden. There were two other men with him and their expressions were such that she feared the worst. She waited while Phillip spoke to them, then they raised their hats to her and hurried away.

Phillip turned to her and his expression was sombre. 'I'm sorry, Becky.'

'Oh, no,' she whispered, her eyes filling with tears. 'Poor Jane! She was so looking forward to telling him he had another son.'

'Both mother and child are well?'

She nodded, gripping her hands tightly together. 'I dread telling her and the children the news.'

'I'm sure you'll find a way,' he said gently, covering her hand with his. 'I have to tell you that we've brought his body here and it lies in his workshop. I did not consider it seemly to bring it in to the house at such a time.'

'Thank you,' she said huskily. 'The priest will be here soon to baptise the baby. I will explain the situation to him. Do you know if Simon received extreme unction?'

'There was no chance of his doing so as he never recovered consciousness,' said Phillip. 'Is there aught else I can do to help?'

Her hand trembled in his grasp. 'I can't think

right now. You've been of great help, both you and Nicholas. Apparently he is having supper with a friend at one of the colleges and had to leave in a hurry. No doubt you know where to find him.'

Phillip nodded, wanting to hold her tightly and to tell her not to worry and that he'd take care of everything for her.

Rebecca turned her tearstained face up to his. 'I really ought to let my brother know what has happened because he is the only man in the family, but I cannot leave Jane and the children now to get a message to him.'

'Of course not.' His tawny brows puckered. 'I deem it best if we wait until the funeral is over before I find him and explain the situation you and Jane now face.'

Rebecca lifted his hand to her face and rubbed it against her cheek. 'Thank you. I'm so grateful.'

'I'm just glad that there is something I can do to help you. Now I must go.' He hugged her. 'I'll see you soon.'

She thanked him again and then, with a sad little smile, she turned and went inside the house.

As Phillip heard the door close he felt at peace with himself now he had definitely made the decision that would change his future. Life was likely to be more complicated, but his happiness lay with Rebecca. But right now his brother would be expecting him at their lodgings. They were to dine with a Master Latimer, a tutor and lecturer in the Greek language and history at Brasenose College, whom Nicholas had met on his travels. Phillip could only hope that their host was not one of those people who made his subject sound as dry as dust.

He found his brother struggling to fasten his shirt and took over the task. As he did so he noticed a clump of Nicholas's hair seemed to be missing. 'How did that happen?' he murmured.

'You might well ask,' grunted Nicholas, 'although you look no better. Have you seen your reflection? Your face is smeared with blood and moss.'

Phillip grimaced. 'That was coming down the tree. What's your excuse?'

Nicholas's mouth tightened. 'I'd rather not talk about,' he said, but then proceeded to tell Phillip all about his participating in the birth of Jane's son.

Afterwards Phillip could only stare at his brother in admiration. 'You are a brave man! Doing all that for a woman you've only just met.'

Nicholas glared at him. 'I had no option but to do as I was told. She really was high-handed and

I was glad to get out of there before her husband returned. Although…' he sighed '…Rebecca told me that she is considering using my name as one of the boy's baptismal names.'

'You must have made a better impression on her than you thought,' said Phillip, then his smile faded. 'The husband—sadly he never recovered consciousness.'

'You mean he's dead!' Nicholas swore.

'My feelings exactly, Brother, although I didn't expect you to react the same way.'

'I can't help but feel some compassion for her and those girls and the lad. They might have been naught but trouble to me, but I'm not an ogre.' He inspected his bound cut hand. 'The eldest girl cleaned it with wine and did all that was necessary. Even so, it makes me glad that soon I'll be settled comfortably behind the walls of Blackfriars priory.'

'What about the premises on Broad Street? Aren't you even going to take a look at them? Because if you aren't interested in the business, I really am prepared to buy your shares.'

Nicholas glanced at him. 'If you're certain about it, then I will sell them to you. I'll write a letter and you can take it to my man of business next time you're in Greenwich. He can get in touch with the Raventons.'

Phillip nodded. 'I won't be returning there until the end of the month, although I'll be leaving Oxford for Worcestershire after the funeral. Becky wants to inform her brother of Simon Caldwell's death.' Phillip began to remove his doublet and shirt before pouring water from a pail into a bowl. Borrowing his brother's soap, he began to laver his upper body.

'You think he will take responsibility for the family?' asked Nicholas.

'I doubt it. His life is music and his career is bound up with the court of the Princess Mary. I can't imagine him giving all that up to support a family that he is not tied to by blood. Becky is a different matter, although I can't see her deserting Jane and the children.'

Nicholas frowned. 'Perhaps the husband left enough money to provide for them. That house—'

'He's recently spent money repairing the roof and part of the upper storey when a tree came down in the storm,' said Phillip, swilling water over his face and neck.

'That must have come as a blow,' said Nicholas. 'Surely he must have a man of business who will be able to sort matters out for Jane Caldwell.'

'Let's hope so.' Phillip finished his *toilette*.

'Now, what have you in your luggage that I can wear to supper this evening?'

Nicholas rolled his eyes, picked up his bag and slung it at him.

Their host, Master Latimer, wasted no time commenting on the brothers' appearance. 'You both look as if you've been in the wars.'

The brothers smiled and skated over the events of that day. He looked grave when he heard about Simon Caldwell's death because he had met the master mason and commented on the difficulty of replacing him. But as they partook of a fine apple cognac that Nicholas had presented to him, he took both brothers by surprise. 'So what say you, Nicholas, to talking to my students about your travels in Greece, especially your sojourn on the island of Rhodes?' he asked.

A weary-looking Nicholas started and spilt a little of his cognac on his doublet. 'You are jesting?'

'No, I'm serious.' The master's snowy brows met over his bulbous nose. 'I'm sure they would find what you have to say about the Grand Masters and the Knights of St John fascinating. You can even mention Saint Paul having landed on the island if you wish, and it would not surprise me if some of the students from the other colleges were interested in what you have to say.'

Nicholas shook his head and sipped his cognac. 'No, I'm sorry, Marcus, but I'm not a gifted orator like you and I would stammer to a halt in no time.'

The other man looked disappointed. 'You could read from your journal.'

Nicholas was adamant. 'You don't understand! I have come here to Oxford to live in seclusion whilst I decide my future. Besides, you are much more knowledgeable on the subject than I am.'

'But your viewpoint will differ from mine,' insisted Marcus, 'and I'm sure they would be just as interested in what you have to say about the Americas,' he added slyly.

Nicholas glanced at Phillip, who raised an eyebrow. 'You could read from your book, as Master Latimer has suggested,' he said.

Marcus beamed and rubbed his hands together. 'Having read it myself, I'm sure plenty of the students who can't afford to purchase it will find it marvellously entertaining. I must admit you fired my enthusiasm for exploration of those new lands across the ocean. The Almighty only knows what could be revealed of their past history if we were able to dig and delve over there.'

'I can't see them having much of a history. Most of the land I saw was virgin forest,' protested Nicholas. 'Anyway, I've told you I'm no orator. My brother is the speaker you need. He had a hand in writing the book and, whilst he's in Oxford, he'll be preparing my latest journal for the printing press, I hope.'

Marcus turned to Phillip with a smile. 'I thought you were a shipbuilder, but if it's true what Nicholas says, then why don't you do what he suggests?'

Nicholas said swiftly, 'I would add that my brother is also a storyteller, playwright and actor. He has performed at court and has recently been writing a play for the king's revels over the twelve days of Christmas.'

'You are, indeed, talented, Master Phillip,' said Marcus, looking delighted. 'Have you ever studied the Greek plays?'

'A little,' said Phillip. 'The man who introduced me to them studied here at Oxford.'

'Then what say you to taking your brother's place, as he suggested?' asked Marcus.

Phillip exchanged glances with Nicholas, who reached for the cognac bottle and grinned. 'It sounds an excellent scheme to me. You become me, brother, and I can disappear happily behind the walls of the priory. What say you?'

'I deem the role could prove interesting,' said Phillip, sipping his cognac.

Marcus nodded vigorously. 'You could disguise yourself with a false beard. Although I doubt that matters because no one here knows either of you. We could even put on a Greek play with your help. I'm sure the students would benefit from it,' he added enthusiastically.

Phillip's searching gaze went from one to another and his eyes were bright as he said, 'Maybe that is worth considering for another occasion. I know of someone who would willingly help with such an undertaking. At the moment I deem it sufficient that I take my brother's place. I will have to read his latest journal. I suggest that the lecture be two weeks from now as I have to visit Worcestershire and, in December, I must return to Greenwich.'

'Then it is settled,' said Marcus, rubbing his hands together. 'I will spread the word and you can be certain we will have a goodly crowd for you to entertain. In the meantime let us have some more of this excellent brandy. You certainly won't taste its like within the cloisters of the Blackfriars, Nicholas.'

It was not until the brothers retired to their bedchamber that Nicholas said, 'You cannot do it.'

Phillip did not need to ask what he referred to. 'Stop worrying! We have no reason to believe that your enemies have followed you to Oxford.' He climbed into bed. 'Anyway, on the morrow you'll be safely interned behind the priory walls.'

'It is not my own safety I am concerned about,' said Nicholas, drawing back the bedcovers and climbing in besides his brother. 'You do realise that Marcus will not stop at spreading the word about this lecture within the colleges?'

Phillip blew out the candle at his side of the bed. 'You don't know that.'

'No, but it's a possibility,' said Nicholas.

'It's true that the king encourages the academics, but I deem he is more interested in pursuing the woman he would have for his latest mistress than what takes place in Oxford. He has yet to endow a college, unlike the queen and his mother before him,' murmured Phillip.

'Exactly—the queen! What of her Spanish visitors and their kin? She probably takes an interest, where he does not.'

'Most likely, but I doubt the news of a lecture by Nicholas Hurst would reach Katherine. She lives quietly with her ladies and household, writing letters to her daughter and finding comfort in her religion, seldom visited by the king.'

Phillip hoped his brother would now go to

sleep and allow him to rest and think his own thoughts. Had Becky managed to break the news of Simon's death to Jane without her having a fit of the hysterics? It was going to be difficult for the household in the coming weeks and he would not be there to help them during all that time. He must see Becky in the morning. On the tail of that thought came Nicholas's voice out of the darkness. 'I've just had an idea, but I think I'll sleep on it.'

'You do that, Brother,' said Phillip, stifling a yawn. 'Goodnight.'

Chapter Eleven

The following morning Phillip woke to find it already light and that his brother was up and dressed. He realised that Nicholas must have fetched food and drink for breakfast, for he was not only sitting at the table with a sheet of paper held down with his broken arm, but was eating, too.

'What's that you're reading?' asked Phillip, wincing as he rose from the bed.

'It was slipped under the door. I discovered it when I arrived back from the baker's,' murmured Nicholas, without looking up.

'What's it say?' Phillip crossed to the table and glanced down at the sheet of paper.

Nicholas looked up at him. 'Rebecca's maiden name was Mortimer, wasn't it?'

'You know it was,' said Phillip, sitting on a stool the other side of the table.

Nicholas nudged the paper towards him. 'Read it! It's addressed to Master Hurst, but it's clearly meant for you.' He rose to his feet and went over to the window and gazed out.

Phillip sat down in his chair and drew the sheet of paper closer and began to scan the lines written there.

I am sending this to you, Master Hurst, because purely by chance I saw you enter this building last evening. Although it is years since I last visited your father's shipyard, I was convinced I had seen you before. I was mistaken. It is your likeness to your father that I recognised. You are very like him when he was your age, so I made enquiries about you at the porter's lodge and discovered who you were. I wish to say that although I do not want to see my twin brother again, I would like to make contact with his wife, Mary, and her daughter Rebecca and son Davy. I am staying at Corpus Christi College with an old friend, so you could leave a message for me at the lodge if you can help me.

Yours hopefully, Anthony Mortimer

When he had finished reading, Phillip lifted his head and stared at his brother. 'I never expected this. I had no idea that he'd ever visited the shipyard.'

'You were probably too young to remember him; besides, if he and his brother were identical twins, then you probably wouldn't have known it was him, anyway,' said Nicholas. 'It's possible I could have seen him when I worked there. Explain to me what this is about? I thought Rebecca's parents were both dead.'

Phillip did not immediately answer, but drummed his fingers on the table and gazed into space. After several minutes had passed he said, 'There is a riddle here and I fear the answer will not be to his liking. Rebecca was told by her father that her mother had deserted the family and run off with her lover. All her life Rebecca has carried the hurt of what she saw as her mother's rejection. Then recently she discovered that the man in question was her father's twin brother, who she didn't even know existed. It made her even angrier towards her mother but also him. Her father was not the best of parents, but she felt they were to blame for the man he became and that she had been robbed not only of a mother's love, but a father's, too.'

'But in that missive Anthony Mortimer is asking after the mother,' pointed out Nicholas.

'I know,' said Phillip softly, 'which makes me question what happened to her.'

'So do you have an answer?' asked Nicholas, coming over and sitting across from Phillip. 'What do you think happened to their mother?'

'I believe their father lied to them and some ill befell Mistress Mortimer—perhaps her husband killed her in a jealous rage.' Phillip sighed, eased back his shoulders and winced as he did so. 'I must arrange to meet Anthony Mortimer.'

Nicholas reached across to him. 'Hold on! You need proof before you go making such accusations.'

'Jane's husband was recently doing some renovation at Draymore Manor House near Witney. During a recent storm, a wall was blown down and they came across a skeleton.' Phillip's expression was grim. 'Davy told me that his grandmother was a Draymore, so the family has a connection with the house. The Mortimers could even have lived there for a while and, if that's so, the skeleton could be that of Rebecca's mother.'

'How are you going to prove it?'

Phillip reached for the jug on the table and poured himself a cup of ale. 'First things, first. I need to talk to Anthony Mortimer and also to the men who found the skeleton. One of whom is here in Oxford.'

Nicholas's eyes held Phillip's. 'You'll not tell Rebecca about all this yet?'

'God's blood, no!' said Phillip vehemently. 'She has enough to cope with right now. I'll see what her uncle has to say and then decide whether it would be best to involve Davy before going further with the matter.' He grimaced. 'It looks as if I might have a travelling companion on the journey to Worcestershire.'

'You could arrange for him to take the message to Davy and save yourself time,' suggested Nicholas. 'You've much to do before returning to Greenwich in December. Don't forget you've the lecture to give.'

'Don't remind me,' said Phillip with a wry smile. 'But one thing is for certain, I don't want Rebecca getting wind of any of this just yet.' He drank some of the ale and then stood up. 'I must dress if I'm to call in at Corpus Christi. Do you know where it is? When are you leaving for the priory? And where are your journals?'

Nicholas did not answer all these questions immediately, but picked up his knife and cut several slices of bread. 'You'd best have some breakfast before you go. I'm wondering if you're going to need my help.'

Phillip raised an eyebrow. 'In what way can you help me?'

'With the women. If Jane Caldwell's husband didn't have a man of business, who's going to make the funeral arrangements? You know that's generally a man's job. Rebecca will be kept busy looking after the children.'

Phillip felt suddenly suspicious about his brother's sudden concern for Rebecca and Jane after what he'd said last evening. 'You're better adhering to your original plan and retreating to the peace of the cloisters,' he said firmly. 'You need to rest that broken arm after fighting off that cur and delivering a baby.'

Nicholas pulled a face. 'Don't remind me. I only want to help, but I can see you wish to do everything yourself.'

Phillip frowned. 'It's not that. I could be mistaken in what I said the other day and we might have been followed here from Greenwich and you're safer behind the priory walls.'

'I think we'd have noticed if we were followed,' said Nicholas shortly. 'But I accept that you're concerned about my safety.'

'Of course I am. I've had months of worry, wondering if you were dead and now you're alive here in Oxford, I want you to stay that way,' said Phillip, slightly ashamed of his suspicion about his brother's motives, but he still found it incredible that Becky should appear to prefer him to his elder brother.

'All right! Although the way you're giving your orders you'd think you were the older brother, not me,' drawled Nicholas, taking a couple of his journals from a box. 'I'll leave you now. I'm not sure when I'll see you again, but I'd appreciate it if you kept me informed about what's happening.' He paused. 'You can always visit me at the priory.'

'I thought the idea was that you have some solitude to consider your calling,' said Phillip lightly.

Nicholas sighed. 'Always the last word with you, Pip.' He nodded in his brother's direction and left without another word.

Phillip guessed he had offended him, but he had no time to dwell upon it and instead dressed and gave the first of the journals a swift perusal as he broke his fast. Then he left the lodgings within the hour.

He discovered from a student that Corpus Christi was situated on Merton Street, which was on the opposite side of High Street from the church of St Mary the Virgin where Simon Caldwell had died. According to the student, the college was much closer to the river. He was walking along the High Street when he saw Rebecca coming towards him with a basket on her arm and James by the hand. She was dressed all in black, but the wind had whipped colour into her cheeks. He knew the moment when she caught sight of him because her features came alive and her pace quickened. He found himself running towards her, stopping inches from her and the boy.

'Becky,' he breathed.

'Phillip!' She beamed up at him. 'I did not think to see you so soon.'

' Nor I, you.' Only by the greatest self-control did he prevent himself from kissing her.

They stared at each other, their eyes locked. Only when her arm was jostled by a passer-by did Rebecca say, 'I am on my way to buy bread and to visit Simon's man of business. Were you on your way to visit us?'

Phillip avoided answering that question by asking, 'How is Jane?'

Rebecca's mouth drooped. 'Yesterday it was as if she has not heard a word I said to her about Simon. This morning it is different. After a storm of weeping, she has pulled herself together and has been telling me what I must do. I have insisted she stay abed, although she fought with me. I have had to leave her in the charge of Maud and her mother. The girl sometimes helps us in the house. I would that we could have Tabitha instead.'

'I will send word,' said Phillip, taking her arm and drawing her aside, out of the way of passers-by. He was aware of James tugging on her hand, but a frown caused the boy to desist. 'I am sure Christopher and his wife will understand your need of her is greater than theirs. No doubt Ned will accompany her.'

Rebecca's eyes brightened. 'You are so kind and I'm sure Jane will prefer that. I left her talking with Maud's mother about sewing Simon's shroud.' The light in her face died and she sighed. 'It is all so sad.'

Phillip pressed her arm gently. 'I hate to ask this, but has she given any thought to when the funeral is to be?'

'I am to ask Simon's man of business to arrange it. We will not attend, of course, but Jane would appreciate it if you and your brother could represent us.'

'Nicholas! She wants Nicholas there!' he exclaimed.

Rebecca nodded. 'Odd, isn't it? I deem it is because he helped deliver baby Simon.'

'Most likely,' said Phillip, wondering if by some miracle he might yet win his wager.

She stared at him, a question in her eyes. 'What is wrong?'

He smiled. 'Not a thing that cannot be put right.'

There came a chime of bells from the church. 'I must go,' said Rebecca. 'I don't like leaving Jane and the girls with Maud and her mother too long. I will see you later?'

'Aye.' He nodded, slipped a groat into James's hand and parted from them.

Phillip had thought that he might only be able to leave a message at the lodge for Anthony Mortimer. Fortunately he was informed that he was available and had left instruction that if a Master Hurst was to call, then he was to be shown up. In a very short time Phillip was escorted to a room on the first floor. Further along the passage he noticed two men. The profile of the younger appeared familiar, but he could not remember where he had seen him before. As for the elder man, he was speaking in Spanish.

'Master Hurst?' The sound of the voice immediately drew Phillip's attention. The door in front of him had opened and he instantly recognised the man who greeted him. The only noticeable physical difference between Anthony Mortimer and his twin, since Phillip had last seen the latter, was that this man's hair was white and there were creases about his eyes and mouth, as well as warmth in the voice that greeted him. He was also dressed well in a dark-blue doublet of fine broadcloth and blue hose.

'Master Hurst, I am so pleased that you have responded so swiftly to my missive.'

'Your message intrigued me, Master Mortimer,' replied Phillip, shaking his hand and noticing the heavy gold signet ring on his left hand.

'Please sit down,' said Anthony, waving him to a seat. 'My friend is giving a lecture, so we have at least an hour in which we can talk.'

'There is a man further along the passage. A Spaniard,' said Phillip. 'Have you any idea who he is?'

'Ah, you must mean Juan Luis Vives,' said Anthony. 'My friend pointed him out to me. He's a man of some eminence. He used to be Reader of Rhetoric here. I believe he's acquainted with the queen and she employed him to draw up a curriculum for her daughter's education.'

Phillip realised he had heard mention of him at court. Apparently Sir Thomas More had met him in Bruges and been impressed with his ideas. This had led to his being invited to England by

Cardinal Wolsey. 'A man of eminence, indeed,' murmured Phillip.

'Please, sit down,' invited Anthony.

Phillip took the stool indicated and accepted the offer of a glass of wine. 'I can tell you, Master Mortimer, that not so long ago we were searching for you.'

Anthony shot him a curious glance as he poured the wine. 'Who is *we?*'

'After your sighting at Minster Draymore and then in here in Oxford, I travelled to Worcestershire with your niece, Rebecca, to speak to her brother, Davy. She had no idea that you existed.'

'What!' Anthony frowned as he handed him a cup of ruby-red wine.

Phillip thought he looked so like his twin when he was displeased that it was uncanny. 'We thought you were your brother's ghost.'

'Ghost! You mean Adam is dead?' He ran a hand through his shock of white hair and took a pace or two about the room. 'When did this happen?'

'Several years ago, now; Master Caldwell sent a message to your agent, but he received no reply.'

Anthony sat down and leaning forwards, rested his arms on his thighs. 'Master Caldwell!

Was he not the mason employed to work on Draymore Manor?'

'Aye! Unfortunately he met with an accident yesterday and was killed,' said Phillip.

'That is bad news! But I can tell you that I am here because I received a missive from my agent's wife, saying he was sick unto death. I have been out of England and that is why I knew none of this. Tell me, what is the connection between Master Caldwell and my nephew Davy?'

'It is your niece, Becky, and Master Caldwell's wife—or widow, should I say—who are connected. Becky was married to her brother, Giles. But she, too, is a widow and has been living with the Caldwells here in Oxford.'

'I see.' Anthony's white bushy brows drew together over his fine nose. 'What of Rebecca's mother, Mary?'

Phillip hesitated. 'Here is a riddle, Master Mortimer—Becky believes her mother to have deserted her when she was only a child, by running away with an unknown man. Only recently was she told that man was you, her father's twin.'

'But that is not true!' Anthony paled beneath his tan and fumbled for his wine, downing it in two gulps. Then he leaned forwards and said, 'You must tell me all you know.'

'Tell me first,' said Phillip, 'whether you were ever Becky's mother's lover?'

'Aye, we were lovers and I believe Rebecca to be my daughter.' He put his head in his hands and said in a muffled voice, 'I met Mary, you see, before Adam did. We fell in love, but I needed to repair the family's fortunes and business took me abroad. My father had been killed at Bosworth Field when Adam and I were only six years old and it was a struggle for my mother to keep the house she had inherited from her father and support the three of us. Anyway, I planned to marry Mary when I returned, hopefully with the family fortunes renewed.' He lifted his head. 'When I eventually came home, it was to discover not only had Mother died in a fire at Draymore Manor, but that my brother and Mary were married with a son and living in the chambers that had not been destroyed by fire. At the time Adam was working away—he had always been good with his hands and was an excellent craftsman—and Mary poured out to me all that had happened. Adam had told her that I had been drowned at sea and persuaded her to marry him. She believed him because there is this belief that twins can sense things happening to the other. I deem that possibly true when twins are close, but not in our case. Adam and I were never emotionally close. Anyway, the love Mary and I had for each other was re-ignited and we became lovers.' Anthony's eyes were damp. 'It had always maddened Adam that I was the elder twin and the heir,' he muttered. 'He knew she was vital to my happiness and that's why he did what he did.'

'So what happened when he eventually returned?'

Anthony's expression hardened. 'What do *you* think, Master Hurst? There was a terrible argument in which all the poison he felt towards me was spilt. I wanted to take her away then, but he would not allow me to see her, so I was in a dilemma. He pleaded with me to give their marriage a chance, saying that after all she was legally bound to him. I allowed myself to be persuaded and for a while I stayed away, but I couldn't do that for ever because I worried about Mary. When next I returned Rebecca was an infant and Mary told me that she believed her to be mine. She was unhappy and full of regrets. I determined not to leave Mary and Rebecca with my brother. By then they were living in Oxford, so we arranged to meet at the manor house, only she did not come at the appointed time. Instead, I received a message from her saying that my brother was her husband in the sight of God and she could not leave him and Davy. So I went abroad and only returned a few months ago.'

'The message was most likely a forgery,' said Phillip, a heaviness inside him. 'I have to tell you, Master Mortimer, that I believe Rebecca's mother to be dead. A skeleton has been found at Draymore Manor and I deem it possible that it could be Mary's earthly remains.'

The two men stared at each other and Anthony jerked upright as if on strings and his face was twisted with grief and rage. 'You deem my brother killed her?'

Phillip nodded. 'I have no proof, but that's what I believe from my knowledge of the man and what you have told me this day.'

Anthony bowed his head and his shoulders shook. Phillip could only sit and wait until Rebecca's father had gained control of his emotions. 'I should have returned long ago,' he said eventually, wiping his eyes with a kerchief. 'All I can do now is to pray that my brother is in hell.'

'You can do more than that,' said Phillip firmly. 'You can tell Becky the truth. She has suffered for years believing the worst of her mother. The record needs to be set straight.'

Anthony's expression lightened and he rose to his feet. 'Where is she?'

Phillip stopped him with a hand. 'Wait! Jane Caldwell is not only newly widowed, but has just given birth. She needs all of Becky's attention at the moment. You must be patient. As it is, your nephew, Davy, came in search of you and Becky thinks he should know of Jane's bereavement. I planned to seek him out after the funeral. If you wish, you can accompany me.'

Anthony agreed to his suggestion and, shortly after, Phillip left the building.

He returned to his lodgings and wrote a missive addressed to Nicholas, informing him of what he had discovered from Anthony Mortimer and also the fact that Jane wished for them both to attend her husband's funeral. He planned to insert the time and date as soon as he knew it. In the meantime, he would seek out the man who'd helped him transport Simon Caldwell's body and see what else he could tell him about the skeleton found at Draymore Manor. After that he would visit Rebecca at home. Even up to the moment he saw her again, Phillip knew that he was going to be in two minds whether to tell her that he had spoken with the man who claimed to be her father. It was only the thought of the questions concerning her mother that made him hesitate to do so.

* * *

'Master Hurst is outside,' said Margaret, turning away from the window in her stepmother's bedchamber and glancing in her aunt's direction. 'Shall I go and let him in?'

'Which Master Hurst is it?' asked Jane, handing the baby to Rebecca.

'The player,' answered Margaret, skipping to the door.

'Stop that,' said Jane, frowning. 'Show a little decorum. This is a house of mourning.'

Rebecca looked at the girl and passed the child to her. 'Put Simon in his cradle. I'll go and let him in.' She wasted no time hurrying downstairs.

It was only when she opened the door that Rebecca remembered what Jane had said about decorum and mourning. Still, she could not prevent a wide smile when she looked up into Phillip's attractive blue eyes. He reached out a hand and she took it, allowing herself to be drawn towards him. He lowered his head and brushed her lips tantalisingly before covering her mouth with his so that her insides melted as the kiss deepened. Then he planted several small kisses on her face before slackening his grip and stepping inside the house, where he kissed her passionately, his hands roaming the contours of her body. After several minutes, when her knees felt so weak and her whole being trembled with longing to couple with him, he freed her abruptly with a sigh. 'I suppose I should have kept my distance.'

'Aye, but I'm pleased you didn't.' She looked up at him and traced the faint scar near his eye with a fingertip. 'At least I know where I stand now, which I didn't after that night we spent together in the stable.'

'I wanted you so badly but there was too much happening.' He captured that wandering finger and nibbled its length. 'It's the same now.'

'I know.' She dimpled up at him and rescued her finger. 'And we should not be doing this because only a short while ago Jane reminded me that this is a house of mourning and there is no room for levity.'

'Poor Jane,' said Phillip.

Rebecca's smile faded. 'Aye. She has much to ponder on in the next few days. Simon's man of business says there is not much money and most likely she will have to sell the house and move to a smaller one.'

'I half-expected that might be the case,' said Phillip. 'What of the funeral?'

'It is to be on the morrow at ten of the clock and a quiet affair. In the circumstances, Jane said that it was pointless inviting all those people he has worked for in the past. Sending messengers would cost money, likewise inviting them to the house and plying them with food and drink.' Rebecca rubbed her forehead where a knot of pain was forming. 'You understand, don't you, Phillip?'

He nodded. 'Does she still want me to ask Nicholas to attend the funeral? For I tell you now, he has already entered the priory. But I am prepared to drop off a missive at the gate informing him of the time of the funeral.'

She gnawed on her lower lip. 'Do not bother. Why should we expect him to attend? After all he didn't know Simon. But you will be there?'

'Aye, and then I'll leave immediately for Worcestershire.'

'I wish I were going with you,' she said wistfully.

'So do I,' he said honestly. 'But you are needed here and I will see that a message gets to Tabitha and Ned.'

Rebecca thanked him and was about to ask him whether he was coming in and having some refreshment when a voice upstairs called to her. 'I must go,' she said.

'Of course. I will see you on my return. I've much to do before I leave.' He wondered if now at least was the time to tell her of his plan to buy Nicholas's shares in the Raventons' company, but that summoning voice came again, so he kissed her briefly and left.

The funeral took place as planned the following day and straight after, Phillip left Oxford in company with Anthony Mortimer. He had taken the time to deliver his missive addressed to Nicholas, having crossed out mention of the funeral, but adding a little of what he had learnt about Jane's affairs from Rebecca. Hopefully by the time he returned, Jane would be up and about and in a state of mind to discuss the future.

'There's a person outside,' said Elizabeth, placing her thumb back in her mouth and turning from the parlour window.

'Not someone you recognise?' asked Rebecca, putting down her sewing. It was ten days since she had seen Phillip and she had been watching out for his return for the last two days.

'He's wearing a black habit,' said Elizabeth, who was peering out of the window again. 'Oh, he's just thrown back his hood. It's Master Hurst—the one with the broken arm.'

Rebecca experienced a deep disappointment, even as she wondered what Nicholas was doing here. She went to open the door, but had trouble doing so because it was sticking with the damp. Without her even asking, Nicholas put his shoulder to the door and pushed. It burst open and he fell inside. She bent to help him to his feet. Once Nicholas had brushed himself down he turned and faced her. 'Why are you wearing a habit?' she asked.

'Disguise,' he said briefly. 'I came to see how the household was faring and whether my brother has returned.'

'No, he hasn't,' said Rebecca. 'Why the disguise? Is it that you've had word of those who tried to harm you?'

'They sought to kill me, Rebecca,' he said grimly.

She hesitated. 'I understand your quarrel with the Spanish sea captain was over a woman.'

He shot her a glance. 'Who told you that? My brother?'

'No, you mentioned something to Jane.'

'I'd forgotten most of what I said to her that day.' He sighed. 'Her name is Louise and I believed myself to be in love with her, but she kept from me that she was already betrothed. She thought he wasn't coming back, you see.' He sighed again. 'May I come in?'

'Of course.' She led the way into the parlour

and waved him to a seat whilst she stood next to the fire. 'So no news of Phillip and my brother,' she said by way of conversation.

'Phillip did deliver a missive to me at the priory,' said Nicholas, holding his hands out to the fire. 'He mentioned visiting you but nothing about your uncle, Master Mortimer. I thought Phillip would have returned by now. I'm hoping no dreadful fate has overtaken him.'

Rebecca's heart seemed to flip over. 'Are you sure you don't mean my brother, Davy, when you mention Master Mortimer?'

Nicholas hesitated before saying, 'No, Master Anthony Mortimer.'

Rebecca froze. 'What do you know of my uncle? What has Phillip told you?'

Nicholas drew a deep breath. 'I should have held my peace, only I thought he might after all have explained some of it to you before he left Oxford. He told me little, but I know that he received a message from him a week or so ago,' said Nicholas, resting his arm on the chair.

There was a long silence and then a tight-lipped Rebecca said, 'Will you excuse me?' and she left the parlour.

Nicholas swore and then heard a voice saying, 'Tut-tut!' and realised that one of Jane's step-daughters was in the room and had been listening to their conversation. 'You've upset her,' said Elizabeth with relish. 'And Mama says there's been enough upset in this house recently and she doesn't think Davy will be able to sort out the mess we're in.'

Nicholas sat down and thought that perhaps here was a way he might be able to compensate for upsetting Rebecca if he could help the family. 'Tell me about it?'

Elizabeth came and leaned against the arm of his chair. 'Papa didn't have as much money as she hoped. He had to use some of it to repair the roof after the storm blew down a tree. We might have to sell up and go and live in a smaller house in Witney.' She rocked backwards and forwards, heel, toe, heel, toe.

'Why Witney?' asked Nicholas.

'Because it's a wool town and is prosperous. Mama used to live there when she was my age and she and her mother used to spin and her father weaved. Then they died and she had to carry on alone for a while and then she married Papa and came to live here.'

'I see,' muttered Nicholas, frowning.

There was a sound at the door and the next moment Jane entered the parlour in a rush. 'Master Hurst, how good to see you,' she said brightly.

Nicholas rose to his feet. 'It is good to see you up and about, Mistress Caldwell,' he said awkwardly.

'Indeed.' She clasped her hands in front of her. 'Rebecca is fetching some refreshments. Your news stunned her and she's very angry with your brother. You will stay, and tell her anything else you know about her uncle, won't you?'

Nicholas did not hesitate to say firmly, 'Perhaps I should leave that to Phillip.'

Jane sat down on the settle in front of the fire. 'Maybe you're wise to do so. I'm sure we both have enough on our minds without getting ourselves tangled up in their affairs. Sooner or later I would like to have Simon baptised in church. My head was in such a muddle the day the priest came here and it was not done properly. I wondered if you'd be prepared to be one of his godfathers?'

Nicholas was stunned and did not know quite how to answer. 'I am honoured that you should ask me, but may I have a little time to consider? I am unsure how much longer I will be here in Oxford.'

'Oh, I thought you had decided to settle here,' said Jane, frowning.

'I came here to ponder my future and…' he shrugged '…I am still undecided. I might have to go away again, but I will stay here until my brother returns. I know he had a good reason for not explaining matters to Rebecca before he left.'

'And what might that be?' said Rebecca, her voice loud as she entered the room, carrying a salver containing a jug and cups. She was followed by Margaret bearing another salver with a platter of wafers and rolls. Bringing up the rear was James with a bowl containing apples from the tree in the garden. 'I'm sure I have a right to know, Master Nicholas, what has passed between my uncle and your brother.' She placed the salver on a small table with a crash and glared at him.

Nicholas squared his shoulders and said firmly, 'I will not discuss it with you. I tell you only that your uncle has gone with him to visit your brother. I didn't come to cause trouble between you and Phillip. You must know that he has your well-being at heart.'

'That's as may be, but he has no right to keep such news from me! I am not a child that I cannot cope with the ills of this world.' Her grey eyes flashed steel. 'He knew my feelings about my uncle and mother and I will find it difficult to forgive him this.'

'Then there is nothing more I can say.' Nicholas stood up and bid them all a good day and left the parlour.

Elizabeth and Margaret pulled faces at each. Then the former said, 'Mama, don't you think—?'

'Hush,' said Jane. 'We must hold our tongues. This is a matter between your Aunt Rebecca and the Masters Hurst.'

'Exactly,' muttered Rebecca, trying to ignore the sound of Nicholas struggling with the front door. She reached for a wafer and bit into it. There was the sheen of tears in her eyes as she gazed across the room. How could Phillip have kissed her the way he did before leaving, knowing he was keeping such an important matter from her? She doubted she could ever look him in the face and smile again.

'You're in trouble!' The voice came out of the darkness and was recognisable.

Even so Phillip left the door ajar, lifting the candle higher so that its flickering flame sent shadows dancing around the walls. It revealed a black-robed figure silhouetted against the window. He closed the door behind him with his hip and placed candlestick and the box under his arm on the table. 'Is that you, Nicholas?'

'Who else?'

Phillip crossed the room and watched his brother throw back his hood. 'What are you doing here? And why are you wearing that habit? What d'you mean *I'm in trouble?*'

Nicholas moved away from the window and perched on the bed. 'I thought you'd have returned earlier than this. Were the roads treacherous?'

Phillip did not answer, but removed his hat and gauntlets and placed them on the table before crossing to the fireplace. 'You could have lit a fire.'

'I wasn't intending staying much longer. I've come here every evening, hoping to find that you had returned.' Nicholas watched as his brother set about getting together the makings of a fire. 'So, did you find Davy Mortimer?'

'He wasn't in Worcestershire, if that's what you mean. The King has had a change of heart and the princess is to be allowed to attend the Christmas festivities and has moved closer to London with her court. We eventually found him, but he could not return to Oxford with us. I was also able to visit our brother in Greenwich and spoke to Tabitha and Ned. They're on their way here now. But tell me, what is this trouble?'

'It's Rebecca. I'm afraid I let slip that you'd met her uncle.'

Phillip swore savagely and snapped a length of kindling. 'Why did you have to visit her?'

'I wanted to find out if they'd heard from you. Did you know that Mistress Caldwell is planning to move to Witney?'

'No!' Phillip stood up abruptly and took a turn around the room. 'Why this sudden interest in the women and the business? I thought your mind was set on taking holy orders.'

'I decided it wasn't for me after all.'

Phillip's eyes narrowed. 'You seemed so set on it. Why the change of heart? Is it that you've realised that Becky is a treasure after all?'

'I can admire her attributes, but it has naught to do with her.' Nicholas gazed at the floor. 'What are you going to do about Becky? Where's the uncle now?'

'Draymore Manor! He's travelling here on the morrow.' Phillip clenched and unclenched a fist. 'It was my intention to accompany him to the house to see Becky, but now I must explain matters to her before he arrives.' He picked up his hat and pulled it down over his head, reached for his gauntlets. 'I presume you won't be here when I return?'

'Probably not. I'm still lodging with the Blackfriars.'

Phillip shook his head in disbelief, took the key from the door and slammed it behind him. He clattered down the stone steps and came out into the quadrangle. Fortunately there was still a faint light in the sky. He managed to avoid the sundial and hurried out into the street and headed towards the river. As he strode along the pathway, he could only hope that Rebecca's anger had abated somewhat since Nicholas had told her the news. He should have asked his brother what exactly he had said to her. Phillip decided the best way he could explain his actions to Rebecca was by starting with her uncle's letter and going on from there. One thing was for certain—the next hour was likely to prove extremely difficult.

The front of the house was all in darkness. Remembering what Nicholas had said about Jane's decision to move to Witney, he wondered if the family had already left and his heart sank. But then he told himself it was surely too soon for them to have done so and he set out around the side of the house to its rear. To his relief he saw light coming from the kitchen and he knocked on the door before putting his hand to the latch. The door did not yield and he realised that it must be bolted. He rattled the latch.

'Who's there?' called a voice. 'I tell you that I'm armed.'

'Becky, is that you?' he shouted, placing his

mouth to the gap between door and frame. 'It's Phillip!'

There was a long silence and then she called, 'Phillip, you say! I know no trustworthy man of that name! I remember how my father kept things from me, treated me as if I were a lack-wit. As if it was not bad enough that my mother had rejected me.'

He winced, but told himself that she was at least talking to him. 'I can explain!'

'Doubtless you will have an explanation, but will it satisfy me, I ask myself?'

'You won't know until you hear me out,' said Phillip. 'Let me in! This is a ridiculous manner in which to have a vitally important conversation!'

'Who are you to tell me that I am being ridiculous?' snapped Rebecca.

He groaned. 'I didn't mean you were ridiculous, just this situation. Let me in, Becky! It's freezing out here and I haven't had an easy time of it.'

'Do you think I have? Since Nicholas mentioned you'd had a missive from my uncle, I've told myself that I was a fool ever to trust you.' Her voice wobbled.

'I kept the news from you because I care for you.'

'It's a very odd way of showing it.'

'Let me in! Let me prove how much I care,' he responded.

There came a different voice. 'By all the saints, Rebecca, let the man in!'

A relieved Phillip heard bolts being drawn and became aware the women were having a struggle to open the door. 'You need a man in this house,' he said, placing his shoulder to the door. 'Step back!' and he pushed. He entered the house and rammed the door shut with a back kick of his booted foot. 'Thank you, Jane,' he said, without looking at her, having eyes only for Rebecca. Her expression was uncompromising and his heart sank.

She stood against the table, her back as stiff as a board and her arms folded across her breasts. 'It is a late hour to come calling, Master Hurst. I don't know how you dare to show your face here!'

'Leave us, Jane,' he said firmly.

'No, don't, Jane,' ordered Rebecca.

Jane took one look at Phillip's determined features. 'I shall give you the time it takes for me to go upstairs and check the children are asleep.' She left the room.

Phillip noticed the sheen of tears on Rebecca's cheeks and he could only think of comforting her. He crossed the floor and slipped an arm around her waist. 'Oh, Becky sweeting, surely you know that you can trust me and it wasn't ever my intention to hurt you?' he said unsteadily, and then he kissed her with a hungry passion, lifting her off her feet and holding her against him.

When eventually Phillip enabled Rebecca to draw breath, she pushed him away and said, 'Do not think you can persuade me with kisses to forgive you? Explain yourself!'

He sighed and released her. Then he pulled out a chair for her and, once she was seated, sat opposite her. He knew how important these next few moments were and prayed he would not make a mess of things. From inside his doublet he took out a folded sheet of paper and handed it to her. 'That was delivered to me the day before the funeral. It provided me with a question as much as an answer.'

Rebecca held the paper towards the fire so that its light fell on it. She began to read what was written there. He could see how stiffly she held herself and longed to take her in his arms again and soothe her. She must have read the message at least three times before lifting her head and staring at Phillip from pain-filled eyes.

'What happened to my mother?' she croaked.

Chapter Twelve

'I wish you could be spared the truth,' said Phillip gently.

Rebecca's throat tightened. For a moment she thought she would choke on the words that rose within her and caused a chill about her heart. Then she managed to swallow and said in a raw voice, 'She's dead, isn't she?'

'I believe so,' he said heavily. 'She never did run away with Anthony, although that was their plan. They were going to take you with them, but when the appointed time came she didn't arrive at their rendezvous. Instead, Anthony received a message saying that she had changed her mind.'

Rebecca gripped her hands tightly together. 'Why did she change her mind? Didn't she love him enough?'

'To all appearances she had written that she was married to his brother in the sight of God and would not break her marriage vows.'

'That makes her more noble than I judged her to be.' Rebecca's voice was strained. 'Why were they going to take me with them and not Davy?'

Phillip covered her hands with both of his. 'Anthony was the elder twin and it was he who first met Mary. They fell in love but he had to go away on business. I gather he was away for quite a while, so Adam told Mary that he'd drowned and she believed him because he spoke of there being a special bond between twins. He persuaded her to marry him. She had Davy and then Anthony returned and, of course, she realised that she had been tricked into marrying the wrong brother.' Phillip felt Rebecca's hands clench beneath his own and raised them to his lips. 'I won't tell you the whole story. I'll leave that to Anthony. But whilst Adam was working away they became lovers. He said you were his daughter because Mary told him that was so.'

There was a long silence.

'You're telling me the truth?' Her voice was uneven.

He frowned. 'Why should I lie?'

'Indeed.' She cleared her throat. 'My head is in a whirl. All this time I have hated my mother for her rejection of me and now…' Rebecca's voice trailed off.

There was another long silence which Phillip was reluctant to break because he knew it would cause her even more pain. As it was Rebecca spoke first. She took a deep breath and without taking her eyes from his face, said, 'Do you think—?' She altered what she had been about to say and burst out, 'Ad-Adam killed my mother?'

Phillip freed a pent-up breath. 'Aye! A skeleton was found at Draymore Manor by Simon's labourers after a wall collapsed during the storm not so long ago. They think there was a tiny hidden chamber behind it. Apparently by the size of the skeleton, it is believed to be that of a woman, but there is no indication how she died. Anthony and I have come to the same conclusion that it is your mother's relic.'

'Oh, holy Mary, Mother of God!' whispered Rebecca, freeing her hands and getting to her feet.

He saw tears seep from beneath her eyelids and instantly hurried round the table towards her, only to have her retreat from him. 'I need some time alone, Phillip, to come to terms with all of this,' she said in a strangled voice. 'Please, don't come any closer. Let yourself out!' She turned and ran from the kitchen before he could prevent her.

He followed after her, but found his way upstairs blocked by Jane, who had the baby cradled against her and held a candle. 'No, Phillip,' she said firmly. 'I don't know what you've told Rebecca, but you will not pass.'

He hesitated, desperate to reach Rebecca, but knowing that he could not set Jane aside whilst she nursed the child. 'I must speak to her,' he insisted.

'Not now. Return in the morning and hopefully you can continue your conversation then.' Jane's expression was resolute.

Phillip was about to agree when he recalled a previous appointment. 'I can't come in the morning,' he groaned. 'I have to speak to the students of Brasenose College. I've given my word and cannot fail Master Latimer, the tutor in Greek history.'

'Then come midday and share a meal with us,' suggested Jane. 'It will give Rebecca more time to collect herself.'

Phillip thanked her and then remembered something else. 'You must tell Becky that her father hopes to arrive in Oxford on the morrow.'

Jane blinked. 'Did you say her father?'

'Aye. Talk to Becky!' he implored. 'Be kind to her.'

Jane gave him a look that spoke volumes. 'I deem it is time for you to leave, Master Hurst. As if I was ever anything other than kind to my brother's widow! I suggest you leave by the kitchen door as I have already locked and bolted the front one.'

Suddenly Phillip felt weary. For almost a fortnight he had been travelling on Rebecca's business and now he couldn't even finish a conversation with her until the morrow. He wanted to blame his brother, but was it his fault? Without another word, he left and made his way to the kitchen. Jane followed him and he heard her bolt the door after him.

As he strode round the side of the house towards the front, his mind was occupied with all that had passed between him and Becky. So it was that when he passed through the gate and on to the path near the river, he did not see the dark figures concealed behind a tree. Not until he was seized from behind was he aware of them. He struggled and managed to bring up an arm and punch one of them in the face. The man gasped and let out a string of words that Phillip didn't understand. Then he felt a blow on the back of his head and everything went black.

* * *

'So what is this about your father?' asked Jane, sitting on Rebecca's bed.

Rebecca's step faltered as she paced the floor and then she went over to the latticed window and gazed out into the dark night. 'Has Phillip gone?'

'Aye, that's what you wanted, wasn't it?'

It wasn't at all what she wanted, thought Rebecca. Not now! Now she needed to be held in his arms and be reassured that he still wanted her and that life could be good again. At the moment so much in her mind was dark and dreadful, wondering if Adam had left her mother to starve to death in that hidden chamber, alone and terrified.

'Phillip would have followed you up here, but I prevented him.' Jane shifted her son to her other shoulder and patted his back. 'But you still haven't answered my question.'

Rebecca turned and stared at Jane. 'So Phillip told you all about my father.'

'He told me nothing! I wouldn't be asking if he had done so,' cried Jane.

The baby whimpered and Rebecca went over and stroked his downy head, finding a little comfort in the act. How she wished she could bear Phillip's child! Pray God, it was not too late.

'Perhaps I should go after him,' she said in a low voice.

'That would be foolish! It is dark and he will well be on his way now,' said Jane.

Rebecca's shoulders sagged. 'I suppose you're right. Did—did he—he mention my mother t-to you?'

'No. He only suggested that I talk to you.'

Tears welled in Rebecca's eyes and she wiped her damp face with the back of her hand. 'I was so angry with him. Yet I do not doubt now that he found it difficult saying what he had to say.' A sob burst from her.

'Hush, sweeting,' said Jane, obviously summoning all her patience. 'What did he have to say?'

Rebecca dabbed her eyes and fought for control. 'That my father wasn't my father but my uncle instead.' Her voice shook.

Jane blinked at her. 'I don't understand.'

'They were twins! My mother Mary apparently met Anthony first and they fell in love but he went away and my father—I mean the man I believed to be my father—told her his twin had been killed and so she married him instead. Then Anthony returned a-and she realised h-her mistake. Later th-they became lovers whilst Ad-Adam was working away.' Rebecca paused to wipe away the tears pouring down her cheeks. 'I—I am the result of that love.'

'Oh, my sainted mother!' said Jane. 'You're a bastard child.'

'Obviously,' said Rebecca, her head drooping. 'I wonder if that is what Phillip is thinking now.' She heaved a deep sigh. 'I feel so tired all of a sudden.'

'Not surprising,' said Jane. 'You've had a tremendous shock and the last few weeks have been dreadful for both of us. Anyway, better a live father if he can help you, than a dead one who deceived you all those years. But it's going to feel strange seeing this man, the double of the one who raised you.'

Rebecca lifted her head and restless fingers pleated the skirt of her gown. 'It's going to feel more than strange. I will keep seeing similarities—I don't know if I can accustom myself to that! What if I find myself hating him?'

Jane rubbed her cheek against her baby's head. 'One can get used to anything if it's part of one's life for long enough. Phillip said I was to tell you that your father will most likely be in Oxford on the morrow.'

'What!' cried Rebecca.

The two women stared at each other, both thinking the same thing. 'We'll have to provide food and there's so little in the house,' said Jane, getting to her feet. 'I did ask Phillip to come at midday and share a meal with us, too.'

'You did!' Rebecca's spirits rose a little. 'You think he'll come?'

'Of course he'll come. He was quite desperate about you. It wouldn't surprise me in the least if he wants to marry you,' said Jane. 'That's why I wasn't having him leaping up the stairs and entering your bedchamber. A hearty thick soup and plenty of bread, I think,' she added seemingly inconsequentially.

'And cheese,' added Rebecca, feeling peculiar. 'If only we could obtain a couple of coneys. Men like meat.' She laughed a mite hysterically. 'I don't know how I can think of food at such a time.'

Jane shrugged. 'Necessity! Let us get a good night's sleep and all will look different in the morning.'

The light died in Rebecca's eyes. 'I would have thought Phillip would have come earlier than midday.'

'I did suggest he call in the morning, but apparently he has given his word to one of the tutors that he will give a lecture to some of the students.'

Rebecca frowned. 'I wonder when that was decided.'

'You will find out soon enough.' Jane touched her lightly on the shoulder. 'Now get some sleep. I must say, it will be interesting meeting your new father.'

Rebecca removed her gown and drew back the covers and climbed into bed. 'I don't know if I'll be able to sleep now I know for certain that my mother is dead.'

Jane stared down at her, a question on the tip of her tongue, then decided not to ask. She sensed the answer might just keep her awake if she were to know.

Phillip groaned as he regained consciousness. His head was aching abominably and he could hear a clanging noise. He opened his eyes with difficulty and peered on to a small space with bare stone walls. He vaguely remembered coming round a couple of times but then drifting off again. The air was freezing cold. He had no notion of where he could be and then he noticed louvred openings in the opposite wall through which a predawn light filtered. Then he realised that the clanging noise was a bell striking the hour. The noise vibrated through his head, causing it to ache even worse. Thank the saints that his hat was firmly clamped to his head so that it deadened the sound somewhat. Still, it was a relief when the noise stopped.

He must get out of here before it struck the next hour. His wrists were tied behind his back, but he was not gagged. Obviously his captors saw no point in it because he was out of earshot of people. Neither were his ankles bound. To all appearances they wanted to keep him alive. He struggled to stand, only to collapse because his feet had gone numb. He set about bringing some warmth and life to them by moving them back and forth. At the same time he struggled with his bonds, trying to loosen them. He wondered about the identity of those who held him prisoner and how long they intended keeping him here. He neither wished to miss his meeting with Rebecca nor the talk he was to give to the students. He felt a desperate anxiety thinking about her pain and his forced parting from her. He so wanted to ease that pain and bring her some release. He had to get out of here, he thought grimly, and doubled his efforts to free himself.

'What's this?' Jane bent and picked up a folded sheet of paper on the floor by the front door.

Rebecca paused in the act of pulling on a glove

and glanced at the paper. 'Perhaps it's from Phillip!' She snatched it from Jane's hand and unfolded the sheet. 'It can't possibly be from him. Here, look! It's written in a foreign tongue.' She thrust it under Jane's nose.

Jane took the paper and gazed at the writing. 'You're right. It must be a mistake. Who would deliver such to a house of two widows and four children?'

Rebecca pursed her lips. 'Let me see it again.'

Jane handed the paper over and this time Rebecca carried it through into the parlour and placed it on the table there. The girls and James glanced across at her, but she ignored them whilst she perused the lines of writing. 'Here is a riddle, Jane. I am certain that the name at the top of the page is that of Nicholas Hurst and I deem the rest of it is written in Latin.'

Jane peered over her shoulder. 'I cannot read Latin.'

'Neither can I, but I can understand the odd word from a book Beth showed me and I recognise those two, but they are not Latin.' Rebecca stabbed the page with a finger.

'What do they say?' asked Jane.

'Phillip Hurst.' Rebecca's breath caught in her throat and for a moment she sat there, tapping the sheet of paper with her fingers. 'I must take this to him,' she said abruptly. 'And he can deliver it to his brother at the priory! Whoever slid this paper beneath our door must not know where Nicholas Hurst is staying, only that he has visited us here recently.'

'I wonder who it is from?' said Jane.

'There appears to be no name at the bottom,' said Rebecca. 'It's as if they assume Nicholas will know who has sent it.' She frowned. 'I must get it to Phillip as soon as possible.'

Jane's gaze washed over Rebecca's pale features. 'You feel well enough to do that? And what of your father's visit? You deem you will return soon?'

Rebecca forced a smile. 'I will be back as soon as I can.'

'You know where to find Phillip?'

Rebecca stared at her in dismay. 'How stupid of me! Did he tell you where he was staying?'

'I only remember him mentioning one of the colleges. A newer one. Brasenose, I think.'

'Then I must go there,' said Rebecca.

'But you can't!' Jane placed a hand on her arm. 'Women aren't allowed in the colleges.'

Rebecca groaned. 'What am I to do? I must see him.'

Jane squeezed her arm. 'I wish I could help

you. If only my husband was still alive. He could go in your place.'

Rebecca seized on the name. 'Simon! You haven't yet sold all his garments?'

'No, why?' Then Jane's eyes widened and she gasped. 'You wouldn't dare!'

Rebecca thought of the times she had watched Phillip disguise himself as a woman and laughed. 'Oh, wouldn't I! If it is acceptable for an actor to dress as women, then why shouldn't I dress as a man? Where have you stowed Simon's clothing? And don't say you don't remember. I have a feeling it is terribly important I get this message to Phillip.'

Phillip had found a place on the wall where the stone was especially rough and he was using it to saw the rope. The method was slow and painful, the stone having rubbed off the skin from part of his wrists. At least he could feel that the rope was fraying. A little more and then a final tug and the strands broke apart and his hands were free. With a sense of exaltation, he made for the trapdoor in the floor. If good fortune was with him, then it would not be locked on the other side. He lifted the trapdoor and it came up with ease, much to his relief. Below was a ladder and fortunately he could see the floor below where it ended. For a moment his head swam and then he gritted his teeth and began the descent. With grim satisfaction he thought how his captors must have had a difficult time of it, carrying him up here. It puzzled him as to how they came to choose such a hiding place.

He wasted no time climbing down the ladder to the floor below and then through an opening that led on to a stone staircase. The door at the bottom was unlocked and led into the main interior of a church. With a lift of the heart he recognised the place and was relieved that the entrance to the bell tower was so close to the entrance on to High Street. A priest was saying mass. Fortunately the congregation's attention was fixed on him. Phillip crossed himself and then made his way silently out of the building.

He drew his cloak tightly about him, shivering in the frosty air, and took a deep breath and gazed to where a wintry sun was rising in a pale blue sky. What should he do? Hang around to see if his attackers came—but how would he know them? There were already people in the church and what if they were amongst them and recognised him when they emerged? He stood there, filled with indecision, then made up his mind what to do.

* * *

Phillip downed the remains of the wine as he undressed in front of a blazing fire and proceeded to don a new cream-coloured linen shirt he had brought with him from Christopher's house. He was reaching for his new blue hose when there came a knock at the door.

He paused in the act. 'Who is there?' he called.

'Phillip, is that you?' came a voice he recognised.

His heart seemed to flip over. Surely he must be mistaken? 'What is it you want with Phillip Hurst?' he asked cautiously.

'It is I, Becky! I know you must be angry with me. But, please, let me in,' she whispered.

He dropped the hose on the floor and hastened to open the door. He stared at her, scarcely able to believe his eyes. Then he grabbed a handful of the doublet she wore and dragged her into the room. He slammed the door shut with his foot and then bolted it with one hand, whilst all the time holding on to her. 'By all that's holy, Becky, what are you playing at dressed like that?' he hissed.

Rebecca clung to his arm with both hands. 'Don't be angry with me!' she pleaded. 'I can't bear it.'

'Angry with you? If only you knew,' he said, lifting her off her feet, so that their faces were only inches apart.

She released her grip on his arm, slipped her hands around his neck and pressed her cheek against his shoulder. 'I beg your pardon for running from you. I so regretted it. But I felt—'

'I know how you felt,' said Phillip gruffly. 'Look at me!'

She lifted her head and stared into his face. His flaxen brows hooded his eyes so that they appeared almost midnight blue. She wasted no time in kissing him, for there was something about his expression that was intensely reassuring. All the need she had of him was expressed in that kiss. She wanted to bury herself into him, become part of him. Never to be separated from him again. When she lifted her head to draw breath, she said, 'The days whilst you have been away have been so empty.'

'I've missed you unbearably,' said Phillip, holding her so close that he could feel her chest rising and falling despite the binding he felt was there, attempting to keep her breasts under control.

'Kiss me again,' she breathed against his mouth. 'I don't want you ever to stop kissing me.'

He laughed and then kissed her, aware of how difficult it was going to be to stop simply at a kiss. He sensed that she knew that because she was behaving with a reckless abandon, which apparently she had adopted along with her male garb. He lifted her off her feet and, mouth to mouth, chest to chest, hip to hip, carried her over to the bed.

They fell on it in a tangle of arms and legs and suddenly she brought their kiss to an end and opened her eyes and gazed at him. 'You—you're not wearing hose.'

'I know.' His eyes gleamed with enjoyment. 'I was in the process of dressing when you knocked on my door.'

She bit on her lip. 'I'm distracting you. Taking your mind off the talk you have to give.'

'You know about that?'

'Aye, and I want to hear you speak.'

'Do you?' He looked gratified and then he nuzzled her neck. 'Let's not talk about that right now. I'm in need of relaxation first.'

She sighed and drew down the neck of her doublet so his lips could touch her collar bone. 'I'm in need of comfort and the sense of security only you seem able to provide me with and I have to ask myself—is it wrong of me to expect so much of you?'

'No,' he said, his nimble fingers reaching for the fastenings on the doublet concealing from him the pleasures of her flesh. 'I want you to feel safe with me.'

'I felt so dreadful last night,' she murmured, moving her hands from the top of her doublet and sliding them beneath his shirt. 'I wanted you in my bed.'

'They're some of the finest words you've ever said to me,' said Phillip, jerking beneath her touch. He pressed down on her hands and groaned. 'Please, don't do that yet.'

She nodded. 'I beg pardon.'

'No need.' He removed the doublet and flicked open the ties on her shirt, slackened them and removed the garment. Then came the bindings, which seemed to take an age to unwind. The breath caught in his chest as he gazed down at her bare breasts. 'Perfectly formed,' he said hoarsely and lowered his head to salute them with his lips.

Rebecca gasped with delight and laced her fingers through his dark gold locks and held his head there. All that had hurt and worried her faded into oblivion. His mouth and hands led her along sensuous paths that tantalised and brought her eventually such exquisite pleasure that he had to silence her with a kiss as his body joined with hers. That such pleasure could reach a higher pitch than earlier brought unexpected tears to her eyes. She so wanted to please him for showing her the height and depth that love could reach and wasted no time in responding to his need. For surely this was love that they were sharing?

Afterwards they lay in each other's arms in naked abandonment, their eyes closed and their heads together. Eventually Phillip stirred. 'I must get dressed and so must you.'

She shot up. 'I had forgotten why I came here!'

He raised an eyebrow and reached for his shirt. 'You didn't come simply because you couldn't wait until noon to see me?' he teased.

'Of course I couldn't wait. But someone slipped a message beneath our door. It's in Latin and I thought most likely you would be able to read it.' She reached for the bindings and her shirt.

'You brought it with you?'

'Of course.' She climbed out of bed and picked up the hose and girdle from the floor. From a pouch attached to the girdle she took a folded sheet of paper and turned to him with it in her hand. He was in the act of pulling on his hose and she just couldn't look away. 'Your legs are so much more muscular than mine,' she burst out. 'I make a scrawny man.'

Phillip laughed. 'But a comely wench. Is that the message?'

She nodded. 'It has your name written halfway down and Nicholas's at the beginning,' she said.

'Ha!' He eased on his doublet and began to drag the laces in the hose through the eyelets at the bottom of the upper garment. 'Were you able to read any more of it?'

'Only the odd word.' She sat down on a stool. 'Is it to do with these foreigners who are trying to kill him? He told me about a woman he was in love with named Louise.'

'He told you!'

She nodded. 'Only because I repeated what he'd told Jane.'

Phillip said, 'I didn't mention it to you because I didn't want you thinking the worst of him. I was wrong. I should have done. I would have done!'

She nodded. 'I forgive you. About last night…'

He glanced at her as he pulled on his boots. 'I understand about last night and we haven't time to discuss matters any further now.'

She looked relieved. 'You are addressing the students. How did that come about?'

'Nicholas is acquainted with one of the tutors.' Phillip seated himself in front of a polished circle of steel so he could see his reflection.

Rebecca watched him reach for what appeared to be a handful of hair. 'What are you doing?'

'Donning a disguise, although I'm not absolutely certain it's a good idea.'

'Do you want me to leave?'

He smiled. 'You're here now, so you might as well stay.'

She watched him adjust what now was obviously a false beard and moustache. With his disguise securely fixed into place, he pulled on a hat and lifted a cloak from its hook before turning to face her. 'Well?' he asked.

She stared at him with an air of disapproval. 'Why do you wish to look like Nicholas?'

'Because I am taking my brother's place and reading from his journals,' said Phillip, picking up his pack containing a change of clothing and what he needed for the lecture. 'He didn't want to do it. Now, where's this message?' She gave it to him and for a moment her fingers clung to his. He read what was written there with a grim smile, then stuffed the paper in his pack.

She stared at him. 'Well?'

'It's nothing for you to worry about.'

'Why will you not tell me?'

'I promise I will explain later.'

'All right! I accept you have a lot on your mind.' She stood on tiptoe and kissed him before moving away.

'I presume that kiss means I'm definitely forgiven for upsetting you last night,' he murmured.

She took a deep breath and turned and faced him. 'Before you went away you told me to trust you. I believe that you did what you thought was best for me, so I have decided to give you all my trust.'

He flashed her that smile of infinite charm and she felt a warm sweetness curl in her gut. 'I appreciate that. Later we'll talk some more. Now we must go.' He made for the door and unbolted it. 'You wanted to hear me lecture to the students, so you must accompany me if you are to be allowed in without a ticket. You must be on your guard and not forget that you are pretending to be a student.'

For a moment Rebecca was uncertain whether she was brazen enough to go into the midst of a crowd of youths and men and pretend to be one of them. He smiled. She took a deep breath. 'This address-lecture-talk—I presume it is in English?'

He stretched out a hand to her and then let it drop. 'Young master, you'll understand every word and I'd appreciate your opinion later.'

'Then you shall have it, Master Hurst,' she said with dignity and followed him down the stone steps and out into the fresh air, attempting, as she did so, to imitate his walk.

Throughout his time in the hall, Phillip did not allow his mind to wander, but kept his attention firmly focused on the words he was reading and the same also when he spoke of his own travels to the island of Rhodes, explaining to his audience how the Knights of St John had built on the Byzantine foundations. He also told them of what he had learnt about the ancient art of Grecian boatbuilding. Despite all this, he was conscious every now and then of Rebecca's eyes fixed on him with a rapt attention and this strengthened his confidence. She had managed to worm herself to the front of the standing students and when he concluded his address, it was she who led the applause.

It was only when he was taking another bow that he realised Rebecca was no longer there. His eyes scanned the crowd frantically, remembering that day in Witney when he had caught sight of her. He remembered chasing after her with his skirts pulled above his ankles. It had been such a relief to find her. God grant that he found her now because he knew he could not live without her. Suddenly he spotted a black-habited friar at the back of the hall making an exit. Was that

Nicholas? He supposed he should talk to him, but it would have to wait. Finding Becky was his priority. Praying that no one had guessed her secret, he gave a final bow and made himself scarce before Marcus Latimer insisted on his joining him for dinner.

To Phillip's relief, he found Rebecca waiting for him across the street from the hall. Instantly, he seized her arm and led her away from the throng of men and youths leaving the building. 'Let's away from here,' he said in a low voice.

'I saw Nicholas,' she said, almost tripping over her feet as she attempted to keep up with Phillip as he hurried along. 'Where are we going?'

'To Jane's house, of course. Fortunately I doubt anyone would have recognised you or Nicholas disguised as you are, unless they heard you speaking.'

Her face blanched. 'I do hope no one overheard us talking! Although, as it was, Nicholas was so shocked when I spoke to him that he barely opened his mouth. When he did, it was only to tell me to wait for him outside.'

'Which you did presumably?'

'Aye. I told him about the message and he suggested you meet him at the Raventons' premises in Broad Street this afternoon.'

Phillip abruptly released her hand. 'What else did he have to say?'

'Only that there was something he must do and then he left,' said Rebecca. 'Why didn't you want me to tell him about the message?'

'Because I'd prefer him not to know. He'd deem he had to protect me.'

'P-protect y-you! Why? I don't understand,' stammered Rebecca. 'What has it to do with the message I gave you?'

'Let's walk on,' said Phillip, taking her arm, again and hurrying her along.

'You're still wearing your disguise,' pointed out Rebecca. 'Should you not remove it? I'd rather you were not mistaken for your brother.'

Phillip caught her worried glance and smiled. 'I have another disguise with me. I thought I might have need of it. Let's find somewhere quiet.'

The quiet place was up an alley behind a broken-down cart. Rebecca was ordered to keep watch whilst he pulled a gown and wig from his pack. 'This is ridiculous,' she said, rolling her eyes. 'You disguising yourself as a woman and me dressed as a youth.'

'Just do as you're told,' said Phillip sternly.

She turned her back and watched for anyone approaching. His experience of having to make swift costume changes meant it was only minutes before he tapped her on the shoulder. She turned and, despite her concern for his safety, she chuckled. 'You've forgotten to remove the moustache.'

He grimaced and carefully peeled it off. Then, after taking a paper and placing it in a book from his pack, he stuffed the other items inside it. 'Let's walk on a little towards the river,' he suggested. 'Put your arm through mine as if we were mother and son.'

She gave him a look. 'Shouldn't I take the pack if I'm pretending to be your son?'

He hesitated and then gave it to her. She swung it on to her shoulder and then they proceeded to the river as if they hadn't a care in the world.

Chapter Thirteen

Once they arrived at the riverbank, Phillip opened the book and from it produced the sheet of paper that Rebecca had given to him earlier. 'Now for the Latin message,' he said.

'You're going to read it again?'

He nodded. 'My Latin isn't as good as my brother's and there were parts I hurried over.'

Her head drew close to his bent one as he opened the paper. He was silent so long that she concluded that he must still be having difficulty in translating it all. Eventually he lifted his head and, after placing the sheet back in Nicholas's journal, he gazed across the water to where a heron stalked a fish. 'Well, what does it say?' she asked, tapping him on the arm.

He reached out and caressed her cheek. 'You

mustn't worry about what I'm about to tell you. After I left Jane's house last night, I was set upon and woke up this morning, my hands bound, in the bell tower of the church on High Street.'

She gripped his hand and held it tightly. 'Obviously, you escaped. Do you—you believe whoever did that to you also sent the message?'

He gave a tight little smile. 'Aye, I did wonder if it was the men who attacked me last time, but this message tells me that is highly unlikely. It is my brother they are really interested in. I admit I was puzzled as to why they chose to hide me up in the bell tower. Surely there are hiding places that are easier to reach?'

'I should imagine scarcely anyone goes up the tower and for that reason alone it shows a certain familiarity with the building,' said Rebecca.

'Which means they have a knowledge of the layout of the church,' said Phillip.

Her brows knit. 'A large number of tutors and students go into that church regularly. It's the university church.'

'Exactly so! And most of the tutors would have some knowledge of written Latin and maybe some would know Spanish. I would swear that one of my attackers spoke in that tongue.'

Her grey eyes flared. 'Do you think these

are the same men who attacked Nicholas in London?'

Phillip nodded. 'The message says that they want my brother to hand himself over to them in exchange for my safe deliverance.'

Rebecca gasped. 'So they know you're brothers! Do you believe they would have set you free if Nicholas did what they wanted?'

'Whatever their intentions, they will not have their way,' said Phillip, his eyes glinting. 'We need to find a member of a college whom they might know.' He returned the book to his pack.

Rebecca's face tensed with worry. 'Why don't you leave Oxford? I'd prefer that to you putting your life in danger in place of your brother.'

'I'm going to leave Oxford sooner rather than later, love,' said Phillip cheerfully. *More cheerfully than Rebecca thought he had a right to be.* 'But I can't just walk away from this. Besides, I need to tie up a few ends here before I go.' He swung the pack up on to his back.

'When did you plan to leave?' said Rebecca.

'Hopefully on the morrow,' he said softly. 'There is the play for the king to finish, rehearse and perform.'

'I wish I could go with you.'

He smiled. 'We'll speak of this again soon. Much depends on what Nicholas has to say.'

'You do intend to discuss this with Nicholas, then?'

'Of course.' He took her hand and kissed it. 'Hopefully when we reach Jane's, Master Mortimer will have already arrived there and you can be acquainted with him. He still remembers when you were little more than a baby.'

They began to walk beside the river.

Rebecca determined not to be apprehensive, but she was fighting a losing battle. She was nervous. 'I understand now why you didn't tell me about meeting him before the funeral,' she said, forcing a smile. 'I would have found it difficult to cope with such news about my mother. Even now I know it is not going to be easy. I will need to ask my uncle—no, my—my father's forgiveness for thinking so badly of him.'

'No, Becky!' Phillip shook his head at her. 'I'm certain he believes it is he who needs your forgiveness for staying away so long. If he had returned years ago, he would have discovered the truth and your life would have been less lacking in love.'

'All right, I accept that, but what of my mother? I find it hard to forgive myself for judging her so harshly,' she said sadly.

'But you weren't to blame,' said Phillip, coming to a halt.

'I know and it's too late to make amends!' Her eyes filled with tears.

'It's never too late, Becky. Look at us!' He stretched out his arms.

She stared at him in his feminine garb and she loved him so much she felt emotion swell inside her, destroying her sadness. 'Aye, I am looking,' she said drily. 'What a pair we make.'

His eyes twinkled. 'I'm sure your mother is looking down on us from heaven and finding pleasure in knowing you and the man she loved finally met and gave to the other that affection between father and daughter of which you were both robbed.'

Rebecca nodded. 'I will believe that. Now let us make haste. If you are to meet Nicholas in Broad Street this afternoon we can't waste any more time.'

'Aye, and don't forget that we are also expecting Ned and Tabitha to arrive in Oxford today.'

As they approached the house, she suddenly remembered they were in disguise. 'What if my father has arrived? I cannot meet him dressed in male garb,' she said in dismay.

Phillip agreed, but had an idea. 'You can change into the gown I'm wearing in Simon's workshop, although it will be too long.'

'Better that than meet my father wearing what

I have on now,' said Rebecca. 'If he is not there, then I can run upstairs and change.'

So she changed into Phillip's gown and if they had not been in such haste, it might have taken her much longer because they could have taken advantage of that time alone.

The meeting with her father was not, after all, the ordeal that Rebecca had feared earlier in the day. Although Anthony's likeness to his twin was frighteningly uncanny, she soon realised his expression lacked the critical appraisal and impatience so often seen in his brother's eyes when he had stared at her.

'You're so like Mary,' said Anthony, his voice rough with emotion. From inside his russet doublet of fine broadcloth, he produced a small object and handed it to her.

Rebecca gazed upon the likeness of the girl painted there and she was deeply touched. 'But she's lovely!' she exclaimed in wonder.

'Aye, and so are you.' He smiled down at her. 'She would have been proud of the woman you have become. As for me, I am delighted with my daughter.'

She reached up and kissed his cheek. Then both were silent as they gazed at the miniature of Mary and Rebecca thought how her mother would always appear young and smiling to her. Any misgivings Rebecca might have still nursed about Anthony Mortimer faded. It was obvious that this man had cared deeply for her mother and for that reason alone she wanted him as her father. She could not pretend that his resemblance to his twin would be easy to cope with, but surely it would improve the more she grew to know him.

He touched only briefly on the tragedy of her mother's death that had so changed all their lives. There was no doubt in his mind that the skeleton was Mary's and Rebecca believed it, too. She knew this would not be the last time they would talk about Mary. At the moment she sensed that Anthony found it extremely painful to discuss her, especially after he had come that morning from seeing her remains buried in the churchyard at Minster Draymore. She promised herself that soon she would visit her mother's grave.

Later, over a simple meal of soup, bread and apples, he talked about the years since he had last seen Mary. She was aware that Phillip was watching her as she listened to her father. She thought how different her life would have been if her parents had run away together, taking her with them. Her life might possibly have been as adventurous as that of Nicholas Hurst's, for her father had travelled far and wide, trying to forget the woman he had loved and lost. Thrice Anthony had been imprisoned in alien lands and four times he had been shipwrecked. Only his quick wits and a kind fate had kept him alive. He had also entertained foreign dignitaries in the exotic courts of oriental princes and become rich. Only when an enemy had tried to poison him did fear and a longing for home bring him back to England. Of course, if Anthony and Mary had run away together and taken her with them, then she would never have met Phillip, thought Rebecca. So perhaps whilst fate was unkind to some, it was kinder to others, she concluded.

It was after the meal was over, and Anthony was talking to the children and Jane, that Rebecca noticed Phillip was missing. She realised he must have left for his meeting with Nicholas. Suddenly she remembered that she was still wearing the gown he had donned as a disguise. She had been so caught up in all her father had to tell her that she had given no thought to her clothing. Now she worried—what if they had been followed and he was recognised by Nicholas's enemies? The thought of losing Phillip caused her to feel as if a cold hand squeezed her heart. She excused herself, hoping that she was mistaken, but determined to go to Broad Street to reassure herself that he had arrived there safely. But first she had to change into a different gown. She had no sooner done so than there came a knocking on the front door and she hurried to answer it.

'It's a decent-sized property,' said Nicholas, standing in the middle of the downstairs front room in Broad Street and gazing about him. 'D'you know when the printing presses are to be delivered?'

'In a sennight,' answered Phillip, folding his arms and leaning against the wall. They had yet to discuss the message. 'I was informed that the master printer will be here in a couple of days. Why the interest? You didn't arrange this meeting to talk business.'

'No,' said Nicholas, placing his hands in the wide sleeves of the habit and staring into space. The silence seemed to go on so long that Phillip cleared his throat, hoping to rouse his brother from his reverie. Nicholas blinked and said abruptly, 'Jane Caldwell asked me to be a godfather to the boy.'

'That must have come as a surprise.'

'You can say that again! I didn't know how to answer her, so I asked for time.'

'Sensible of you. Have you made up your mind yet? I have to tell you that I've changed mine about buying your shares,' drawled Phillip. 'I'm going to ask Becky to marry me. I'm also planning on having living quarters and a disguising house built here in Oxford where my troupe can perform plays for the students and the good people of this town.'

'If you have the funds, that could be an excellent notion,' said Nicholas. 'I know Marcus was eager for you to put on Greek tragedies for the students.'

'I am glad my idea meets with your approval,' said Phillip, inclining his head in his brother's direction. 'I know I'll have to pay you two gold coins if Rebecca accepts my proposal of marriage and I'm pretty certain she will.'

'I wasn't thinking of our wager.' Nicholas straightened up from the wall on the other side of the room and his expression was stern as he walked over to Phillip. 'You will need every penny you have managed to save. Now shall we get to the real reason we're here. If you're going to marry Becky, you can stop right now pretending to be me and remove that beard.'

Phillip removed the beard and rubbed his

chin. 'Last night I lacked a disguise and was hit on the head and taken captive, but I managed to escape as you can see,' he added swiftly at his brother's intake of breath. 'I suspect my attackers were Spanish and that they have a contact in one of the colleges.'

'What! This is what I feared,' said Nicholas angrily.

'Will you calm down?' snapped Phillip. 'Their plan was that Becky deliver the message to you, suggesting that you present yourself at a certain meeting place and they'd set me free in exchange for you. Well, that idea failed, but I had hopes that they might mistake me for you if they saw me on the streets this afternoon and follow me here. We'd get a look at them and you could see if you recognised any of them. Best viewpoint is upstairs. If you continue to wear your friar's disguise, you'll be safe.'

Nicholas scratched his neck and did not speak for several minutes, then he shook his head. 'These habits really itch if you don't wear sensible garb underneath.' He began to unfasten the rope that served as a girdle and dropped it on the floor before dragging the habit over his head. He was fully dressed in shirt, hose and doublet beneath the garment. 'I'm going to see Marcus. Perhaps he knows of a Spanish tutor or student.

Then I'm off to the priory to return the habit and collect my baggage and after that I'll return here. I've decided your idea's a good one. If my enemies haven't noticed you, then perhaps they'll notice me and make their move.'

Phillip said far more mildly than he felt, 'You're really mad! I begin to fear you have a death wish!'

Nicholas frowned. 'I cannot understand why they are so keen to be rid of me. I thought the Spanish captain had settled his score with me when we fought in Flanders. We both had wounds to nurse, so honour should have been satisfied. I can only believe that he discovered that Louise was carrying my child.'

'What's this about a child?' exclaimed a startled Phillip.

'Louise told me she was almost certain she was with child and I was the father,' said Nicholas, scratching his neck again. 'I put it out of my mind when we parted. Only then I was involved with helping at the birth of Jane Caldwell's son and after that came the news that Becky and her real father had been separated when she was only a child, leaving her to be reared by his twin, who ill-treated her.'

Phillip stared at him. 'Don't tell me, you've got to find out if there is a child.'

'Aye, because if so then I do not want it reared by that Spanish sea captain. I want to be responsible for it myself.'

Phillip scowled. 'I can understand how you feel, but you'll be walking into danger. He wants you dead.'

'I know that and also that Louise deceived me, so how can I ever trust her again?'

'That's for you to decide. I cannot give you easy answers,' said Phillip. 'Anyway, right now we have your enemies here to deal with. I'm going upstairs to see if I can see anyone who might be hovering around suspiciously. Coming?'

'Give me a few moments,' said Nicholas, so Phillip left him and went upstairs. He was gazing out of an upper window overlooking the busy street when he saw his brother cross the thoroughfare in the direction of Brasenose College. He stiffened, wondering what his brother thought he was doing. Moments later he saw a man emerge from beneath the overhanging window where he stood. The man went in the same direction as Nicholas. Phillip watched him glance over his shoulder and his heart began to thud. The man's complexion was swarthy and the hair beneath his hat was the colour of jet. There was also something familiar about him. Suddenly

Phillip recognised him and wasted no time making his way downstairs and out of the building. He could be mistaken in believing his quarry was involved in Nicholas's affairs, but he was not taking any chances.

'Isn't that Phillip?' said Rebecca, seizing Ned's arm as they came on to Broad Street. For it was he, and Tabitha, who had been standing on the path when she had opened the front door. Instantly she had told him that he must go with her and sensible man that he was, there had been no argument from him.

'Where's he going?' asked Ned.

'Not into one of the colleges, I hope,' said Rebecca in dismay. 'I cannot follow him there.'

'Look,' said Ned. 'He's running!'

'Then let's go after him,' cried Rebecca, picking up her skirts and racing in Phillip's direction.

Ned's legs were longer than hers and he soon overtook her, but they were both some distance away when they saw Phillip take a flying leap on to a man's back. He staggered and a dagger fell from his hand. At the same time they recognised the man who turned and punched the would-be assassin as Nicholas. The man collapsed against Phillip and slid to the ground.

The pair of them walked the last few yards

and stared down at the assailant. ‘Why, I’ve seen him before!’ gasped Rebecca.

Both brothers glanced her way. ‘What are you doing here, Becky?’ asked Phillip, startled.

‘I was concerned about you going out without a disguise. Do you realise who this man is?’

‘Aye! If I’m not mistaken, we heard him singing in the church in Ludlow,’ replied Phillip.

‘I’ve seen him before, too,’ said Nicholas, looking pale beneath his tan. ‘His name is Tomas Vives and he’s some kind of kin to Louise’s sea captain. He sings like an angel.’

Tomas’s eyelids flickered open and he groaned. ‘He’s not sounding much like an angel now,’ said Ned.

‘I wonder if Davy knows the kind of person he’s associating with,’ said Rebecca.

‘We’ll see what our singing angel has to say,’ said Phillip grimly. ‘It’s possible he wasn’t involved in the first attack on Nicholas as he was with Davy in Ludlow. Still, it’s likely he can provide us with the names of his compatriots. I have a feeling I know of one of them who has friends in high places.’

‘High places or not,’ said Rebecca firmly, ‘he should be brought to justice.’

‘I think Ned should escort Rebecca home and

leave this to us,' said Nicholas, blowing on his knuckles. 'We'll take him back to Broad Street.'

She looked at Phillip, who said, 'You go, love. Your father will be missing you.'

Reluctantly she agreed and went with Ned, suspecting that her presence might inhibit the brothers in their questioning.

The rest of the afternoon passed incredibly slowly and Rebecca wished she had not been so acquiescent in obeying Phillip. On returning to the house she had found Jane and Anthony in deep conversation about the wool trade and, not wanting to interrupt them, she had gone into the kitchen to talk to Tabitha about her sojourn in Greenwich. As they gossiped, they prepared a more filling meal for supper than the one set before her father at midday.

It was dusk by the time Phillip arrived at the house and he drew Rebecca aside and shooed Tabitha out of the kitchen. Whilst a couple of coneys stewed with vegetables and barley in a pot over the fire, he told her all they had discovered from Tomas.

'Apparently Louise's sea captain died of the wounds inflicted on him in the fight with Nicholas,' he said. 'So a couple of his kinsmen pledged to avenge his death whilst in their cups after the funeral. They knew Tomas, another of their cousins, and a more distinguished member of the family were in England, so they thought they'd rope them in. The one of distinction refused to have anything to do with the scheme. But Tomas, who had visited him in Oxford and sang in the church…' Phillip paused to take a gulp of ale '…was of much more help to them. By sheer coincidence or, as they believed, the hand of God, he knew of the Hurst brothers through Davy. The other two kinsmen had lost track of Nicholas after he left London, so they were pleased when I visited Ludlow with you and through Davy learnt where his sister lived in Oxford.'

'So it is my fault that you and Nicholas almost got yourselves killed,' sighed Rebecca.

Phillip frowned. 'Of course it's not your fault. The visit to Ludlow proved useful and lucrative to me. Especially now we have something on Master Tomas Vives.'

'What do you mean?'

Phillip took her hand between his own. 'I mentioned that he had friends in high places, but Tomas and his cousins will not leave the country until Cardinal Wolsey has had a talk with them.'

She frowned. 'What have you to do with the

Cardinal? Is he not an enemy of Princess Mary's guardian?'

Phillip hesitated, then decided it was probably wisest that they had no secrets between them. 'Aye, he pays me handsomely for keeping him informed about any unrest or gossip where'er my troupe visits.'

'I see. As if being a player, writer and a ship-builder was not enough for you, you must be a spy as well to satisfy your taste for adventure,' she said drily. 'Does this mean those who tried to kill Nicholas will escape justice in exchange for information?'

Phillip's brow knitted. 'Most likely and they will be kept prisoners for now. Nicholas plans to return to Flanders in search of Louise and his enemies are best kept out of the way.'

She felt a twinge of disappointment. 'Is he planning to marry this woman?'

'That I do not know. I deem my brother's life is extremely complicated at this moment; besides, he could be thinking it would affect our wager.' He drew Rebecca into his arms.

She stilled. 'What is this about a wager?'

'The other year Nick and I bet the other two gold coins against who would marry the first. I also pitched another two gold coins into the pot not so long ago, saying I thought he would be chasing after a woman before Christmas.' He added ruefully, 'I thought then he had a chance with you, although I really wanted to lose our wager because I wanted you for myself.'

'I see,' said Rebecca softly.

'Do you? By the way, did you know that Jane has asked Nicholas to be Simon's godfather?'

She gasped. 'Now that surprises me, although—'

'What? Did you think like me for a brief moment that they might suit?'

'To be frank, I thought the children were taken with him and he would have found a proper home with them and Jane. All I can say now is that I hope Nicholas finds his heart's desire, for I have found mine.' She looked up at Phillip with love in her eyes.

'And I, too,' said Phillip, his voice rough with emotion. 'I love you, Becky, far deeper than I can ever express.'

She rubbed her cheek against his. 'I love you, too. Frighteningly so.'

'Frighteningly?' His lips brushed hers.

'I couldn't bear it if I were to lose you.'

'Then we must make certain we don't lose each other,' said Phillip quietly. 'Which seems the right time to ask you to marry me.'

'I want to marry you,' she said instantly. 'Only—'

'I'm not accepting any excuses,' he interrupted, tilting her chin and kissing her again. 'I deem you'll be able to voice three objections at least to a hasty marriage.'

She gazed into his blue eyes and felt as if he could see into her very soul. 'You know what they are?'

'Jane and the children and your father.'

He made to kiss her again, but she held him off. 'You haven't cited living in a wagon and travelling around the country in terrible weather?'

'That's because I have in mind a better way of life for you and our children. A home-cum-disguising house in Oxford, which means you will be able to continue to see Jane and the children and your father as often as you wish.'

Rebecca's face lit up. 'Then I will marry you.' He would have drawn her close, but again she held him off with a hand against his chest. 'Wait! You have made no mention of my being a bastard child. Are you sure you want to marry me?'

'Who am I to judge your father or you? My mother was a king's bastard,' said Phillip.

Her eyes widened and she opened her mouth to speak. 'But that's another story,' he said, and silenced her with a kiss.

* * * * *